H
K

D1616038

WHISPERING RANGE

Also by Ernest Haycox
in Thorndike Large Print ®

The Wild Bunch
Sundown Jim
Long Storm

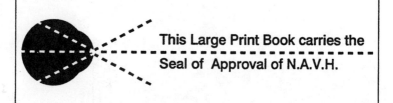

This Large Print Book carries the
Seal of Approval of N.A.V.H.

WHISPERING RANGE

ERNEST HAYCOX

Thorndike Press • Thorndike, Maine

356053

Published in 1994 by arrangement with Golden West Literary
Agency.

Thorndike Large Print ® Western Series.

The tree indicium is a trademark of Thorndike Press.

The text of this Large Print edition is unabridged.
Other aspects of the book may vary from the original edition.

Set in 16 pt. News Plantin by Minnie B Raven.

Printed in the United States on acid-free, high opacity paper. ∞

Library of Congress Cataloging in Publication Data

Haycox, Ernest, 1899–1950.
    Whispering range / Ernest Haycox.
      p.   cm.
    ISBN 0-7862-0200-9 (alk. paper : lg. print)
    1. Large type books. I. Title.
  [PS3515.A9327W5   1994]
  813'.52—dc20   94-5670

WHISPERING RANGE

CHAPTER I

SUNDOWN

Eve Leverage came out of the hotel like a boy — swiftly, carelessly, and her lips pursed in the attitude of whistling. Her gray eyes quested along the street with a level expectancy; her tip-tilted nose made a wrinkling gesture against the hot sun. Two gangling punchers who seemed to have collapsed to semi-consciousness on the porch steps gathered themselves together foot by foot and rose before her, muttering, "G'mornin', Miss Eve," in unison. Eve's thoughtful preoccupation vanished before a frank, glinting smile. "Hello, Pete. Hello, Buck. Busy as usual, I see." Then she stopped so abruptly that one of the men threw out his hand, thinking she was about to trip on the steps. Eve never noticed the gesture. Her glance, going on down the street, had reached its mark. David Denver appeared through the crowd and strolled leisurely forward. A coral pink appeared on Eve's cheeks; she looked again at Messrs. Buck Meems and Pete Wango, and she looked into her purse.

"What became of that letter?" she asked these two shiftless sons of the prairie. "I had it in my hands just a moment ago."

The gentlemen flinched, as if accused of stealing it. Wango, having a chew in his mouth, remained stolidly dumb. But Meems was a more versatile man and made a stab at intelligent conversation. "Was it — uh — important, ma'am?"

"You have no idea," said Eve mysteriously. "Now, I've got to find it." She turned to the door, cast a quick look around, and stopped half inside the opening to watch Denver; to her the street, dusty and sprawling and hot, had become suddenly eventful.

David Denver — Black Dave Denver — approached in comfortable idleness. He had his hat tipped back and his face turned toward Cal Steele who walked alongside and told some kind of a story with much gesturing of arm. Denver nodded, the somber gravity of his features lighting up. Rather wistfully the girl wished she knew the kind of a story Cal Steele related, for there were few people who could make Dave Denver smile. Steele, in fact, was almost the only man who had the power of lifting Denver out of those strange and darkly taciturn moods that so often descended upon him.

The two of them stopped. Al Niland came

8

across to join in, and presently Steve Steers emerged from Grogan's Western Star. So the four of them drew together as they inevitably did when in the same neighborhood. Dissimilar in so many respects and sharply varied in personalities, there yet was some common quality that cemented a deep friendship between them. The girl often had wondered about it, and at this moment she puzzled over the problem again. Al Niland was a lawyer who liked to take poor men's cases and fight with an ironical energy. Steve Steers was a roving puncher who, though welcome on any ranch, preferred to ride free and solitary through the hills. Cal Steele owned a small outfit near Dave Denver's D Slash ranch, and of the group this man was the most brilliant, the most volatile, and the most prodigal of his energy and talents. They were all young, and they were all fighters. But the girl, seeking deeper reasons, knew some deeper trait was shared by them. They were restless, nonconforming men; each a strong individualist and without illusions. Dave Denver's streak of clear-sighted grimness could be found likewise in the others.

The girl sighed a little as she saw Denver's smile fade and his bold features settle. The others were grinning amiably at some wild tale told by Steve Steers; but Denver's moment

9

of forgetfulness was past, and he reverted again to the stormy, unsettled side of his nature. The first hot sun of the young year reached nooning and flashed down on the shackling, paint blistered buildings of the town, on the pine false fronts, on the whitewashed 'dobe walls, on the stone turret of the courthouse, on the drawn curtains of the second-story windows. A dinner bell rang. Buck Meems was drawling at his partner.

" 'S funny thing, Pete. Ev'body considers Denver a big man. You do, I do, ev'body does. But look at him standin' beside Al Niland, not an inch taller ner a pound heavier. Al ain't more'n five feet eleven, and he don't weigh a hunnerd-seventy on the hocks. See what I mean? Denver ain't rully a big man when yuh git him among others. It's only when he's off by hisself that he looks like a young house movin' down the street. Funny, ain't it, Pete?"

"I could die of laughin'," muttered the drowsing Wango. "Ever have him slap yuh on the back?"

"Nuh."

"Take a try sometime and see if they's anything humorous about that."

Buck Meems was not a man lightly to cast aside an idea. He pursued this one doggedly, his mind almost audibly creaking from the strain of unaccustomed thinking. "Reason he

10

looms so big alone is because we sorter expect him to be big. Git my idee, Pete? I mean big things is done by big men in a big sorter way. Folla me?"

"I'm limpin' after yuh," admitted Pete.

"He's big," insisted Buck Meems, attempting to wring the last drop of significance from his thought, "because even though he ain't actually big nev'less he's big on account o' the big way he does big —"

"Gawd's sake," groaned Wango, "roll over and get it offen yore chest."

Meems, silenced, brooded darkly. "I bet," he finally announced, "that if somebody put a bullet in yore coco it'd rattle like a nickel in a tin cup. Le's eat."

"Why, thanks fer offerin' to pay my dinner," said Wango and rose instantly.

"Who said anything about —" exploded Meems and became conscious of the girl's presence. The two stalked past her into the hotel, and she heard the murmur of their argument floating back. Denver broke away from his friends and sauntered on, at which the rose color on Eve Leverage's cheeks began to deepen. She moved casually across the porch. Denver turned in and met her with a slow lift of his hat. The girl, who knew this man's temper better than he would ever realize, saw the small crinkling furrows of pleasure spring around his eyes, and because of that signal her chin lifted gayly.

"This is a Thursday," he mused in an even, drawling voice, "and what brings you to town during the middle of the week?"

"Dad had business, so I rode along with him. But," and she assumed a mock deference, "if you don't want me in Sundown I shall of course get right in the wagon and drive home."

"Not a good idea," he decided. "You were meant to be right on this spot at this minute to cheer a dull man on a dull day."

"The king speaks," sighed Eve, "and the poor maid trembles in fear. What is your will, my good and great lord?"

He put his head aside and scowled at her. "That," he reflected, "has all the earmarks of a muffled knock. Little girls ought to have more respect for age."

"Oh, my training has all been wrong, Mister Denver. But don't you think it's almost time for you to throw away the notion I'm still a little girl? You've been thinking that for ten years. People do grow."

He studied her with perfect gravity and over so long a period that she began to lose her cool ease of manner. This man could make a mask of his face, and one seldom knew if he were serious or if behind the ruggedly modeled features there lay a soft laugh.

"You might be surprised," he observed finally, "just how often I change my mind about you, Eve."

"Now that's interesting. Tell me more."

"Just like a woman. Do you ever eat?"

"I have been known to."

"Well, you look hungry right now, and I feel charitable."

"I shall eat a great deal and run up a big bill," she warned him. "And you must order a whole jar of pickles for me. I expect that of gentlemen who take me to dine."

"Pickles for a grown lady," agreed Dave Denver solemnly and followed her into the dining room. They took a table in one corner and watched a hungry Sundown citizenry file through the door. Denver's glance roamed across the room, and Eve, experiencing a queer twinge of feeling that was half pride and half jealousy, saw that one of the waitresses had abandoned the big table and was coming over. Somehow this man had the power of creating loyalty. Men spoke to him in passing by, spoke to him with that soft slurring courtesy of equal to equal. His three strong friends sauntered in; but though there was room at the table for them, they only nodded and passed on to another, giving him the privacy he seemed to desire. Colonel Fear

13

Langdell paused a moment, bowed at Eve, and spoke quietly to Dave Denver. "Meeting of the Association at two, Dave." Denver nodded, and Langdell walked away, a thin, straight ramrod of a man, quite conscious of his power. Eve, eating with the unashamed vigor of youth, knew that it was not every man nor many men for whom Fear Langdell would take extra steps; and this thought brought out another. No matter what company Dave Denver was in, and no matter how quietly he sat back, the effect of his presence would be felt as it was in the dining room.

Remembering Buck Meems's talk, she studied Denver candidly. The puncher was right. Denver was not overly large. Her own father was as tall and as heavy. The comparison somehow surprised her, for she had always thought of Denver as being much the bulkier. The difference, she discovered, lay elsewhere — in Denver's big-boned wrists, in his sweep of shoulders, in the unsymmetrical boldness of his face. A scar shaped like a crescent lay on one dark cheek, black hair ran rebelliously along his head, and his eyes sat deep, violet eyes with flecks of other coloring in them. There lay the difference — there was the seat of that power which stamped him so definitely.

"When you get through with the inquest,"

14

he drawled, "I'd like to know the verdict."

She caught herself and looked down. "Apparently you read minds, David."

The shadows left his features; humor flashed from his eyes. "No, but I can read little girls' faces."

"Big girl in this case."

"Big girl it is, then." He leaned forward. "Why are you so all-fired anxious to grow up?"

"I have already grown up. I am twenty and as old and wise as I ever shall be. You ought to know that about women."

"Yeah? Where would I be getting my information?"

"I have been told you were rather successful with women," said Eve looking squarely at him. The shot struck him dead on. The deeply set eyes turned stormy and then swiftly cleared.

"Believe nothing you hear and only half of what you see," he replied enigmatically. "And that doesn't sound good, coming from you, Eve."

"Oh, fiddlesticks!" exclaimed the girl. "Do you think I am a little dummy wrapped up in five yards of cloth? But I suppose I must be meek or get sent away from the table."

He chuckled. "I reckon you have grown up, for you've learned the trick of drawing a man off the trail. I asked you what was your all-fired hurry to blossom out as a lady. Ain't there grief enough in this world without hurryin' to meet it?"

"I think," said Eve, far more sober than she had been thus far, "I shall not tell you. Some day possibly you may learn for yourself."

"After I get more education?" he countered grimly.

Eve's father, Jake Leverage, came into the dining room and walked over to them. "One o' you two is in bad company," he observed amiably, "but I wouldn't swear which." He sat down and reached for a platter. "Goin' to beef much stuff this spring, Dave?"

"No. Market's too shot. Hold over until later."

"When a man talks that independent I reco'nize he ain't got any mortgages to worry about," grunted Leverage, parting his whiskers.

"I let the bankers do that worryin'," was Denver's dry response. "They seem to thrive and get rich doin' it, so why not let 'em?"

"You allus was a hand to run your own show," agreed Leverage. "But the more immediate question is, have you lost any stock through strange disappearance?"

"Rustlers don't seem to like my beef, Jake."

"Yeah? Well, yore lucky. I don't know what

16

this country's comin' to. Somethin's got to be done to somebody. I ain't mentionin' any names but —"

"Do you happen to know of any names you might mention?"

Leverage looked a little uncomfortable, and Eve watched Denver with a wrinkle of thought on her forehead.

"Folks can do some pretty close guessin'," grunted Leverage. "And when fifteen-twenty people guess the same I'd say there must be a foundation o' fact. You goin' to the Association meetin'?"

"I'll listen in," assented Denver idly.

"There's got to be more'n just listenin' this time. You know as well as I do that this sort of horseplay can't go on. It comes right down to a proposition of who is goin' to run this country, the roughs and the toughs or the ranchers. It is a fine state of affairs when honest men raise beef for crooks to steal. I ain't in business for my health, ner I don't propose to play Santy Claus for Mister —" He checked himself from indiscretion and reddened.

"I see you have a particular gentleman in mind," suggested Denver.

"And his whole damned ring," added Leverage stoutly. "It's up to us to play a little game of root, hawg, or die."

"Takes three things to hang a man," opined

Denver. "You've got to catch him, convict him, and find a big enough rope to hold him."

"The second item can be allowed as done right now. A good-sized posse can do the other two. I'll go so far as to furnish the rope myself. But you don't seem totally sold on the idee, Dave. Don't it mean nothin' to you? It had oughta. Yore eatin' pie from the same dish as the rest of us ranchers. It ain't no time to back and fill."

Denver looked at Eve, once more displaying the old temper of somber disbelief. "I believe in playin' my game and lettin' the other man play his. If the time comes when I've got a chore to do against a rustler I'll do it alone without askin' for help. Half of the big cattlemen in this county got their start by means of a quick rope and a careless brandin' iron. Now that these same dudes have got rich and turned honest they send up a tinhorn squawk every time they lose a calf. Let 'em haze their own rustlers instead of puttin' the chore on others."

"Wouldn't you hang a proved rustler?" demanded Leverage.

"I'd have to think about it," was Denver's slow reply. "A man would have to be considerably smaller and meaner than me — which is sayin' considerable — before I'd want to haul him out on a limb."

Leverage shook his head. "Hate to hear you say that. It's worse than a case of some fellow nibblin' a few head here and a few head there. It's organized outlawry we're goin' to have to fight. Root, hawg, or die. We run our business or they run us. I ain't able to get very soft-hearted over a crook under them circumstances."

"I guess I'll have to be pinched before I shout," drawled Denver, eyes following across the dining room. A man came in with a printed broadside and tacked it to the wall; black type announced to Sundown city the following entertainment:

LOLA MONTEREY!

AND THE WESTERN OPERA COMPANY
WILL PRESENT AT OUR OPERA HOUSE
THIS EVENING
AN OLD FAVORITE
CAVALIER OF SPAIN!

LOLA, SUNDOWN'S OWN SINGING
BEAUTY,
COMES BACK TO HER BIRTHPLACE
AFTER A TRIUMPHAL TOUR
OF EUROPE TO PLEASE THE FOLKS
OF THE OLD HOME TOWN
TO-NIGHT!

Jake Leverage scanned the notice. "They sure got the country plastered with them notices. I see 'em on every juniper shrub along the road. Been three years since we saw Lola in a play, ain't it, Eve? What's she want to come back to this sun-cooked scope of alkali-crusted land for, anyhow? I got no admiration for foreign places like Yurrup, but if I was a gal with Lola's talents I sure wouldn't waste no time around here. I'd go away and stay away."

Eve tried to catch her father's attention, but he went on blandly. "A great girl. I'm no hand for this fa-so-la music as a rule, but it was a genuine pleasure to sit back in the old Palace and hear her sing. Yes, sir. Well, I reckon you got to go to that, uh, Eve?"

He turned to his daughter and received in full measure the impact of her warning glance. She shook her head slightly, at which the old man muttered under his breath and combed back his mustache to drink the rest of his coffee. Eve's clear face seemed sharp and troubled as she watched Dave Denver. He had turned to the notice and was staring at it, all features caught up in a brooding, stormy expression. For a time he appeared to forget all others in the room, to forget that there were people around who might be interested in observing his reaction to Lola Monterey's name.

Eve lowered her eyes to the table, knowing very well how many quick and covert glances were thrown toward Dave Denver. Lola was back, bringing with her a breath of the old story and the old gossip.

Denver squared himself to the table and reached for his cigarette papers. "Yeah," he observed casually, "she always had a fine voice. The outside world was her place."

"Then why should she come back?" Leverage wanted to know and received a kick on his booted leg under the table.

"I couldn't say," mused Denver. "Probably Lola doesn't know herself. That's the way she does things."

"All wimmen's alike," grunted Leverage and scowled on his daughter. His leg hurt.

Outside was the jangle and clatter of the Ysabel Junction stage making the right-angle turn from Prairie Street to Main. By common consent the people in the dining room adjourned dinner and headed for the door. Denver walked behind Leverage and Eve; the girl, never knowing why she should let herself say such a thing, spoke over her shoulder.

"Old times for you, David. Aren't you glad?"

She was instantly sorry, and a little ashamed when she heard Denver's slow answer come gently forward.

21

"You've convinced me you're no longer a little girl, Eve. I'm not sure I like the change."

"And why?"

"Little girls are more charitable minded than big ones."

They were on the porch. The stages — there were three of them this trip instead of one — veered up to the hotel porch and stopped. Some courteous citizen opened the door of the front coach and lifted his hat. A woman stepped daintily down, and there was a flash of even teeth as she smiled on the crowd. Eve's small fists tightened; she threw a glance behind her, but Dave Denver had disappeared from the porch and was not to be seen. Eve thought Lola Monterey's eyes went through the ranks of the assembled Sundowners with more than passing interest, but if the woman was disappointed she was too accomplished an actress to reveal it. Old man Leverage muttered, "By Jodey, the girl's pretty, Eve. She's got beyond Sundown."

Eve nodded, a small ache in her heart. The tempestuous, flamboyant dance-hall girl of three years ago had returned from her conquests with the veneer of fine manners and proud self-confidence. Her jet-black hair bobbed in the sun, and the slim, pointed face, showing the satin smoothness of Spanish blood, had the stirring dignity of actual beauty. Moving up the steps

22

with the same lithe grace that had brought her out of poverty and mean surroundings, she paused, swung around, and smiled again on Sundown. Soft and husky words fell into the silence with a queer vitality.

"I am home — and glad."

Then she passed into the hotel, the rest of the opera company following after. A traveling salesman, calling heartily to his friends, swept past. And at the end of the procession strolled an extremely tall man with the jaw and the nose and the eye of England. He seemed weary, bored, puzzled. At the door he paused to ask a plaintive question of a bystander, and those nearest him caught the full fragrance of a broad and richly blurred speech freshly blown from Albion's misty shores.

"I say, my friend, one of my bally braces has burst a stitching. Can you direct me to the local haberdashery?"

The crowd was dissolving. Leverage turned on his daughter. "I reckon you'll be wantin' to see the show tonight, uh?"

"I do," said Eve, "but why in the world did you mention it in front of David? It made me feel as small as —"

"Good grief, why?" demanded the astonished Leverage. "It ain't a crime."

"Do you think I want him to believe I was fishing for an invitation? And you shouldn't

23

have mentioned Lola around him, Dad."

Leverage shook his head. "Wimmen beat me. Danged if they don't. Now a kid like you has got to go and join the ranks. Well, we'll stay over then."

"We'll go right home," said Eve, "so I can get into some clothes. Folks don't go to shows in gingham dresses, and there's Mother."

"Imagine that," grinned Leverage. "Well, don't forget that the most important ceremony you been through so far, which was bein' born, didn't call for no clothes at all. And I have et with three Senators and a governor with nothin' better than overalls on which had a red flannel patch in the seat. But you can go home and come back, though Ma won't want to come. I know better'n to argue. Wait till I get Joe Peake to take you in a rig. I got to stay over for the Association meetin'."

Eve smiled at her father and strolled down the street, leaving the porch deserted except for two lackadaisical gentlemen who somehow had witnessed all the recent excitement from the comfortable vantage point of the porch rockers.

"Buck," said Wango, "whut's that brace business which the Englishman was cryin' over?"

"I heard somewhere that those fellas called suspenders braces," replied Meems.

"Hell, ain't that peculiar? And whut's a habadashery, anyhow?"

"Your turn to guess," drawled Meems. "I done my share."

"Well," growled Wango, "he ain't a-gunta git by with no foreign hooch-a-ma-cooch like that around here."

"Lola sure has got pritty," reflected Meems.

"Yeah. Reckon Denver figgers so."

"Shut up," admonished Meems without heat. "Don't drag in dead cats."

"Ain't you a moral son of a gun? Pardon me for chewin' tobacco in yore presence. But what I'm wonderin' is how the stage got through without excitement to-day. Yuh know, they's supposed to be money in the Wells-Fargo box this trip."

"Don't be mellerdramatic, Wango. Who'd bring money into a joint like Sundown?"

"I heard," said Meems lazily. "Well, mebbe Lou Redmain was asleep at the switch."

Buck Meems rose from the depths of the rocker and stared at his partner with a penetrating eye and said very coldly, "Was I you, Pete, I'd git me some packthread and sew up that four-cornered thing yuh call a mouth."

"Well —"

"Shut up," stated Meems succinctly. "It's too hard to git partners, an' I don't want yuh shot down until I git back what yuh owe me.

25

As for the gent whose name yuh was so careless as to mention out loud — don't do it no more. You don't know him. You never heard of him, see? Let yore betters worry about that business. You and me is humble folks with an itch to keep on breathin'."

"Trouble's comin', nev'less," maintained Wango.

"Comin' hell a-riot," agreed Meems. "That's what the Association is meetin' for. That's why yuh see Dave Denver stalkin' around the streets lookin' about as hard as I ever saw him. But you and me is out of it, see? Or have I got to spell the words?"

"Oh, well," breathed Wango and cast a sidewise glance at his partner. "How about a drink?"

"Thanks for the invite," said Meems, and rose instantly.

"I never said nothin' about an invite —"

"And it was nice of yuh to offer to pay my way," broke in Meems firmly. "Come on."

CHAPTER II
STORM WARNING

Dave Denver and Al Niland stood at one corner of Grogan's hundred-foot bar and downed an after-dinner whisky neat, as was the custom. The men of Sundown drifted in, took their liquor, and swapped unhurried talk. Denver looked around the room, nodding here and there at ranchers he hadn't seen during the winter. Niland leaned closer.

"Did you see the same fellow I happened to see get off the third stage?"

"Stinger Dann?"

"The same," grunted Niland. "Since when's he taken to payin' fare?"

"Maybe he's run all his good horses to death," suggested Denver.

"Somebody's doin' a lot of night ridin', that's certain," mused Niland. "It's a funny thing how this county reacts to the hint of trouble. All winter we've been quiet. Nothing's happened much. All of a sudden folks get a little skittish and quit talkin' out loud. The underground telegraph starts workin'. Look around the room and see how many men are swappin' conversation real close together and tryin' to appear aboveboard. I never saw the signs fail. Pretty soon something will break loose."

"Which brings us back to Stinger Dann," drawled Denver. "He's enterin' for his liquor. Where's he been the last few weeks?"

Niland spared a short, quick glance at a man with a burly frame and raw-red cheeks cruising toward the bar; Stinger Dann was scowling straight ahead and paying heed to nobody, as was his characteristic way of moving through life.

"Looks nowhere and sees everything," muttered Niland. "I don't know where he's been holin' up, Dave. You tell me where Redmain's been, and I'll tell you where Dann's been. Same place. He's probably here to cover the interests of his beloved chief in the Association meeting."

Dave Denver chuckled. "That would be just the nervy thing Lou Redmain might think of."

"There was some trouble over beyond Sky Peak a week ago. Will Wire's men ran into lead one night when they was crosscuttin' their range for home."

Denver considered the news thoughtfully. "That's gettin' a little closer to Sundown, ain't it? Usually the boys do their stealin' farther off."

"The time may come when we'll have to do some shootin' on our own account," prophesied Niland.

"Let's wait till the wolf howls first. All I seem to hear at present is a lot of bear talk. Enter Mister Steers, looking very sad. Which foot did the horse step on, Steve?"

"Aw, hell," grunted Steve and reached for a bottle.

"Expressive but vague," was Niland's ironic comment. "Somebody must of hurt your feelin's to the extent of offerin' you a job."

The compact, sandy-haired Steve Steers drank his potion and shuddered. "I don't never seem to get a break, men. Consider this item. I shore want to take in the show to-night, just for old time's sake. But Debbie's off up in Mogul country with her folks on a visit so I can't take her. And if I dared go to see Lola Monterey alone I never would hear the last of it. Nossir, I never seem to get a break."

"Wear false whiskers," suggested Niland.

"They'd fall off," mournfully remarked Steve Steers. "That's my luck. And somebody like Miz Jim Coldfoot would see me and go tell Debbie."

"Love," reflected Niland judicially, "is a mighty purifier of mortal man."

Denver, standing slightly aside and watching Steve out of grave eyes, drawled idly, "Depends on the man, Al. I reckon love would have to be some stronger than hydrochloric acid to purify Steve."

"Love," said Mister Steers. "Ha-ha."

Niland winked discreetly at Denver. "After you're married, Steve, it'll be better."

"Or worse," groaned Steve. "Let's have another drink of this here panther spit."

Stinger Dann was walking flat-footedly away from the bar. In the center of the room he threw a quick glance back to where Dave Denver stood, and his rude, cold eyes seemed to contain a definite challenge. So marked was the gesture that a lull came to Grogan's saloon, and two men standing beyond Dann moved out of range. Denver never stirred. A flare of stronger light flickered up to meet the gunman's challenge, and the rugged features hardened perceptibly. Dann moved on and left the saloon.

"That had all the earmarks of an opening play," said Niland quietly. "Didn't I tell you things was smokin' up hereabouts?"

"Let 'em smoke," mused Denver. "I'm mindin' my own business and having a good time doing it. Maybe I won't always be doin' that, but we'll wait and see."

Cal Steele rolled into the saloon. He marched up to his partners with a flashing, nervous smile. "Well, congratulate me."

"Where yuh been?" demanded Steve Steers.

"Reviving some very pleasant memories," said Steele. He poured himself a drink and tipped the glass to the rest, standing quite erect; undeniably he had a carriage and a polish to him the others lacked. Somewhere along an unknown and carefully concealed past he had lived in gentle and scholarly surroundings, and the reflection of it was on his manners, his acts, and on the features that so easily shifted from high gayety to most bitter cynicism. "I drink, boys, to beauty, to talent, to the eternal flame that is woman — to Lola Monterey!"

Both Niland and Steers looked a little anxiously at the unsmiling Denver. But he nodded his head. "As usual, Cal, you get closer to the actual truth than any man I ever knew. You have described Lola. She is just that."

Cal put down his glass and laid an arm on Denver's shoulder. "And what good does truth do me, or fine talk? You spoil the game for all of us, Dave. She sent me here. She wants to see you."

Denver's eyes smiled. "And that is a command."

"Association meetin' in a few minutes," grumbled Niland, frowning at Steele.

"I'll see you there," said Denver and went out. Niland spoke his mind to Steele. "Been

31

better if you hadn't brought such a message. Dave ain't the man to cool his feet in Lola's string. They ain't the same kind of people at all."

But Cal Steele shook his head thoughtfully. "I know Lola. She's my kind. Up in the clouds, down in the mud, never still, never happy, easy angered, easy hurt. And" — he looked up — "though she is the most selfish woman in the world, she would give her life for a man she wanted to love. Sounds a little odd, doesn't it, boys? I know. She's my kind. And I happen to know she wants Dave."

"Get out," snorted Steve.

"She told you?" asked Niland skeptically.

"I'm not blind," murmured Cal Steele, face darkly shadowed. "Though I wish I were sometimes. I want her myself. Damned funny, isn't it? Let's drink to Dave and Lola."

Some of the more impatient ranchers were already aiming for the opera house, which had been designated as the meeting place for the Association, when David Denver swung toward the hotel. He heard one of them say rather angrily, "I don't give a damn who it is or how strong his wild bunch may be, we've got to stop it. There's too many people riding around in the dark. If they ain't disposed to sleep at night, then, by the eternal, we'd better give 'em somethin' that'll induce a permanent sleep." But this party seemed the only talkative one; the others were moodily silent, saving their words for formal delivery. Denver's glance swept Sundown slowly and deliberately as he advanced, and his mind registered this and that detail with a photographic distinctness that would, in moments of leisure, serve to help him build up his shrewd judgment of people and events. Stinger Dann had taken post against a wall of the Palace, shaded by the overhanging gallery. By the stable the Ysabel Junction stage was making up for a return trip. Eve Leverage stepped boyishly out of a dry-goods store and smiled at the world. Denver went into the hotel and climbed the stairs with a cloudy restlessness on his cheeks. Swinging down the hall he paused at Number One — the best room of the house — and heard Lola humming huskily inside. For one long interval he stared at the floor; then knocked. The humming stopped, the girl's voice rose with an eager, throaty "come in." Denver pushed the door before him, stepped through, and closed it.

He could not realize as he paused there, studying her with half a frown, rebellious hair tousled on his head, and a somber flare of emotion in the deep wells of his eyes, that he was the exact and unchanged picture of the man she had carried with her for three years; nor could he know that his blunt, "Here I am, Lola," was the exact phrase she felt David Denver would greet her with. But he did know that the old-time belle of the Palace had become a mature beauty. She stood in the center of the room, fine lacework clinging to her breast, jet hair tied severely back, and her lips pursed upon a smile or a cry. A mature beauty, yet still the same vital Lola Monterey, still with a queer, unfathomed glow in those eyes dusted with velvet coloring. She tipped her chin, laughed softly, and then caught her lip between her teeth.

"Here you are, David. You were scowling when I went away. You are scowling now. Is that all you have for me?"

"I suppose other men have told you that you're beautiful, Lola?"

"I suppose. But I have never listened to men as I listen to you. You know that."

"Then I'll say it. Something's rounded you out. There's something inside that body of yours —"

"Misery, maybe. They say it is good for people." She came over to him, brushed her finger tips across her own mouth and placed them on Denver's cheeks. "From me to you. That is my welcome — as I think you know it would always be. I have heard a thousand gallant speeches from men whose gallantry I

34

doubted. It is good to know one man I never have to doubt — and wouldn't doubt even if I had reason. Come, sit down." She put an arm through his elbow and led him to a chair, then crossed and sat facing him.

"You have not changed," she went on swiftly. "And I'm glad — and sorry."

His face cleared and a piece of a smile came to his eyes. "That sounds just like you."

"Well, isn't it nice to come home and find the same landmarks? That makes me happy. But you are still stormy, still unhappy, still savage with yourself. That makes me sad."

"Let's talk about you for a change, Lola."

She shook her slim head so vigorously that the jade earrings danced against the satin of her skin. "Let other men talk about me. You and I — we will talk about you. You know about me — all about me. There is nothing to add for these three years. I am still that hungry little girl of the Palace whose body never grew up to her temper. You have prospered, David?"

"The ranch has grown," he admitted.

"You have a big ranch house now, facing down Starlight Canyon — and you sit on the porch at night and look across the prairie, alone."

"Who told you that?" demanded Denver.

"I made Cal Steele tell me everything that

had happened to you in three years. I know about that scar on your cheek, I know about the arm you broke, the battles you have fought. So I have the history of David Denver, cattleman, gentleman. From poor Cal, who wanted to talk of himself and me."

"Cal," said Denver, "is the best friend I ever hope to have. He's in love with you, Lola. You couldn't find a better man —"

Her swift smile interrupted him. "You will not get rid of me that easy, David!"

Suddenly the old temper returned to him. His big hands closed. "Why did you run away, Lola?"

The answer came swift and straight. "Because I loved you too much!"

"Then why in God's name have you returned?"

"Because," said she just above a whisper, "because I loved you too much."

"We were better off apart. All the struggle and misery —"

Instantly she was fire and flame. "Don't I know? You were born to hurt me. You always will. And I will always try to find a smile in your unhappy eyes! Always, even when you have cut my pride to pieces! I am just a beggar, asking for something I think I never will get! Lola Monterey doing that! David, my dear, there's no woman born who will ever be able to hold you. No woman will ever be able to smooth away that sadness and bitterness. But —"

She caught her breath and watched him. He said nothing; only looked steadily back to her.

"— but I have been able to make you forget yourself and think of me, just for little spells of time. I can lift you to me, make you smile. That is enough for me — it is more than another woman has done. You see — I still hope."

He rose, speaking gently. "I reckon I'd cut off my arm rather than hear you say that. You've got beyond Sundown now, Lola. To-night you'll play for us. To-morrow you'll be gone. And that will be the end, for us. I'll not be seeing you again. I remember Lola Monterey of the Palace, and I don't think I want to see Lola Monterey of —"

"You will be there to-night, David," she broke in softly. "I know you better."

"If so, I'll not be near enough to say good-bye. So I'll say it now."

But she shook her head. "No. To-night I sing. To-morrow the company goes on without me. I am staying here, David. I have thought about it for a year. It is arranged. I think I might go higher still in my work. I love it. But I love something else better, and so Sundown is home for me again."

"You are making a mistake."

She came toward the door and touched his arm with the tip of her fingers. "I am always making them, David. I always will. Didn't I say I was a beggar? Beggars cannot be choosers. When I am hurt, which is so often, I must smile and think that I came from nothing and should be glad. Who wants to see Lola Monterey crying? But I often wonder what happiness is like. Perhaps some day I shall know, perhaps not. Now go along. And, tonight, when you hear me sing, remember that I sing to you."

The gentle pressure of her fingers put him in the hall. He had a glimpse of her velvet eyes, round and shining, and then the door closed, and he walked heavily down the stairs to the street. Somebody spoke to him. Colonel Fear Langdell dropped in step, talking crisply. "Let's get the ball rolling. I have been waiting around for you. Expect you to influence a great many of the weak hearted, Dave. In fact, I expect you to take the leadership in a disagreeable chore. Men will ride for you who wouldn't ride for anybody else."

The two passed into the opera house, and thus engaged Denver failed to see Eve Leverage pass in a rig driven by Joe Peake. But Eve had seen him come out of the hotel just as she had seen him go in previously. And she knew where he had spent the intervening minutes. Sitting very straight and sober beside Peake, she stared bleakly across the sloping hills, saying to herself over and over again, "That old story about them is true. It is true, all of it. But what difference does it make? I don't care — I don't care! I can't find fault with David!"

There were about sixty men in the opera house, part of them owners, part of them foremen, and a few belonging to the more responsible trading element of Sundown. Niland and Steele and Steers were sitting together, and as Denver took a seat beside them Niland bent a rather ironic glance at him. "The vested interests of this county," he whispered cynically, "are on their ears. Bet you ten dollars Langdell mentions the sacred rights of the Constitution and the sanctity of property." Dave Denver nodded and swept the assembled men gravely. They were not talking much; they were sitting rather stiffly upright, jaws set and arms folded. This was the attitude of people who already had settled their minds and arrived at conclusions. Denver knew that no matter what argument developed and no matter what minority opposition rose, the Association would come to but one decision. That thought caused him to frown stubbornly. It was a part of his lonely, rebellious nature to despise mass action. He hated the manner in which the big cattlemen had so cannily and insistently pressed their will on the rank and file, had brought pressure to bear upon the smaller owners, had circulated rumors and hair-raising tales about outlawry until the whole region, from Sky Peak to the Rim and from Ysabel Flats to the Mogul Hills was astir with fear and excitement. His dominant individualism detested all this, and he stared unfavorably at Colonel Fear Langdell as the latter rose on the stage and lifted a rather imperious hand.

"This being a special meeting of the Association," said Langdell in a cold clipped voice, "I suggest we dispense with roll call and minutes."

The motion was put and passed. Al Niland moved restlessly and grunted. He had crossed swords with Langdell, also a lawyer, in court many times, and he had little love for the man. Langdell, involved in all kinds of land deals and commercial enterprises, never failed to represent the close conservatism of the county and seldom let an opportunity pass to call Niland a firebrand. Standing on the stage, stiff and spare and confident, Langdell turned his sharp, shrewd face around the hall to build up an expectant silence. Into this silence he placed his words like sharp javelins.

"Perhaps as presiding officer I ought not assume the right of expressing the purpose of this meeting. But I feel we are all conscious that the sense of the meeting is to come immediately to one question and settle it for once and all. And I shall take the liberty of saying that question is — what are we going to do about the damnable and increasingly arrogant banditry of the crooked elements that infest Yellow Hill County? For two years we have sat still and let outlawry grow under the false sentiment that every man is entitled to his fling before settlin' down. I say false sentiment because those kind of men never settle down. Property is property whether fixed in a building or moving on hoof. The owner's right is absolute and never should be violated. What is the record for the past two years? Four men shot down, approximately a thousand head of stock lost, banditry organized, and every trail and stage road in the county made unsafe for peaceable riders. There have been three stage hold-ups and one driver murdered because he had the guts to resist, and I say we ought to build a monument to that kind of a fellow. Instead of that, what do we do? We catch a few isolated rustlers, a sentimental jury tries them and lets them out to rustle again. Well, what are we going to do about it?"

"He forgot the Constitution," whispered

41

Niland humorously. Cal Steele slumped in his seat with closed eyes and a faint boredom on his face. Fleabite Wilgus, enormously wealthy operator of the Gate ranch, was on his feet and talking in a whining voice few could hear. Threadbare and dirty, he appeared to worse advantage than the most shiftless rider around Sundown. One of his phrases reached through the room.

"I'm a kindly man, as everybody knows. But if I had my way I'd give no shrift to a caught rustler, and I wouldn't waste the time of bringin' him to jail. That's me."

Steve Steers leaned indignantly forward and muttered. "Kindly, is he? Say, I worked on his spread a week and I wouldn't repeat for all the money on God's footstool. Actually, he counted out the sugar for the table and fired one cook for cookin' three slices extra bacon."

"My boy," said Niland sardonically, "you don't understand the humble duty of a wealthy man toward his wealth. It's a sacred trust."

Leverage was up and wasting no words. Everybody liked Leverage and listened carefully. "When I was twenty years younger in this country we didn't have any law, and we did have a pack of trouble makers. There was just one way of gettin' at the solution, which was rope and gun. I'm frank to say I didn't much like it, for some fairly good men got strung up with the bad ones, and I was mighty glad to see the legal way come to Yellow Hill. I still prefer the legal way — when it works. But it don't seem to be workin' very good now, and it hasn't for some time. I cast no reflections on judges or law officers, but I'm frank to say there always seems to be one man on a jury who'll hang it and I've got my own private opinions as to how that occurs. So, since influences outside the law get around justice, my belief is that influences outside the law must bring justice back. In case that ain't plain enough, I mean vigilantes!"

There was a sharp and instant applause. Somebody yelled, "And hangin' on the spot of capture!"

Leverage looked thoughtful. "I suppose so. I dislike takin' life thataway. But one or two heavy doses of medicine will go a long way toward doin' away with the necessity of a ridin' committee. After that, let us confine our job to catchin' and provin' a rustler guilty, and let the court pronounce sentence."

Fee, of the Flying F spoke briefly. Short-ridge, another large owner, was just as brief but a great deal more vehement. Then there was a lull in which Fear Langdell waited for further war talk. Denver realized that Lang-dell expected some fighting speech that would weld everybody together and actually put the vigilante proposal into enthusiastic commission. Leverage, by his slight touch of reasonable hesitancy, had just missed setting off the spark, and the increasing delay served somehow to dampen the meeting. Langdell looked about to find the proper man. His eyes lighted on Denver.

"Dave, you've been silent a long while. Get up and say your mind."

"I'm listenin'," drawled Denver.

"Let others do the listenin'," countered Langdell impatiently. "We expect you to talk."

Denver rose, feeling the eyes of his three partners boring into him curiously. Niland had turned nervous, and Steve Steers hitched forward; but Cal Steele had a queerly set cast to his cheeks and had dropped his pose of sleepiness.

"Maybe you expect me to talk," stated Denver coolly, "but you can't expect me to follow the piper. I'm not built that way. Granting most of your bear talk to be true, and granting the necessity for fighting back, I'm sorry to say I can't see this vigilante stuff and won't be a party to it."

"Why not?" snapped Langdell angrily.

"If a man rustled me," went on Dave, "I'd personally go out and hunt him, and I'd per-

44

sonally settle the account. I wouldn't ask anybody else to do it. I wouldn't shove such a chore on the shoulders of a whole community. I wouldn't ask another man to be my catspaw, and I'm damned if I'll be catspaw for a few men who are well able to keep their own range clean."

"Afraid of lead, uh?" demanded Langdell sarcastically.

"You know my record better," said Dave softly, "and I take exception to the remark. Are you willing to stand accountable for it, Colonel Langdell?"

The drawling question fell flatly across the utter silence. Rather abruptly Langdell made amends. "I did not mean that personally, Denver. But you make a mistake. This is not a one-man affair. The whole country is interested."

"I'm not. None of my beef's been borrowed. For that matter, nobody within ten miles of Sundown's been bothered. The night ridin' so far is all across Sky Peak. Why don't the gentlemen yonder do their own hangin'? I say I don't understand all the steam and smoke certain parties have been throwin' out lately. This vigilante business is too dangerous. Ridin' committees never know when to quit, and they don't always use good judgment. I'll admit the stage robberies hit nearer home —

but that is distinctly a matter for the sheriff. And if the present one doesn't work, why not get another? That's also a matter that gets me to wonderin'."

A voice from the back of the room boomed out. "By God, I don't know as I'll accept them remarks, Denver!"

It was the sheriff, Magnus Ortez. Denver turned to him. "You're a public official and open to public discussion, Ortez. And I never make a remark I'm not willing to stand by."

He had touched off the long-suppressed anger of the aggrieved ranchers and the war-like ones. The opera house began to sing with the rising clamor. Here and there Denver saw men who sat still and refused to join, but he felt he had played into Langdell's hand unconsciously, had served as a whip. Langdell was tightly triumphant and shouted another question:

"You believe in coddlin' these outlaws, uh? You believe in lettin' crookedness get by?"

"I believe in mindin' my own business until other people won't let me. I run my affairs. Let others do the same. As for crooks, that's an open question. Quite a few very respectable citizens in the West made their strictly honest fortune out of a half-dozen stray cattle. I don't consider myself any fit judge of honesty. Put up a million dollars for the man able to take it — and who will be so damned honest then? You wanted to hear me talk — and you got your wish."

"I move," shouted a voice, "we establish a vigilante committee and name a leader who is to choose his own men, work in his own way, and receive our full sanction and support!"

"Second!"

"Vote it!"

They rose to vote. Denver and his three partners kept their seats: Steers a little awkward but absolutely loyal to Denver; Niland contemptuous of the whole affair; Cal Steele with his eyes closed and his face entirely passive. Niland muttered, "They are as crazy as loons!"

"Passed!" shouted Langdell. "And I make this motion, even if it is not my place to do so! I move Jake Leverage to be ridin' boss of the vigilantes with absolute authority and all our resources to call on!"

"Vote it!"

Leverage's voice rose futilely against the rising tumult. The Association, with at last a course of aggressiveness suggested, let itself go.

"Stampede!" whooped Niland, grinning.

"Everything said about outlaws here to-day is right," muttered Denver, "but there's something rotten about it, and I can't seem to get straightened out. All I know is I'll be no party to it."

Cal Steele opened his eyes and said briefly, "You're right, Dave."

"I do what you boys do," affirmed Steers. "All the same to me."

The clamor subsided. Leverage was on his feet. "I didn't ask for this," he said. "I don't like the responsibility, either. But I'm not the kind to bellyache and then lay down when my hand's called. All I want to say is I'll go through to the best of my ability, and I'll gather my men. I want your support. And I don't want any of you fellows to be unfriendly with me, even if you don't approve my course. I'll be as fair as I can."

"As fair as the pack will let him be," muttered Denver, and turned out of the hall. "I hate to see old Jake Leverage the goat," he told the others when they came abreast of him.

An elderly man hurried up and spoke quietly to Denver. "I'd of gone in if you had," said he. "But you changed my mind, as well as a few others. So just remember, you've got support."

"Thanks," said Denver and studied the street.

Stinger Dann still stood under the Palace gallery, sullen and indifferent. The sight of

48

him roused Denver's thoughts to a different angle, and he began to look more carefully about him. There was a strange rider loitering by the blacksmith shop, and another man he knew only by reputation posted at Grogan's. The arrangement of the three drew his brows together.

"I think it's time for a drink," suggested Niland.

Cal Steele roused himself from his distrait moodiness. "Any time's time for a drink."

Meems and Wango were conferring earnestly at the entrance to Grogan's, and Meems winked heavily at Denver. "It ain't possible, it ain't even natural, but the fact remains, nev'less."

"All right," agreed Denver, "I'll bite. What is it?"

"That Englishman's got a name that's the original stem-winder of all monickers I ever heard. It takes two to git a bit on it. Ready, Pete?"

"Ahuh, shoot!"

Meems drew a deep breath. "Almaric —"

"St. Jennifer —" lisped Wango in turn.

"Crevecœur —"

"Nightingale!"

Cal Steele repeated it rather gently to himself. "Almaric St. Jennifer Crevecœur Nightingale. His father and mother loved him.

Where'd you find out, Buck?"

"It's on the hotel register," asseverated Meems. "Took two lines to get it all in."

"I think," crooned Cal Steele, "we shall have to conduct a surgical operation on that name and get it down to homely Western proportions. He may stay with us awhile, and I doubt if Sundown could clamp its jaws around the original." He closed his eyes a moment, smiling faintly. "Yes, indeed. The inevitable contraction would be — Jenny's Nighty."

The group howled. Denver chuckled and looked up at the mention of his name. Dr. Williamson drew alongside the walk with his buckboard. "Dave, you going toward your ranch pretty soon?"

"I thought I might stay over here to-night," replied Denver. "But if there's anything you want just ask it."

The doctor, weathered and lined with the years of his service, took a decent chew of tobacco. "Well, one of Fee's riders was coming along Copperhead River and saw old man Jesson across the stream. Jesson spelled 'doctor' in the air with his hands, the river makin' too much noise to hear a thing. So the rider came right to me. I calculate it's Jesson's wife needing me. It's about time. Copperhead's pretty high, and I might not be able to ford it, but I don't want to waste time by taking the twenty-mile detour to the bridge. If I could get some help I might —"

"Right with you," said Denver, and motioned for Steve Steers. "Let's sift. We'll be back in time for the show."

Together they crossed to the stable for their horses and then followed Doc Williamson down Prairie Street to the rolling ridges beyond. Denver looked back once. Stinger Dann was staring at him. The two others — those Denver had noticed stationed by the stable and Grogan's — were drifting toward the gunman. Some sort of signal passed between the three. Then they disappeared into the Palace.

"Layin' for somebody," mused Denver. His jaws hardened. "Possibly me. They shall have their chance to-night."

CHAPTER III
THE ROARING COPPERHEAD

Prairie Street emerged from Sundown and became the Ysabel Junction stage road winding south to the steel ribbon that made a dividing line between the rolling contours of Yellow Hill County and the open immensity of the lower prairies. Also in that direction, leagues ahead, was the state capital; Sundowners occasionally visited the capital and came back with the feeling they had been on a long journey, such being the isolation of the land. The stage road, already turning to powdered dust from the early spring sunshine, had not been fashioned by men who cared much for easy grades; it went straightaway up the slopes and coasted directly down into the numerous little valleys. Where so bold an attack was impossible, it zigzagged weirdly along cliff faces or shot around high rock points. But always it took the short way in preference to the easy one, a matter-of-fact reminder that here horses were cheaper than time.

Dr. Williamson knew his country very well after thirty years of practice in it. Sitting taciturnly in the buggy seat, coat tails flapping, he put the team to a stiff trot and covered the distance. About five miles from town he abandoned the stage road for a stock trail that wavered up along the backbone of a pine-studded ridge; this threatened to peter out presently, but the good doctor only took another morsel of tobacco and drove ahead. A windfall lay across the way; he looked sharply to either side for an alternative trail and, failing to find it, whipped the horses over the obstruction, buggy springing violently. Ahead was a steep climb. Without comment Denver spurred beside the rig, shook his loop over an angle iron on the dashboard, and towed the vehicle to the crest. From this eminence many small valleys and holes were to be seen puckered between the rising ridges. Cattle grazed along the lush areas, a line cabin stood here and there, and far below a patch of river surface flashed in the afternoon sun. There was no distinct trail downward, but the trees were thin and the ground open. Denver dropped back, rope still holding the buggy, to act as a drag, and the doctor drove down with a sort of reckless wisdom, choosing his openings on the run, vehicle teetering and hubs scraping against tree trunks. Presently a road shot around the hill, and the doctor took it. Denver cast off; the party set ahead on the run. Copperhead River and Copperhead Valley lay below, and in five more minutes of headlong driving Dr. Williamson drew up to the very margin of the water and stepped stiffly down. Across the river was a cabin, and out on the bank a man moved back and forth, wringing his hands. "It's Miz Jesson, all right," grunted the doctor. "I told her a month ago she ought to move into Sundown for this event."

"River's a little wild," said Denver dubiously.

"So the Fee man told me," observed Williamson. "But the detour's too long. I'd be too late. There's a baby bein' born yonder, and we got to cross."

"That's different," was Denver's laconic reply. He ran his eyes along the turbulent stream. Normally this particular spot was a safe and shallow ford with sloping sandy sides. To-day the Copperhead, swollen by rain and melting snow, came charging out of its upper gorges and threw itself turbulently across what once had been a slack area. Even as they watched, the teeth of the current bit out vast chunks of the bank and swept them down. Jesson was apparently shouting at the top of his voice and making no impression against the sheering, crackling sound of the current.

"Damned if I see how it's any different,"

was Steve Steers's gloomy thought. "It ain't fordable."

Denver's attention stopped at a cottonwood beside him. "If we could tie a rope to one of the upper branches of that tree — and get the rope yonder — you might be able to slide to Jesson monkey fashion, Doc."

"Try it," said Williamson. "I carry fifty foot of rope in the buggy."

Steve Steers got that piece and joined it to his own rope. Denver made another tie with his. "That's about a hundred and fifty feet to operate on."

"Why anchor this end clear up the tree?" questioned Steve. "More solid down at the base."

"Got to keep it out of the water," said Denver. "Once the current catches the bight of this line it'll jerk the eye teeth out of the man that tries to hold it. Shin up."

Steve took an end of the combined rope, shinnied halfway up the cottonwood, and made it stoutly secure. Denver, meanwhile, had advanced to the water's edge and was coiling part of the free end for a throw. Jesson waved his hands and stepped a few feet into the river. Denver swung the loop mightily and let go. Jesson jumped, but the line fell short and was whipped downstream. Denver swore softly, wading farther from shore while Steve hauled the rope back and handed it out to his partner. The lash of the current curled around Denver's hips, and he rocked with the impact. Jesson had advanced as far as he dared. Once again Denver put his whole strength into the cast — and knew that he had failed. Jesson stumbled and clawed for dry ground, shaking his head like a crazy man. Steve hauled in the dripping rope and said nothing. Denver got back to shore and stared across to the cabin so near and still so unattainable. Misery lived in that cabin; life flickered while the iron claw of nature pressed destructively down. Once again Denver found himself fighting against the primal, brute forces of the land as he had been doing all the years, and once again the black temper of the man came whipping across his face, and his violet eyes flared with the morose desire to check and defeat that overwhelming, inevitable power under the shadow of which all men walked. Burning sun, blizzard, miring mud, snow-choked trails, thirst, starvation — he had fought these things doggedly, and now he found the same grim, impersonal enemy in front of him again, shaped as a swollen river.

He swung up to his saddle and reached for the coil of rope. "I'll try a little farther out," he told Steve.

"We're not gettin' much of anywhere. It's

too long a toss."

A rider came loping down the road, followed a short cut, and advanced on the group. Steve muttered something under his breath, but Denver nodded gravely. The newcomer was slim, willowy; a black hat shaded a dark, triangular face — rather expressive face with sleepy, watchful eyes. Those eyes took in the scene, detail by detail. A pleasant voice drawled.

"Howdy, boys. What's the caper?"

"River to cross, Lou," said Denver and pushed his horse into the stream. The animal bunched and halted. Denver set his spurs and forced it on until the curling surface rose to the beast's belly. Jesson was posted again. Denver canted his body to get a long sweep into his throw, shot the rope high and swift, and felt his mount lose footing. There was nothing to do but let the animal have free head; it had been overbalanced by the current and, fighting for a hold on the slippery gravel, it swung and slowly slid down the stream. The current lifted it bodily, and then, in the space of a moment, man and horse were so much helpless drift in the angry flood.

"Easy now," muttered Denver and put a little pressure into one knee. The horse responded, pointing its head toward the sliding shore. Steve was racing abreast; the newcomer shot past, shaking out his rope. Denver lifted one arm as a target for that throw, but at the same instant a contrary boil of the river shunted his mount circularly toward the bank. Denver felt the pony strike bottom, slide, and get a surer grip. Cautiously he worked out of it and reached land. The newcomer shook his head.

"Bad situation."

"Listen," grunted Steve, "use yore head. Once yuh get beyond depth yuh might as well sing a hymn. We got to dope another way of crossin' this drink."

"I'd offer to take a throw," put in the newcomer, "but if you can't reach it I can't do any better."

"Comin' from you, Lou," remarked Denver, "that's handsome."

"Just so. I hate to admit any man's better than me."

Denver rode back to the cottonwood and signaled Jesson. By considerable wigwagging he conveyed the idea he wanted Jesson to saddle a horse and bring it to the river; Jesson nodded and ran back behind the cabin. Denver dismounted, removing his own saddle.

"Now what?" asked Steve.

"Got another idea. I almost made that throw. Another five feet and the thing's done."

"Yeah?" was Steve's skeptical reply. "Another five feet and yore sunk. Don't consider it."

Denver studied the river. "There's an offsetting current right above us. If a man rode into it he'd be carried out a considerable distance — close enough to make a sure toss of the rope."

Steve stared at his partner. The newcomer rode away to inspect the possibilities. Steve cleared his throat. "Tell you what, Dave. Yore throwin' arm is some weary. Supposin' I do the water-walkin' act yuh got in mind."

"You climb up in that cottonwood and keep an eye on the rope."

The newcomer rode back. "It'll carry you down the river pretty fast, Dave."

"I suppose so."

"Well, I'll ride along the bank with a loop shook out."

"Obliged, Lou," said Denver and rode bareback to the spot he intended embarking from. Steve paid out the line to him, and then both he and the newcomer placed themselves in a position to hold it from the water. Jesson rode hurriedly down from the cabin. Denver signaled his purpose, and Jesson pantomimed his understanding. He made his horse breast into the current and turned it broadside to Denver, lifting both hands above his head.

Denver built his loop, at the same time holding the shore end as high as he could. Steve and the newcomer watched him with fixed attention; Williamson's leather cheeks were gravely clamped around a section of tobacco. Denver eased the horse into the water and made it go straight forward until its belly touched. Immediately the pressure of the current shot the beast beyond footing and Denver, gripping with his knees, began to swing the loop. The far shore shot past with queer rapidity, the pony began to roll, and the man knew that when he made his last throw he would be too far off balance ever to recover. Jesson's upraised arm came abreast, the loop went like a bullet; Denver, plunging into the stream to keep from dragging against the bight, saw Jesson catch and snub the loop in frenzied haste. Then Denver went down like a rock with a roar and a rumble in his ears.

When he came up, strangling out water, he saw his horse's head bobbing in the distance. He saw, too, a blurred and panoramic strip of shore and Lou Redmain spurring along it. After that some resurgent wave slapped him in the face, upset his coolness, and sent him down; and all he knew was that his arms and feet were struggling aimlessly against the smother of the river. He broke the surface a second time and fought to maintain himself, no longer finding the shore. White spearheads reared jaggedly, his breath was shut off. Something struck him on the temple; instinctively he hooked an arm above his head, feeling a counter current pressing him back. He thought Redmain had missed, and he made the attempt to clear his head and at least coast on the surface; but the same counter current that had stopped him now rolled him over, and he descended into the queer night of drowning. And it was with a very dim consciousness that he felt a tightening around his body and a stiff pressure. Purely by reflex he wound his arms about the rope; and so was hauled ashore.

He was not out, but Williamson had him straddled and was pressing the water of the Copperhead from his lungs. Presently the hunger for air left, and he drew a full breath. Williamson stood up. "All right, Dave. You did your job, now I'll do mine."

"Think you can wangle acrost on that rope, Doc?" Steve Steers wanted to know.

"I'm seventy years old," stated Williamson, "and I've done everything but the tight-rope act. I guess I'm not too old to do that. But I'm damned if I'll come back the same way. I'll ride one of Jesson's horses around by the bridge. Dave, you take my team and buggy to your place, and I'll pick it up later."

61

While talking he had somehow lashed his pill bag to his chest. Getting on his feet, Denver looked across the river. Jesson had backed his horse from the water and, by paying out the rope, had swung to a higher section of the shore. Thus, if the tension was maintained, Williamson could cross dry. The doctor climbed in front of Lou Redmain; the latter rode out into the river underneath the rope. Williamson stood up, grasped the rope and swung clear, feet and arms wrapped around it.

"I bet," said Steve Steers nervously, "he wishes he was closer to his monkey ancestors."

Williamson, swinging beneath the rope, moved rapidly and by degrees reached midstream. At this point the line let him down until his pendant coat tails skipped on the surface of the racing Copperhead. Jesson, keeping the far end snubbed around his saddle horn, apparently did not dare to place too great a strain on the rope; and he seemed to have some little trouble in holding his horse steady. Williamson halted, advanced a few feet beyond the middle point, and seemed to tire. So he stopped again while the three watchers on the west shore stood profoundly silent. Then the doctor crawled on, foot at a time, passed the most dangerous spot and elected to drop down in the shallow edge of the river rather than haul himself all the way to the high bank. He waded ashore and without stopping ran into the cabin.

Lou Redmain reached for his cigarette papers, casting a short, bright glance at Denver. "Doc," he muttered, "is all right."

"They ought to name the kid after him," stated Steve solemnly.

Denver chuckled. "Half the kids in Yellow Hill are named after him already."

"What is his first name, anyhow?" asked Steve.

"Stephen Burt Williamson."

"What?" exclaimed Steve. "Hell, them names is my names!"

"Sure," agreed Denver. "And the doc brought you into this vale of tears, likewise."

"I be damned!"

Jesson cast off the rope, and it snaked into the current. Steve hauled it in. Jesson was pointing toward the south, on his own side of the river, and Denver, looking in that direction, found his horse grazing a half mile down. Jesson made some more Indian talk and rode after the pony. "I'd figured it was fifty-fifty with that brute," mused Denver. Lou Redmain idled, giving Denver an opportunity to drawl his thanks. "I'm obliged. When your loop hit me I'd took in about all the liquid I was able to stand."

63

"Always glad to give you a hand," said Redmain politely. "Or Williamson."

Steve wandered off to the buggy. Denver watched Redmain's face when he put his sudden question. "Not tryin' to pry into your affairs, Lou, but Stinger Dann's in Sundown this afternoon."

"Perhaps," replied Redmain enigmatically, "I sent him there. Or perhaps he went of his own accord."

"He seems to be nursin' a grudge," went on Denver.

"I never knew him to be without one," said Redmain, lip curling.

"I was just wondering," drawled Denver, "if he happened to be pointed my way."

"I haven't put him on your trail," Redmain was quick to answer.

"That's all I wanted to know."

But Redmain pressed the point. "I've got no reason or desire to cause you trouble, Dave. And if that damned fool is figurin' to get on the prod I'll yank him back into the bushes."

"Let him have his fun," said Denver soberly. "He always has considered me to be his brand of poison, and it'd be just as well to let him try his hand. I don't like to watch men circle around me."

"He'll make no play against you," stated Redmain flatly. "In the first place, he's got to do what I tell him. In the second place, he's useful to me and I don't want him shot up."

"Yeah," mused Denver, "I always felt you regarded him as a right bower."

Redmain gathered his reins. "Got to be traveling. By the way, is that opera outfit in town?"

"Lola's there," said Denver quietly, "which is what you wanted to know."

For a moment a dark, wild flash of emotion flamed in Redmain's eyes, and the narrow face became taut and pale around the nostrils: here was a killer, a man without compassion or conscience emerging swiftly from a deceptive shell of manners. But with equal swiftness Redmain recovered himself and stared inscrutably down at Denver. Then he whirled and raced away from the river, pony hoofs making a rapid tattoo over the ground. Steve had mounted. Denver threw his saddle into the buggy, took the seat, and started off. Together the partners angled into the higher land. Purple crusted shadows folded about the ridges; the team's clatter rang far along the still ravines. Night settled down, bringing with it the pervading loneliness and mystery of a country yet untamed.

This was a busy season of the year, but Denver earlier in the day had given the crew leave to hit Sundown for the show and its pursuant revelry. So when he drew into the long avenue of poplars and came by the bunkhouse he found a strangely unnatural stillness pervading home quarters. The crew had eaten beforehand and departed, leaving behind only those recluse spirits who seemed to enjoy solitude. One of these stopped his fiddle in the dead center of a weird harmony and came out to take over the team. Lights winked from the main-house, water bubbled melodiously from a spring pipe, and the spiced scent of the hills swirled across the yard. Denver left an order with the hand.

"My saddle's back of the buggy. Slap it on that gray gelding, Shad."

Going to the house, Denver and Steve ate a quick snack; then Steve stretched himself in a front-room chair while Denver shaved and changed clothes. Rather facetiously the sandy-haired puncher hailed the transformation.

"Doggone it, Dave, yore beginnin' to drift out of my class. When a man barbecues his whiskers every day he ain't common folks no more."

"Fellow ought to show a clean face at the opera house, shouldn't he? You going?"

"Well, I'm driftin' back to Sundown,"

opined Steve, "but I ain't goin' to the show. Not by a jugful. Debbie would raise a ruckus if she heard."

Denver chuckled over a cigarette. "For an engaged man you sure take life serious. Why not wait until you get married before assumin' this pallbearin' atmosphere?"

Steve's lazy, quizzical features were puckered solemnly. "You don't know nothin' about it. When a man's married he knows where he stands. The judge has thrown the book at him, the knot's tied, and there ain't any question about it. Which I mean when a fellow's married he's plumb arrived somewhere. But this engagement business, what is it, anyhow? You ain't one thing and you ain't another. One minute yore hot as hell, and the next minute yore cold all over. You dunno what to say, what to do, or how to act. Dave, it's awful."

"When's the ceremony going to be?"

"Hah!" snorted the perplexed Steve. "There's another item. How in hell do I know? Listen, you got a great experience comin' to yuh, Dave. Before you pop the question yore high card. Nothin's too good. You sit in the best parlor chair, the old man hands out his best cigars, and the lady leans on yore arm as if she couldn't do without yore big, handsome carcass. But afterward — then what? All of a sudden you ain't nothin' but a future husband. The girl gets a far-off cast to her eyes and considers clothes and etiquette and such stuff; the old man considers the expenses and don't pass out no more cigars. The parlor chair's sent back to the attic, and nobody's got time to talk to yuh atall. I don't know nothin' about it. I suppose I'll get a notice some day to appear at such and such a church for the event — and otherwise I'm just hangin' out on a limb waitin' to be sawed down."

Denver spoke rather gently at his partner. "I wouldn't want you to think I was casting any cold water on matrimony, and I think Debbie Lunt's a fine girl. But I recall when you and I used to ride fifty miles to a dance and have a pretty sizable time. Also I recall the occasion when you and I switched all the teams at Fee's barn raisin'. You seem to have lost some starch lately, Steve."

"I ain't had an idea of my own since I proposed," reflected Steve, weltering in gloom. "I thought that was sure a bright idea at the time. I ain't so sure any more."

"Then why get married?" grunted Denver.

"Well, I figgers it out this way. How will life be thirty years from now with Debbie? Terrible — awful. I shudders to think of it. A bath every week, no smokin' in the house, no liquor, no poker, no roamin'. No nothin'. It'll be, come here, Steve, and go there, Steve, and, Steve, mind the mud on yore shoes. Likewise, Steve, put a muffler on yore neck against the cold and, Steve, dear, I will take care of yore month's pay, so shell it over and don't bat them eyes on me like that. Oh, my Gawd!"

"If that's the way you feel," stated Denver, "why not bunch the proposition?"

"Well," sighed Steve, "I figgers that thisaway. How will life be thirty years from now if I ain't got her? Hell, Dave, there ain't any other woman who wants me. I'd be a single galoot. Batchin' in a shanty full of holes. Mendin' my own socks and cookin' my own beans. Nobody to talk to and nobody who gives a damn what happens to me. Bein' old and useless without a fambly is shore a sorrowful thing. So I considers. I shudders to think of bein' married to Debbie and I shudders to consider I'll lose her. Upon mature reflection I calculate I shudder hardest when I think of losin' her. Therefore, marriage is the ticket."

"Ought to be glad you got it fought to a standstill," offered Denver dryly.

"Yeah," muttered Steve and stared across the room. There was an enormous lack of enthusiasm in his answer, a kind of mortal weariness. "Oh, yeah. Uhuh."

69

"Let's go," said Denver, leading out. They got their horses and turned back on the trail. Beyond the poplars Denver stopped. "Listen, I sort of want to get a little information for my own personal use. Let's split here. You take the short way into town. I'll go round by the toe of Starlight."

Steve Steers was alert. "Lookin' for anybody in particular?"

"No, but I'd like to know if the population of Yellow Hill County is shiftin' across the Copperhead to-night. Stinger Dann has sort of put a bug in my bonnet."

"It's an idea," mused Steve, "and might bear fruit."

"Said fruit, if any, is for our own nourishment exclusively," warned Dave.

"I heard yuh the first time," stated Steve. "Let's slope. And better hurry, or yuh won't get to show that shave."

He spurred on down the trail. Denver cut around his ranch quarters, ascended a stiff pathway, and plunged into the sudden gloom of a pine belt. The lights from D Slash winked and were cut off; the pines spread away before an upland meadow swimming with fog, and this tilted into a narrow ravine that struck straight for leveler land to the south. Denver, with a comparatively free trail in front, urged a more rapid pace.

As he traveled he reviewed the affair at Copperhead crossing. Ever since that remote boyhood day when he became conscious for the first time that the placid world held a thousand threats he had been fighting savagely against the dominant elements. His whole life had been fashioned and tempered by these struggles and so now in manhood David Denver looked on the wild forces of nature as a pagan would, endowing these forces almost with living personalities. He had been fighting them too long to regard them any other way. Thus he felt a grim sort of satisfaction in knowing that he had whipped the river and won another engagement in that everlasting skirmish with the earth. Yet when he considered that but for the swift accuracy of Lou Redmain's lariat he would now be nothing more than a bit of senseless rubbish rolling along the turbid stream, all the rebellious instincts in him rose up, and he scowled at the night.

"No man can survive a thousand chances," he thought to himself, "and I've taken a great many already. Some day this country will get me. Like it got my dad. Like it's got others. I reckon I'll always be battling, and one of these times my foot is going to slip. When that happens I'm gone."

But he knew he would never quit, never fail to throw his strength into the contest.

71

He galloped down the incline with a slumbering shoulder of Starlight Canyon on his left. The stage road came sweeping past, and he turned into it, the gray gelding stretching out to a long free gallop. Below and beyond the prairie lay like a calm ocean, surface overlain with the misting fog. There was a moon somewhere above, but its pale light refracting against the heaving banks of atmosphere made only a shimmering corona that revealed nothing. The thick air cut through his shirt, and all the dampened incense of the countryside slid sluggishly across the highway. A coyote barked, and away below the road the bell of some homesteader's milk cow tinkled. Unconsciously Dave Denver's mood softened under the spell of a world fermenting with new life.

He crossed an open bridge, the boom of his pony's shod hoofs echoing away. Down a long and level grade he traveled, and up another rise. At the throat of some dim gully he stopped, dismounted, and applied a match to the wet side trail. But it was blank of riding signs, and he went on; past Dead Axle Hill, along the hairpin descent into Sundown Valley, and beside the foreboding wall of Shoshone Dome. Somewhere in the distance he caught the tremor of hasting riders; instantly he left the road and paused in a black crevice of the dome. The sound swelled out of the western side of the valley and suddenly dropped off.

"Comin' through the soft meadow stretch," he decided.

Presently the party achieved the sharper underfooting of the road and swept forward. Denver leaned over and placed his hand across the gelding's muzzle. Shadow and shadow flashed by, a bare twenty feet removed; silent shadows riding two abreast and swaying with the speed of their passage. Fire glinted from a flailing hoof, and then these nocturnal birds of passage had melted into the distance, and the reverberation was absorbed by the vast night. Denver regained the road.

"They started from the Wells," he reflected, "not from Sundown. And they're hell-bent for somewhere, as they usually are. My guess was wrong. Redmain's already pulled them out of the Sky Peak country. As always, when lightnin' strikes he's miles away. A wise man if not a good one." So plunged in thought, he let the gelding go and in a half hour picked up the lights of Sundown. Music came from the opera house; the show already had begun. He racked his horse in front of Grogan's and entered to find Steve at the bar.

CHAPTER IV
A GENTLEMAN'S GAME

"Nothin'," said Steve softly.

"I had better luck," was Denver's rejoinder. Grogan himself, an overbearing man with a spurious smile of good humor, came down the bar, and Steve changed the subject.

"Well, go see the show, and what do I care? I'll play poker." Then, remembering this was also one of those pastimes an engaged man should not participate in, he hastily qualified. "I mean I can spend a large evenin' lookin' on."

"It certainly sounds violent," jeered Denver and strolled out. Instead of going directly across the street to the opera house, he mixed rather casually with the tide of aimless punchers and so was carried as far as the hotel porch. He stopped short of the strong light coming out of that hostelry and stepped into the mouth of an alley. A man drifted by, went up the hotel porch and inside. Presently he came out and halted to light his cigarette; by the glow of the match Denver saw puzzlement on the fellow's features.

74

"I thought so," grunted Denver. "Same man that Stinger Dann had posted by the stable this afternoon. Don't know him. Redmain's got a lot of fresh blood in his band lately. Now what is the present idea?"

The man crossed the street quickly and shouldered through the crowd, dropping out of sight somewhere near the Palace. On impulse Denver withdrew into obscurity, made a wide circle of town, and crept through the back lots of the north side. He found himself suddenly arrested by the half-open door of the opera house; Lola Monterey was singing, and her tempestuous, throbbing cadences swept away the years of her absence and brought him back once more to the days when he had watched her dancing in the Palace — a slim, scarlet figure cutting through the smoke haze of the hall. Always, he recalled, there had been in her songs something to remind him life was short and sad; always there was that haunting appeal to stir him profoundly and the direct glance of her dark, glowing eyes to set his own wild blood racing.

Half angry, he drew himself away from the door. "Old times, old ways. She's changed in some ways. She's no longer a hungry little girl, half scared, half savage. She's fought her way up, she's sure and confident — she's a matured woman. But her heart is the same.

Women like her never change that way."

A murmur of sound put all this introspection out of his head. Somewhere in the farther blackness men were talking discreetly, hurriedly. Rising on his toes Denver advanced, skirted the blind wall of the Palace, paused beside the adjoining butcher shop, and slid quietly near the last building in the north line. Below was a harness shop; above was Colonel Fear Langdell's law office, reached by an outside stairway. Boots scuffed against the steps. There was more talk.

". . . how in hell do I know?"

"Yuh ought to."

"Well, I don't. And there's apt to be a bullet in this for somebody."

"Will be if yuh keep on blattin' our location to the wide world. Now go on up there."

"Bad business, I tell you!"

"You do as I say or get out of the country, see? I thought you was tough . . ."

Denver crouched to the ground, grimly amused; one of these nighthawks was shuffling up the stairway toward Langdell's dark office, prodded on by the taut sarcasm of the man below. "If they're tryin' to set a trap for Langdell," he reflected, "they're apt to find hard luck. He's had his eye teeth cut on trick stuff."

The exploring one had arrived at the top

landing. A knob squealed. Silence settled down. Denver grinned in the darkness, and his hand closed around a loose stone the size of a grape. Rising in his tracks he tossed the stone toward the building and dropped to the earth again as it struck and rattled down the stairway, sounding like an avalanche in the utter quiet. The man in Langdell's office ran out, made a clean jump, and hit the ground with a belch of air.

"For Gawd's sake — !"

Both of them were running clumsily off. Denver hurried back to the nearest alley and came out on the street in time to see Stinger Dann go along the sidewalk with a mighty scowl on his face; and a little afterward the man who had followed him to the hotel appeared. Both of them drifted into Grogan's.

"Cheap way of havin' a good time," grunted Denver, trying to fathom Dann's purpose. He walked to the opera house and put his head inside the door, getting the attention of the nearest man in the jammed lobby. "Dell, you seen Langdell in here?"

"Ahuh. Down front somewheres. Want him?"

"No, thanks," said Denver retreating. The more he considered the more he became interested. Stinger Dann was not a man to move without purpose. So thinking, he ambled onward and ran into Jake Leverage, who immediately pulled him out of the crowd.

"Want to see you, Dave."

"I'll lend you money, go on your bail, brand your strays, or furnish character reference for you at the bank," drawled Dave, "but nothing doing as far as this vigilante business is concerned."

"I counted on you," stated Leverage gravely. "If I'm goin' to be useful I've got to have support. You're interested in this."

"I sang my song at the meetin'," returned Dave. "You heard the tune and the words."

"Tell me straight," demanded Leverage, "what's the matter with this business that you won't touch it? Your influence has kept quite a few fellows out of it, and that ain't right."

"I don't like to trail with a herd just to have company," said Dave. "And who do you think you're doing this dirty work for, Jake?"

"For Yellow Hill — for the Association — for me and my family," was Leverage's sober answer.

"And for a bunch of big fellows plenty able to shoulder their own grief," added Dave. "It don't seem right. I hate to see you draw down all the enmity of the wild bunch, which is just what will happen when you hit 'em."

"What's right is right," responded Leverage, somewhat nettled. "I won't back out of trouble."

"Good enough — but the big boys were damned quick to back out of it and let you inherit the grief. No, sir. I'm not buyin' any chips."

"Is that your whole reason?" pressed Leverage.

Denver hesitated and stared toward Grogan's, eyes narrowing down in thought. "No-no, it isn't. But I never make a statement I can't prove, and these other reasons of mine are beyond proof at the present moment. I'll just say I'm not satisfied with the layout. Let it go like that."

"Let me tell you this," remarked Leverage earnestly. "When the scrappin' comes there won't be any neutrals. I foresee that. Black or white is the colors. And don't let your slim hunches maneuver you over to the wrong side. It'll cause you trouble."

"In other words, I'm apt to get hazed down for mindin' my own strict business?" Denver's face darkened. "That happens to be one of the things about mob action I don't like. I'll take care of myself, and I'll see that I am let alone. That applies to the wild bunch, and that applies to any vigilante who tries to make me swap opinions."

"That's exactly what I'm afraid of," exclaimed Leverage. "I have known you since you was a kid. You're as independent as a hog on ice. You don't bend. And I foresee difficulties. I have been through these rustlin' wars before. I know just what happens. Everybody lines up, for or against. And if you stand back somebody's going to suggest you're lined up with the rustlers. Then it's too bad."

"The pack will howl at my heels, is that it?" suggested Denver, rugged face somber and unpleasant.

"I foresee it."

"Then the pack will get a dose of lead," snapped Denver. "I make no distinction between an outlaw who tries to steal my cattle and a red-eyed fanatic who tries to change my mind for me."

Leverage shook his head sadly and turned away. "No hard feelin's, Dave?"

"Not between you and me, Jake. I'm just thinkin' of the buzzards who will go hog-wild and want to shoot everybody on sight."

Leverage moved away. Denver stood still, mastering his temper. Of a sudden the even thread of life had become snarled with knots. Standing aloof he became at once the target of both factions. More than that, he found himself wondering how he should deal with Jake Leverage, who was one of his best friends. He knew things Leverage ought to know for the sake of personal safety. Yet in telling Leverage he became a partisan of the vigilantes. Rather irritably he headed for Grogan's and bought a drink. Through the crowd he saw Steve sitting in at a poker game and went over to find a seat; but the table was full, and so he contented himself with looking on.

It was an odd company. Directly across from Steve was Stinger Dann, who ventured a sullen half glance at Dave Denver and snapped his cards together. Niland and Cal Steele were in the game, and Buck Meems; and the sixth man was the newly arrived Englishman, Almaric St. Jennifer Crevecœur Nightingale, whose ruddy cheeks and sky-blue eyes mirrored a certain puzzlement with the game. Cal Steele, possessing under all circumstances the manners of a gentleman, laid down his hand momentarily.

"You fellows ought to know each other. Nightingale, this is Dave Denver, owner of a spread known as D Slash. Nightingale has bought out the Bucket range from the administrator of old Lindersleeve's estate, Dave."

Nightingale rose slowly and stretched his loose frame to substantial height. The two shook hands. Nightingale's slurred and casual "pleasure'm'sure," seemed lackluster, but his steady, square glance contained something

81

that struck Denver pleasantly.

"Any time you want advice or help," went on Steele, "go to Denver. I pass the information on to you because I understand how a newcomer feels. Was one myself, and I considered it a lucky break to have had Dave to steer me through the early rough spots." Then Steele smiled, fine handsome face lighting. "So if I have taken the easy and evil road it is not because I didn't have sound advice."

"We will now pray," drawled Denver. "You'll have to learn the difference between that man's truthfulness and alleged humore, Nightingale. I see you play our pastime."

Nightingale was dealing and doing it rather awkwardly. "Poker? Well, y'know, I heard it was the thing out here, so I took pains to purchase a book by a fella and read the rudiments. Hoyle — that was the chappie's name. I read his strictures on the game. Seems simple though entertainin'."

Eyebrows drooped around the circle of watchers. "Call it that," grumbled Steve. "I got a different sentiment."

"See you slopped over on your resolution," accused Dave.

Steve thumped the table to indicate he could not open and stared at Denver. "Yeah. Debbie come to town to see the show. How in hell was I to know she was a-goin' to come? She sends for me. I goes. I gets the hide blistered off me for not bein' cleaned up and good clothes on. I asks yuh again, how was I to know? She wouldn't let me take her to the show, wouldn't be seen walkin' beside a dirty son of a gun like me. Cast me to the outer shadders. Ha!"

Niland and Meems likewise passed, though Meems expressed audible grief that he wasn't permitted to open on four good-looking clubs. Steele shook his head; at which Stinger Dann, calculating a pile of ante chips grown healthy by several infertile rounds, shoved out a stiff opener. Nightingale studied his cards for so long a time that Stinger Dann grew heavily sarcastic.

"Didn't Hoyle tell yuh how to read the spots?"

Nightingale was apologetic and entered his chips with the air of a man somewhat flustered. The percentage being rather sweet, all the others took a flyer, and Nightingale slowly thumbed out the draw cards. Niland had been prospecting, and he threw down out of his turn, studying the Englishman with sharp attention as if he were finding angles of the man that intrigued his legal mind. Dann having opened, it was his first bet, and he was about to shove out a stiff one when the Englishman exclaimed plaintively:

"These ruddy sequences and combinations elude one damnably. Let's stop a minute while I get this clear. Purely hypothetical question, y'understand. I have no such hand, but just what relative value do five of the same color and suit possess? Mind, it's purely hypothetical."

Someone in the back of the crowd guffawed, at which Dann bellowed irately: "If some of you damned monkeys don't quit breathin' down my neck I'll bust yuh!" He drew back his tentative bet and snapped at Nightingale. "Supposin' you bet."

"But, I say —"

"The unique situation of which you speak," drawled Denver, deriving considerable pleasure from the scene, "is known as a flush and generally considered easy to look at. Among honest men, such as these present, it tops a straight but not a full house."

Dann's heavy eyes flicked dangerously across Denver's face and settled on the Englishman. He, feeling the weight of both players and spectators upon him, grew plainly flustered. "But I haven't got a flush, gentlemen," he muttered and pushed a bet into the center. Meems instantly laid down with an exaggerated politeness. "I'll just take yore word for it, Nightingale. I won't contribute to no painful knowledge." Cal Steele smiled broadly and likewise threw his cards away. Dann studied the Englishman at length, more and more belligerent. In the end he hurled his cards across the table without so much as showing openers.

"Take the pot, you!" he snapped. "I despise playin' with a beginner that's got fool luck!"

"Do I gather the stakes are mine?" asked Nightingale humbly.

Dann swore brutally and brushed the chips into the Englishman's lap at one violent sweep of his arm. The spectators fell quite silent, some edging off from the table. Nightingale seemed oblivious of the insult. "How odd," he remarked. "I believe you thought I had a flush." And he laid down, face up, five cards of no related poker value at all. Then he reached for his fallen chips.

Cal Steele exploded in laughter. "You'll never work that one again, Nightingale! But it was good acting while it lasted!" And Niland nodded as if some guess he had made to himself was verified. Stinger Dann swore again and reached over to tear Nightingale's discarded hand into fragments. "Damn you, Englishman, don't try to make a fool out of me!"

Denver's suddenly cold rebuke fell into the expectant quiet. "Don't you know better than to haze a stranger, Dann?"

Dann, still seated, thrust his long jaw up

at Denver. "Who asked you to butt into this affair, Mister Denver?"

"I usually act on my own judgment, as you well know," replied Denver coolly, "and I dislike Nightingale to think your poker manners are the manners of Sundown in general."

"Pretty damn proud of yore manners, ain't you?" cried Dann.

"They're better than yours, which is sayin' little enough."

Dann's full cheeks slowly purpled, and his big neck began to swell at the collar. "Maybe you'd like to give me a lesson," he sneered.

"You might not like my price for teachin'," was Denver's level reply. He had never stirred, never moved his fists from their hooked position in his belt. All the sounds of Grogan's saloon had ceased to the uttermost corners of the room; and as if by invisible command the spectators drifted clear of the table, leaving a wide alley down which the two men stared. Those sitting at the table kept their places, very grave. Cal Steele's cheeks slowly drained to pale gray, and he tried to catch Denver's attention.

"When I pay you," shouted Dann, "it will be a long cold day! You know my regards as to you! It's public knowledge and yores for the havin'! Any time yuh want to take exception, just go ahead!"

"My idea exactly," said Denver. "You've been stampin' around Sundown all day tryin' to start something. What it may be I don't know. But I'm tired of havin' to watch you. Takes up too much of my time, and you're not worth it. It's a pretty cheap way of gettin' a reputation for bein' a bad man — this business of standin' on street corners and scowling at peaceful people. If you are pointed my way, I suggest you get up from your chair and start forward."

As quiet as the words were, each one of them fell across the table like the lash of a whip and stung Dann's savage, undisciplined temper. The kick of his foot against his chair shot through the room, and his great body sprang forward. At the same time Cal Steele leaped in front of him, crying, "Stop that!" and Steele's hand plunged down to check Dann's draw. "Stop it! This is no night for gunplay!"

Dann cursed wildly and by a heave of his shoulders threw Steele aside; but the moment of attack was past. Denver's unmoving position somehow took the edge off gunplay, as also did his next drawling suggestion.

"You took a chance, Cal, but maybe you're right. However, we've got to satisfy this amateur bad man before the night's over. Unbuckle your belt, Dann, and I'll do the same. We'll give the boys a treat."

Dann ripped his gun belt free and threw it aside, rolling out from the table into the center of the room. Denver dropped his own belt and moved to meet him. Somebody cried a suggestion that fell on deaf ears. In the flash of a second Stinger Dann yelled, "I'll kill you — I'll break your neck with my fists!" and lunged into Denver. His bare head struck Denver on a shoulder blade, and the sharp impact cracked across the circle; Denver's up-swinging fist smashed into Dann's lowered face, drove it back, and set the gunman on his heels; and in that brief respite Denver saw the common passions of mankind staring at him from all those faces ringed around; savagery glittering out from gluttonous eyes and flaring lips; fear pinching the cheeks of the craven hearted; and the lust and car-nivorous instincts of those who watched their own desires to crush and kill being here played out second hand. Then Dann ran in again, unmercifully beating down Denver's rapier jabs, disregarding them, knocking them aside. He roared. His hot breath belched in Denver's nostrils, and his black face became two great bloodshot eyes. Denver felt his backbone snapping to pressure; a stabbing weight stamped down the arch of his foot; he was backheeled, overbalanced, and he went sprawling through the air and struck the resilient flesh of those onlookers who were baled into so tight a mass. A long rolling pain surged through his body, and he saw blood, his blood, sprinkled on the floor. Dann's brute roar challenged him. His head cleared, and he was up, beating back another relentless rush.

Dann's face was a crimson, dripping disk, and Dann's arms reached again for that bone-crushing grip. Denver stepped aside, pounded at the gunman's face, crashed a blow into the gunman's exposed temple, and swerved to attack again. The temple blow confused Dann, and he stopped to find his opponent, head tipping on the huge muscles of his neck. There was no more for Denver to ask; he had turned tiger, he had unleashed all those wild, primal impulses that stirred in him and were subdued by gentler rules of society. Tonight he was no better than a man of the Stone Age, and through the welter of this conflict the crimson target of Dann's head, the shimmer of pale faces all around, the sharp bursts of pain, the feel of a body giving way — through this his mind ran clearly, sharply, exultantly. If he were no better than a savage, then thank God he was still enough of one to meet savagery and beat it down. Dann had found him uncertainly and lumbered in. Denver heard himself laughing — the sound of it like jagged metals conflicting. He struck aside the groping arms, he pounded the staring face, ripped blows into the swaying body, and sank his fist into a bull neck that rolled away from him and sank down.

Like a man coming out of ether, he stood back to watch Grogan's saloon and all roundabout objects grow clear. The mist fell away; men became something more than blurred outlines, and he was again David Denver instead of a body twisting and swerving under the impulse of a stark, single-celled will. Dann rolled on the floor and shuddered; climbed to his knees and gained his feet. He looked apathetically at Denver, not yet clear headed.

"I said the lesson in manners might cost you something," stated Denver. "My advice is you ride out of town and stay out for awhile."

"It's a mistake I ain't apt to repeat," muttered Dann without emotion. "I never will use my fists on yuh again, Denver. I'll set for you — don't make any mistake on the subject. But it will be with a gun — remember it." Gradually the venom returned to him. "Mebbe I paid a steep price, but, by God, you'll regret this night's work the last day of your life! And on that day I'll show yuh how a white man can rip the livin' heart out of yuh and laugh when he does it!"

"When you ride to-night," said Denver, "take those two strays you been nursin' along with you. They're around somewhere."

The crowd was disturbed by a man shouldering impatiently through. It was Lou Redmain.

"You through with Dann?" he asked Denver. "Had your pleasure with him?"

There was again in Grogan's dropping off of talk, a premonitory chill. Denver nodded somberly. "I'm finished. He's yours."

"Then," said Redmain, pointing a finger at Dann as he would have beckoned a dog, "get out of town within two minutes. And if you ever disobey my orders again I shall shoot you down. Go on, get out." He confronted Denver. "I want you to know this is not my doing. You've got my word on that point."

Dann rolled down the lane made for him and disappeared through the door. Denver, knowing every word of his was witnessed and would be carried far, spoke deliberately.

"Your word is good with me, Lou. When you give it I never doubt it. I have nothing against you now. You are not my kind of a man — you see things considerably different. The day may come when we will have to scrap. Until then consider me as a neutral minding my own business. I expect to mind my own business; I expect others to allow me to mind

91

my own business. If they don't, that will be another story. Supposin' we drink on that?"

"Agreeable," said Redmain. They walked to the bar. Grogan set out the glasses and bottle, and in perfect silence they downed the liquor. A slight flush appeared on Redmain's triangular face as he turned to the crowd. Nodding again at Denver, he walked quickly from the place. Talk sprang up on his departure like air rushing into a vacuum. Nightingale came forward, with Steve Steers and Steele and Niland. The Englishman's bright blue eyes held some reserved, remote expression.

"Thanks," he drawled, "for the timely intervention. Y'know, I gen'rally take care of my own sorrows. Would have done so this evenin', but things moved so blasted fast that I scarcely had puckered my mouth to say something than it was all over. I shall have to be a little — er — quicker on the trigger, as it were. Now, I wonder if the proper move in the circumstances isn't to have a little spirituous stimulant? Not so?"

"Any time's time to drink," observed Cal Steele.

"My judgment is that your poker technique was derived from other sources beside Hoyle," grinned Denver.

"I have played — a game or two," drawled

Nightingale; and it seemed to Denver that somewhere behind those remarkably azure eyes there was a cheerful grin.

"Here's to sin," observed Steve Steers; and so they christened a friendship.

"Do I look bad?" questioned Denver.

"Yore spine may be crooked," said Niland, "but he didn't reach your face at all. However, that shirt will do you no further good. Button up your coat."

"I will do same and depart," agreed Denver. "See you in church."

"Stick around," adjured Steve. "The night's but a pup."

"It'll be a long-haired dog before you drag out of here," said Denver and walked down the hall, stiff from the pounding he had received. Nightingale looked thoughtfully at the rugged back and made a quiet observation.

"A most cur'ous combination of dynamite, the irresist'ble force, nine hungry leopards, and Vesuvius in eruption. I take it he was rather angry with this Stinger Dann. Am I right?"

"That's approximately correct," chuckled Cal Steele.

"I like the beggar," stated Nightingale three drinks later, "and trust the feeling may presently be reciprocated."

"Hold on," broke in Steve Steers coldly. "No man can say that word in my presence. I want you to understand I'm a lady."

Denver walked out to his horse and led it down as far as the hotel, where he discovered the Leverage family gathered. Jake Leverage appealed to him. "I've got to stay over tonight, Dave, and Ma is too tired to go back this evenin'. But Eve figgers she wants to drift home."

"I'm heading that way," said Denver, "and came to offer my company."

"It's three miles out of your way," observed Eve. "I can go alone."

"Would it be the first time I took the long way home with you, Eve?" drawled Denver. The girl blushed and drew up the collar of her coat against the encroaching cold. Mrs. Leverage smiled knowingly. The crowd, released from the show, eddied around them, and there was a general shifting to make room on the porch. Lola Monterey walked swiftly by, smiling through a pale and weary face. Dave lifted his hat. Lola's husky "Good-night, Dave" floated gently over the assembled people; then she was gone. Dave tied his pony to the Leverage buggy and helped Eve to the seat, wrapping the robe about her feet. When he settled beside her and gathered the reins she leaned nearer to him, to speak just above a whisper.

"She's beautiful, David."

"I have always thought so," he replied, and looked more closely at the clear, frank face turned up to him. "So are you, Eve."

"I think," said she, smiling wistfully, "this is going to be the nicest part of the evening."

He turned the buggy in the choked street and drew aside. Dr. Williamson reined in on a borrowed horse, heavy eyed. "It was a boy, Dave, and the Jessons said to thank you."

"Another young Stephen to buck the world, I reckon," mused Dave.

Williamson looked at the pair with solemn approval. "Tuck the robe higher on Eve's throat. It's raw to-night. Don't drive too fast goin' home. It's a fine evenin' — for young people." As he swung away he added another phrase. "No, they named the baby David, which I thought fit and proper."

"The first David named after me," said Denver uncomfortably and maneuvered down Prairie Street. The damp, swirling darkness of the stage road absorbed them. Eve stirred slightly, and he put his arm about her to catch up the robe — and left it there.

"A brotherly interest, David?" asked Eve, softly.

"Sometimes I'm not so sure of that, Eve."

95

"Well, it makes no difference. It helps to keep the cold away."

He thought she was smiling to herself. So in comfortable silence they jogged along.

CHAPTER V
THE EASY EVIL TRAIL

When Lola Monterey climbed the stairs and turned toward her room a slim man in a black hat stepped from the obscurity of the hall's end.

"I wanted to see you, Lola," said he quietly.

The girl stopped with a breath of surprise. "Lou — you come like a ghost."

He drew off his hat, smiling with pleasure. "A ghost out of the past — a not pleasant past?" The dark and triangular face of the man studied her with quick pride. She rested against the wall, eyes half shut, passive. "I had to see you," he went on.

She motioned to her door. "Go in, then. Five minutes, no more."

He shook his head. "I wouldn't do that. It's too late at night."

"You have not changed," she observed gently. "You still protect me."

"You've changed."

"For better or worse?"

"Better for you — worse for me. Once you were Peter Monterey's daughter in a knock-down shack, and I fed you rustled beef to keep that fire in your eyes. Now you are a fine lady and past my help. Maybe you have forgotten."

"Never! Why should I forget? I am not ashamed of my past, Lou. I am proud that this sand nourished me. There is only one thing I'm not proud of."

"What's that?" he asked, sharp and intent.

"For ever leaving. Tell me, is David serious with Eve Leverage?"

Redmain's expressive face darkened. "I wish to God I knew!"

Her luminous eyes widened on him. "So — it is that way with you?"

"It is," was his short answer. "I have wanted that girl since she was out of pigtails. She doesn't know it. Nobody knows it but you, *chiquita*. And you are keeping it to yourself."

"As you once kept my secrets," she promised him, "away back when I was fighting to be a fine and great lady. Ah, Lou, I am sorry for you. But he is not happy."

"Who, Dave? I suppose not. Neither am I, neither are you. Neither is anybody in this world who's got mind enough to see how crooked the whole game is and blood enough to fight back."

"You never have quarreled with him, Lou?" she asked, worry in her eyes.

"Never yet. I like the man as much as it is in me to like anybody, which is sayin' little."

"I never want you to quarrel with him."

He shrugged his shoulders. "Who knows what's to come? Things are pretty badly tangled in Yellow Hill. He and I step around each other politely. How long that continues only God knows."

"You are bitter," she remarked. "What could happen that would make you two have trouble?"

But he laughed shortly and changed the subject. "I had to see you for a minute. One of the few things I look back on with considerable satisfaction, Lola, is that I was a friend of yours and never let you down. Reckon it'll be a long time until —"

"No. I am staying here. This is home for me from now on."

He said nothing for several moments, but his lips tightened as he watched the changing color of her eyes. "I reckon," he said finally, "we are all fools. But what of it? Well, I'll see you again, then. Meantime, don't believe too much you hear about me. Good-night."

"Good-night, Lou."

He went slowly down the stairs to the street. Families and riding outfits were departing, leaving Sundown in the hands of the more reckless spirits; Grogan's was noisy, and the

Palace piano, muted during the show, threw a rakish tune into the semidarkness. The night marshal passed by, cast a quick glance at Redmain, and spoke courteously. "Good-evenin' to you, Redmain."

Redmain nodded, the curve of his lip increasingly sardonic. He reached his horse, swung to the saddle, and went racking down Prairie Street. As the lights of town winked out one by one behind him he lifted his head and laughed bitterly. "By God, life's funny enough to make a man cry. If she stays she'll find out what I've turned into — she'll find out that from a plain harum-scarum fellow I've got to be a crook, a rustler, a leader of outlaws — a renegade with enough reputation to make the night marshal act polite! I'd rather cut off my arm than to have her know it — but she will. Eve Leverage already knows it. Everybody I want to be friends with knows it. So now there ain't a damned soul in the world I can mix with as an ordinary, decent human bein'!"

He swept rapidly along the road, passing slower rigs that were but shapeless outlines in the dark. Drowsy calls were thrown at him but he kept still, both from pride and purpose; for with the coming night he resumed the traits of his trade — secrecy, swiftness, and vigilance. The knowledge he shifted rôles so abruptly added to the kindling fire of his temper.

"Nobody to blame but myself. I chose this business, and I reckon I've prospered. Why have regrets? Why weaken now and fall away from the big prizes? I despise a quitter; I hate a man that will not live up to his talents whether crooked or honest. And if there's no longer a soul in Yellow Hill I can trust or go to for help — then why not throw overboard every damned last scruple I've got and turn wolf? Why not?"

Unconsciously he had shouted that question into the night, and the muffled echo came down the dripping side of Shoshone Dome like the answer of fate. It stiffened him in the saddle as he went racing onward; it roused his gambler's superstitions. These black shadows, within which he spent so much of his life, had replied. It was his dark destiny speaking, it was one clear call in a career of uncertainty. Flashes of realization raced through his agile mind; he was successful and powerful because he had veered from set ways of honesty. He had cut through, he had gone ahead, each step more daring and ruthless and confident. So there was left him only one course — to carry this cold and swift relentlessness of purpose to its ultimate conclusion. Trust no one, bend to no one, never let his heart hold kindness, never let his mind be bound by a promise.

He skimmed through the fog-damp countryside, ran by the toe of Starlight and on into the southern reaches. At a point where the stage road hit a direct and descending line into the open prairie he slackened speed and turned up a lesser trail, winding between the funereal gloom of overshadowing pines. A creek dashed down grade, and the pitch of the trail sharpened. Light flashed covertly at him from a summit cabin; somebody moved in front and challenged softly:

"Who's that?"

"Dann here yet?"

"Waitin' for yuh."

He dismounted, led his horse slightly to one side of the cabin, and went back, entering the place with a swift and sidewise motion that exposed him very briefly to the outer world. Two men sat beside a stove, and a third, Stinger Dann, lolled on the adjacent bunk, holding his swollen head between his hands.

"Next time," said Redmain, "you'll know better."

Dann rose. "Next time I'll kill him!"

"Not while you're in my outfit, Dann. You'll behave. You'll take my orders, and you'll never lift a finger unless I say so."

102

"Then," cried Dann, "I'll pull out of yore damned outfit!"

Redmain's eyes burned into Dann while the trembling moments passed by. Dann's bulk overshadowed him, and Dann's evilly stamped features made the slim chief seem juvenile by comparison. Yet Lou Redmain's will swelled through that cramped cabin room like sun's heat. "You will never leave my outfit, Dann. You threw in with me voluntarily. I made you a partner in this business. You know my secrets. There will never be any getting away for you. You stick."

Dann squared himself defensively. The arrogant, bullying strength in him crumbled before Redmain's superior power. "What yuh tryin' to tell me? I'm a free man! I'm not no damned peon, Lou! I come and I go!"

"Only when I tell you," droned Redmain, and the narrow face moved with anger. "I say you stick or you take the consequences. Make up your mind here and now. I've got a good medicine for herd jumpers like you. Well, what is it to be?"

"I ain't m'self," muttered Dann. "I feel bad, I feel awful. Don't haze me around like that. Can't a man blow off steam once in a while?"

Redmain laughed contemptuously. "I'm glad we have settled it. And I want you to

103

understand this once and for all — never cross Dave Denver, never make a play for him unless I give you orders on the subject. What made you think your draw was as fast as his, anyhow? Why, you fool, he can beat any man's bullet in this country except mine. You'd be dead now if Cal Steele hadn't stopped your play. And what were you doing in Sundown tonight? I didn't tell you to be there."

"Just rode over from the Wells to have a little fun," mumbled Dann, not meeting Redmain's glance.

"You lie," retorted the chief coolly. "You had some nutty idea in your head. Trying to be tough on your own account. If you didn't have my name standing behind you, Dann, somebody would have put a bullet in that clumsy body of yours long ago. I'll tolerate no more foolishness!"

Dann took the lashing in silence; the other two stared at the floor. Redmain turned to one of them impatiently. "The job done, Gus?"

"Yeah," said Gus. "We took twenty cows and calves, run 'em acrost the bridge and stopped near the road. Now what?"

Redmain considered it briefly. "As soon as the travel from Sundown slacks off, put the stuff over the road in a hurry and drive into Tom's Hole. Dann, you go along with the bunch and camp with them. Don't come back to the Wells until I send for you. To-morrow I want the calves branded and the cows blotted. Take your time and do a good job."

"What brand yuh goin' to use this time?"

"Same we've been using lately." Redmain rolled a cigarette, lips compressing. A flare of slight excitement moved across his eyes. "So far, I have played a fifty-fifty game. Half crooked and half honest. It's no good. I'm out for blood. You take one of those cows and switch the brand to Denver's D Slash. Make a bunglin' amateur job of it that anybody could see. To-morrow night drive it into Denver's range and leave it."

"Plantin' somethin' on him, huh?" was Dann's exclamation.

Voices rose outside the cabin. Redmain warned the others. "Keep your mouths shut about this." Then the door opened, and another man entered, smiling sleepily.

It was Cal Steele. "You're late," said Redmain.

"What of it?" drawled Steele. "I might have been still later. I might not have come at all."

"In our business we've got to move fast," grunted Redmain.

"So you ascribe your success in life to the fact you are always punctual," jeered Steele.

"Ten minutes," Redmain reminded him

grimly, "may make the difference of our bein' alive or hung. Don't forget that."

"Is it so important to be alive?" countered Steele wearily. He pointed his finger at Dann and spoke with an angry accent. "As for you, my friend, you nearly got your cursed head beat off, and I wish Dave had finished the job. You'll have to get up earlier to make a sucker out of that boy. What is more, if you had plugged him I would have plugged you. I've said before I won't stand for this crowd monkeyin' with Dave Denver. He is my best friend. Though," and Steele turned morosely unpleasant, "he wouldn't be if he knew what a double-faced misfit I really am."

"So you find friendship begins to sour?" said Redmain.

"A man such as myself deserves no friends," Steele muttered.

"Neither deserves them nor has them," replied Redmain. "I made the same discovery tonight, Cal. So what does that leave us? Why, kick all the fine sentiment overboard and be what we were meant to be."

Steele frowned. "The logical outcome of that belief is published notoriety and sooner or later a posse on our heels. And a cottonwood tree for a springboard."

"They can't beat me. They've got nothing definite on me. Nor on you."

"Nothing is secret forever," murmured Steele. "Public notoriety will do for you or Dann, but I've got enough left in me to need decent friends. Oh, well — what is the situation now?"

"We took some beef to-night. It'll be changed over to your brand to-morrow and be kept hidden until the new burns are healed. Then we'll drive it to your range. Meanwhile I've got about thirty head ready for you now. They've gone through the aging process for two months. To-morrow night I'll have them thrown into your upper range. Better see to it all your riders are elsewhere."

"Be careful about that brand blotting," warned Steele. "I want no slips."

"Gus is an expert," said Redmain. "You couldn't tell the difference with a razor and a microscope. You're safe. Better ship early this year. I need money."

"Whose stuff did you take to-night?"

"Fee's," returned Redmain. "Our last operation over beyond Sky Peak. We're going to work this side durin' the year. That Englishman don't know anything. I'm going to milk him dry."

"Dirty business," grunted Steele. "I like the fellow."

"Something you ought to've thought of a long time ago," retorted Redmain. "No chance to change now. You've got your hands soiled."

"I think I know that better than you do," said Steele and rose to leave. "You've heard about the Association going in for vigilantes with Leverage at the head of 'em?"

Redmain laughed. "He couldn't catch a cold. I'll run him ragged. The poor devil doesn't know —" Then he caught himself. The two men exchanged significant glances. Steele said:

"You're a careful cuss, and you've got brains. Don't overplay your hand."

Redmain closed one fist and spoke with a suppressed exultance. "I am going the limit, Steele!"

"Be careful. And leave Denver strictly alone. I'll string along with you up to that point. Then I draw out. I won't be a party to any doublecross of Dave." Steele went out. Redmain stared at the other men for a long interval.

"Get going, all of you. And keep your mouths shut."

They departed, leaving him alone by the stove, wrapped in his dark thoughts. One by one he explored the alleys of opportunity before him; man by man he considered his outfit, the weak and the strong, the faithful and the treacherous. And from there he began to calculate the power of those ranged against him, his own individual strength set beside that of other individuals and his own outfit matched with the vigilantes. Never before had he let his mind run free as to-night, and never before had he caught so clear a view of the mastery that might be his if he were only bold enough to strike quickly and hard. It flushed him, it fed the latent ambition within him. Out of all this emerged his conclusions. "Denver I shall some day have to meet. Steele will never approve of what I aim to do. He must go down. Soon."

CHAPTER VI
WHISPERING RANGE

Occasionally the women of the district answered the vagrant call of social impulse, and this afternoon a dozen of them were informally gathered together in the shade of the long galleried Leverage porch. The sun, dipping westward, began to desert the emerald ridges but still made a bright yellow glare in the open prairie that rolled away from the foothills into the dazzling distance. It was high time to pack up and go, but the ladies lingered, some reluctant to depart, some waiting for the men folk to come after them.

"Men," stated Mrs. Jim Coldfoot, biting off her thread, "are all the same and none of 'em too good. When I look about Yellow Hill and consider the specimens wearing pants I'm plumb reminded of a rummage counter with all the good cloth already took."

The circle smiled, knowing Mrs. Jim Coldfoot well. Her heart was sound, but her inquisitive mind pried into all things, her ears missed nothing, and her tongue readily dealt in scandal.

"Well," observed a Mrs. Roberts gently, "I dare say some of the poor dears would like to say the same of us."

"They're scared to," observed Mrs. Jim Coldfoot acidly. "All they can do is look humble as pie, and mutter to themselves. Like I've told Coldfoot time and again, if he's got any mutterin' to do for land sakes go behind the woodshed and do it alone. You can't teach 'em anything, you can't get 'em to admit anything. And they'll lie for each other 'sif they belonged to a lodge. Strange to me women can't stick together like that. Men call it honor not to tell on the other fellow. I call it a universal sense of guilt."

"What of it?" Mrs. Casper Flood wanted to know. "Women are free to take men or leave them alone, aren't they?"

"We ain't got that much sense," retorted Mrs. Jim Coldfoot. "I married Coldfoot because he pestered me to death. Sometimes I think he's sorry for it, though heaven knows I'm good to him."

One of the ladies hid her face behind a piece of quilt work and coughed delicately. Deborah Lunt, who had returned from the Sky Peak country, listened wide eyed to this devastatingly frank comment of the older women. Distinctly a pretty girl, she had a manner of drawing her mouth primly together when she

111

was shocked or displeased.

"I believe," said she emphatically, "a woman should not let a man be too familiar. He won't respect her."

Mrs. Jim Coldfoot peered over her glasses with quick interest. "When you and Steve going to get married?"

Debbie flushed. "I don't — that is, the date isn't set yet."

"Don't let him dangle too long or you'll lose him," advised Mrs. Jim.

Debbie's flush deepened. "I wouldn't hold him a minute if he didn't want to marry me. I'm not that kind."

"Ha," contradicted Mrs. Jim. "I've heard lots of 'em say that. It ain't so. All of us sisters fight tooth and toe nail to get a husband. Lessee, you've been engaged six months. No, six months and a half. I recall when I heard the news. Well, that's time enough to let anybody suffer. Ought to have your mind made up by now. No matter how bad you think he is now, he'll be worse when you look at him over the breakfast table with his whiskers in the coffee."

Debbie's deepening flush became scarlet storm signals. "There's nothing bad about him! He's a fine, good man!"

Eve, silent thus far, broke in smoothly. "Debbie, don't let Mrs. Jim fluster you like

112

that. She just loves to disturb us."

"I've got ears and eyes," responded Mrs. Jim tersely. "Anyhow, with Lola Monterey back, I wouldn't trust no man around the corner. I —"

The ladies looked at Mrs. Jim with varying expressions of warning and significance. Mrs. Casper Flood tried to change the subject. "I heard the funniest story about —"

But Mrs. Jim had the bit in her teeth and was not to be stopped. "You can't make nothing out of nothing. Lola's the daughter of a Spanish woman and a white man, which is bad. She learned her trade in a dance hall, and that ain't any help to her. She's been all over the world singing and Lord knows that's nothing to brag about either. I'll admit she's got a way with her, but good looks and nice clothes mean nothing to me even if it does set every man under seventy on his ears."

"I think she is beautiful," said Eve quietly, feeling the united scrutiny of the group.

"Ain't you worried?" challenged Mrs. Jim.

"Over what?" Eve asked innocently.

"Well, goodness sakes," exclaimed Mrs. Jim, "whose man is Dave Denver, anyhow?"

"Now, isn't it queer? — I have forgotten to ask him that."

Approval of this faint rebuke fairly exuded from the other women. But Mrs. Jim didn't know a rebuke from an invitation to dinner. The restless brightness of her glance skittered over Eve's boyish, half smiling countenance. And she plumped out an eager question.

"Would you marry him at the chance?"

Eve laughed outright. "I never answer direct questions on Tuesdays."

Mrs. Jim put away her knitting, seeing Coldfoot approaching with a buggy. "Well," she sighed, "you're a good actor anyhow. Though it ain't any of my business, I'll say I think you're crazy if you're not interested in him. But if you are interested in him there's enough between him and Lola Monterey to cause you many a sleepless night. Girls, I just had an elegant time." She smiled all around and turned to her husband, who waited in subdued silence.

"You're late," said she with some asperity.

"Yes, Mama," agreed Coldfoot and snapped one of his suspenders.

"Don't mumble at me with all that tobacco in your mouth. If you've got to spit, then spit." She climbed vigorously into the buggy and they went swaying out to the road. Mrs. Casper Flood collapsed in her rocker and laughed so hard she almost cried. Mrs. Roberts rose to end her visit. "After a scene like that," she remarked, "I always go home a better woman and cook something special for the men. Nellie, are you riding with me?"

The group broke up. More buggies came down the road to claim the errant housewives. Mrs. Casper Flood stepped to the saddle of a waiting pony and went out of the yard on the gallop; and as the last of them left a man rounded the bend of the ridge, sitting slack and indolent, and pointed for the yard. Eve waved an arm at which Debbie Lunt showed surprise.

"You've got awfully good eyes, Eve. Who is it?"

"Dave."

"Well, no wonder." She wrinkled her pert nose impatiently. "If Steve dawdled along like that when he knew I was waiting for him I most certainly would lecture him."

"Not if Steve were Dave," said Eve softly, "and not if you were me."

Dave cut across the yard and reined in beside the porch. He did not immediately get down, but lifted his hat and studied the two girls quizzically. "Now here is a picture worth travelin' to see," he drawled. "But, hold on, it ain't quite perfect. One of these fair damsels looks like she's too proud to scowl at me and too stubborn to smile. Debbie, I ain't stolen your Stevie boy."

Debbie flushed and tipped her chin defiantly. In her heart she was a little afraid of Denver and a little jealous. The fear, queerly

115

enough, was the fear of a little girl facing a man whose explosive fighting qualities had been talked about in the country for years. Yet it was not altogether that; Debbie always instinctively tried to cover her feelings when his deep and direct and slightly ironic glance rested on her. She felt he was reading her, prying out her intrinsic worth, and finding her lacking. As for the jealousy, she hated the thought that anybody had the power of swaying Steve Steers's loyalty and affection; and she knew Denver had this power.

"You're making fun of me," said she, despising herself for going on the defensive.

"No, sir, not me, Debbie. I never laugh at pretty girls. And where is that human dynamo on wheels — in other words, Mister Stephen Burt Steers?"

"He's supposed to be here now, to take me home," said Debbie with a faint inflection of tartness. Dave looked lazily at Eve and understanding passed between. Eve crooked her finger at him.

"Get down and wait. I see a party coming off the prairie, and Dad's probably in it."

"What makes you think I didn't come to see you instead of your dad?" challenged Dave, stepping to the ground.

"I know you better."

"You don't know me at all," he grumbled

and sat on the porch steps. Debbie frowned vainly at the empty road and walked into the house. Dave chuckled, and Eve winked at him. "No," pursued Dave, "you don't know me at all. I may not be so doggone brotherly. Maybe my intentions are honorable."

She had walked to a porch table. Her answer came over her shoulder, cool and skeptical. "I'm sure your intentions are honorable, Dave — whatever they may be and whichever way they may be directed."

"That remark sounds simple," he mused, "but there's a delayed punch in it."

"Never mind. Here's a cup of tea, stone cold but good for thirst, anyhow."

He took it, stirred the sugar absently, and drank. Eve sat down beside him. "I heard this afternoon why the Jessons named the baby after you."

He colored a little, self-contained man as he was. "That fool of a Steve —"

"Don't you know by now," she broke in quietly, "there's very little you do that escapes Yellow Hill? People wonder about you and talk about you — and they always will. I have heard other things concerning you — about Dann and about — well, many things."

"Mrs. Jim Coldfoot must have been here," said he.

"Yes."

"I reckon it's impossible to keep folks from trying to guess what they don't know," he muttered.

"No, Dave. But some of those guesses are kind." She drew a breath and added wistfully, "Mine are."

"It's possible they oughtn't be too kind, Eve. I say that to you — and never another soul — because I figure you ought to know. Don't consider me too bad. Don't consider me too good."

"Whatever you were, I doubt if it could change my opinion of you," said she, and turned from the subject. "There's Dad and some of the boys — and the Englishman."

The party trotted up. Leverage looked enormously grave and disturbed; something had shaken his usual carriage. He got heavily down and turned first to his daughter. "You see that some sort of chuck is put on the table right off, Eve. I've got to go out again. Dave, come over to the sheds with me. I want to speak with you."

They walked away from the house. "I came up to tell you my men have cut out about twenty of your drift," said Denver. "We're not too pressed for help, and if you are short handed I'll just keep your stuff separate until the country's covered, then shoot it over."

"Thanks," grunted Leverage and stopped,

casting a glance back. "Dave, I have feared this for a long while, and now it's come. An open break between them and us, nothin' less. They've called our challenge. They mean to make it a bloody mess. Lorn Rue was killed sometime last night over on the Henry trail, about three miles south of the Wells. We just found him an hour ago."

"He was one of your picked men?"

"He was. Somehow or other they knew he was and laid for him. It just means this — there's a leak already in the vigilantes. It means also that they've got the country so well honeycombed that they catch every move we make. Rue was placed carefully to watch the Wells; he went into the country after dead dark. And still they got him! That bothers me."

"You had him in there to watch what the outlaws were going to do?"

"I wanted to get a good fresh trail to follow," admitted Leverage. "That's their nest. They go from the Wells to rustle, and they come back to the Wells to carouse. It's the right place to begin our attack. But," and Leverage ran a hand over his harried cheeks, "my job is going to be plain useless if I can't keep things secret."

"Find any tracks around him?"

Leverage shook his head. "He was right in

119

the trail. All sorts of old tracks and fresh tracks running up and down. Everything mixed up; no help there."

"He must have run into something," reflected Denver, "and they shot him to keep his mouth shut."

"We scouted the ground all ways from his body and didn't get a smell."

"Sure," replied Denver. "If he got too close to some choice spot of theirs they'd lug his body off a considerable distance and drop it."

"I hadn't considered that," grunted Leverage. "Confound it, I need a good man to go in there and scout."

"Rue was a good man — while he lasted," said Denver moodily. "That's the hell of this vigilante business. Rue dies because he's lookin' for somebody that took somebody else's cattle. He didn't have a dime in the transaction. And the fellows who ought to be fighting their own battles are sittin' down this minute to a good dinner. It ain't right, Jake. Pretty soon everybody will be livin' under gunshot law because the Fees and the Clandrys and the Remingtons are either too afraid or too lazy to take care of their own individual affairs. It's a rotten business!"

"I hate to hear you talk thataway," protested Leverage. "It's a common fight. If these rustlers hit the big ranchers and get away with it they'll hit the little ones."

"The rustlers wouldn't get away with it if these aforesaid big ranchers didn't hang back," retorted Denver.

"I wish you was in this with me," sighed Leverage. "There ain't anybody else who could strike a warm trail like you."

Denver considered it silently, violet eyes bent on the distance. "Rue was a friend of mine. I hate to see him go. It ain't easy for me to consider that there'll be other friends knocked down. And it ain't easy to consider that you yourself may be the next."

"I'm in it and I'll stay in it," responded Leverage doggedly. "I consider it a duty."

"Maybe I would, too, if I was able to satisfy myself as to the exact beginnin' of this vigilante idea," mused Denver.

"Listen," broke in Leverage irritably, "are you tryin' to tell me this whole vigilante business was started to throw a smoke cloud over something crooked? Why, that's crazy. The Association voted it. No single man got it going."

"There's always a beginning to an idea — usually in one man's head," was Denver's thoughtful reply. "And I'd never fight for any idea or any man unless I knew more about the preliminary hocus-pocus. But what's the use of our arguin'? If it wouldn't be violating any oath of secrecy, I wish you'd tell me where you intended to concentrate your investigation."

"I'm going into the Sky Peak country."

Denver leaned forward. "I'll say this to you alone and nobody else. Don't. The rustlers have pulled out of it."

"How do you know?" demanded Leverage.

Denver's face lightened. "Maybe I'm not a good enough citizen to join in a public posse, Jake, but I'm at least good enough to keep my ear on the ground. And for the love of heaven don't ride alone in this country. Never. Daylight or dark."

Leverage shrugged his shoulders, and they turned back to the house. The Englishman sat on the steps twirling his hat. When Leverage went inside Nightingale looked at Denver. "Seems to be a touch of the dismal in the air, which reminds me I need some of that honest advice Cal Steele said you were duly competent to render."

"Shoot," drawled Denver, noting another rider appear on the far curve of the road. "I'm good at spendin' other people's money and time."

"I find," said Nightingale, "I have inherited a crew along with a ranch. Nice playful boys, but they seem to think Englishmen are fair game for all sorts of sporty tricks. I also have

— or rather had — a foreman who took a sudden dislike to the idea of workin' under a bloomin' foreigner. Rather a queer egg. He is no longer with me."

"Mean you fired Toughy Pound?" asked Denver.

"Well — yes. But somewhat informally."

Denver chuckled. "It'd be Toughy's style to walk out on you. A hard number."

"He didn't walk out," casually corrected Nightingale. "He limped out. Rather a queer custom you have hereabouts as to discharging people. He stated that he was loath to leave unless bounced three times on the seat of his pants, and wouldn't I kindly attempt to do same."

"And so you did?" queried Denver, grinning broadly.

The Englishman flicked the ashes off his cigarette. "Well, y'know, if that is the custom of the country, it's naturally up to me to oblige. Not so? Therefore, to make the ceremony quite effective and proper, I bounced him four times. Now I need a new foreman. I will cheerfully bend to your suggestions."

Denver studied the approaching rider. "You want a good man, a man that understands the country and the cattle business. You want a fellow able to swing the work of the ranch on his own hook and also able to polish off any scissorbill puncher. Also, and most important, you want a fellow who is proud enough to do his job without unnecessary advice from you."

"Is there such a man?" asked Nightingale. "If so, I'll give him the bloomin' ranch and go fishin'."

"Behold the man," said Denver, pointing to the advancing Steers. "He looks good, and he's better than he looks."

Steve Steers jingled across the yard, casting an apprehensive glance through Leverage's front door.

"You got a job," announced Denver.

Steve's countenance expressed dismay. "Shucks, Dave, I just had a job. Where's Debbie?"

"Listen to me, you homely bunchgrass biter," stated Denver firmly, "this is a job. You are now foreman of Mr. Nightingale's Bucket outfit. Your pay is eighty dollars. You run the ranch and everybody that's on it, high, wide, and handsome. No interference. I'm responsible for the suggestion, and, by golly, you've got to sweat!"

"Accept the nomination," said Steve.

"Seems settled," remarked Nightingale calmly and rose to depart. "Now, ah, Steve — should I ask a few questions around my ranch or call on you for an occasional pony to ride, I trust I shan't be considered as intrudin'." With that he galloped off.

Eve and Debbie Lunt came from the house. Debbie went to her waiting mount and was seated in the saddle before the ambling Steve could get around to help her. She looked sweetly at him and with equal sweetness remarked:

"You're a little late, Steve."

"Yeah, Debbie," he muttered.

Together they rode away, Steve looking straight ahead, the girl stiffly erect and silent. Watching them depart, Eve shook her head. "That sounded too much like Mrs. Jim and her husband. Debbie's not wise to carry on so, and Steve's not wise to let her."

"The girl's not bad," reflected Dave, "but she figures she's got to hold the whip on a man to make him mind. One of these days she'll slap him a little too hard."

Eve was surprised at his accurate knowledge of Deborah Lunt and said so. "I'm afraid you know more about women than you ought, Dave. You're staying to supper?"

"Wish I could. But the day's almost gone, and I want to look at a stretch of country before it gets too dark." He got astride his horse, half puzzled, half smiling. "Eve, you're like the drink habit on a man. Seems like I always calm down and forget the grief of a weary world when you're around."

She put an arm around a porch post and lifted her face; some small breath of wind ruffled the curling hair at her temples, and suddenly a foreboding anxiety lay darkly in her eyes. "David, it is none of my business, but you are too strong a man not to have enemies. No matter how aloof you try to keep from the quarrel in Yellow Hill, you will always be in danger. I know how you feel. Dad's told me. And I'm not trying to change your mind. All I say is you never will be able to keep free of trouble — and I wish you would be a little more careful. These last few months I have had a horrible feeling of things about to happen."

"I know," he agreed slowly. "And I hate to see your dad makin' a target out of himself for other people. But remember this, Eve: No matter how much I keep away from this business, I'm always ready to help the Leverage family. If anything should happen to your dad I'd never sleep until I found the man who was responsible for it. I don't agree with the vigilante business, and sometimes I actually can sympathize with these poor fools makin' a living by stealing beef. But there's a line none of them can step over, as far as I'm concerned. If they do, then I'll be ridin'. Not with any committee, but on my own account."

126

"You don't have to tell me," said she. "I have known it a long time. It's a queer thing to say, but sometimes at night I have the feeling that you are not far away — out in the night somewhere, taking care of us."

He looked sharply at her. "How long have you been thinking that?" was his quick question.

"Oh, for the last three or four nights. Why?"

He shook his head. "Just wondered. See you later." Raising his hat he cantered away. Eve rested against the post and watched him go, with grave attention. Long after, when he reached the high bend of the road and was about to swing from sight, he turned and lifted an arm; and she answered the farewell hail with quick pleasure. As he disappeared the last ray of sun drew away from the hills, and purple twilight shaded the land. She turned inside.

Dave Denver did not go directly home. Instead he paced along the curving road for a few miles and left it to climb a tall ridge adjoining. From the summit he commanded a good view of the cupped-in pockets and the narrow valleys roundabout. Here was a house, there a bunch of cattle, and occasionally a rider questing down some trail. Yet as high up as he was he could not gain a clear sweep of the hills; the broken land formed a thousand dark and isolated patches, and ridges kept cutting in to shield whatever went on yonder.

"Perfect layout for the wild bunch," reflected Denver. "There's spots in this country yet unsurveyed and untouched." Rolling a cigarette he considered Eve Leverage's last remark. The intuitive truth in it had startled him; twice in the last few nights he had made a night patrol around the Leverage section. "Two things," he mused thoughtfully, "I never will understand if I live to be a thousand. First, the whispers that cross this country like light flashes. Second, the way of a woman's mind."

There was but a brief interval of evening left him, and so he brought his mind back to its original thought. To his right, or east, ran the stage road; to his left and nine miles deeper in this cut-up country, lay the Wells. At some point Redmain's renegade riders, driving out of the Sky Peak country, had crossed the highway and headed for the evil shell of a town that was their stronghold. He wanted to find the marks of their path to satisfy his own curiosity and to answer a question slowly forming in his head.

"They were out on a hunt the other evenin'," he murmured. "What did they take home with 'em? I might hit straight for the

Dome and look around; but I doubt if they'd return the same way they came. That'd require too much ridin' on the stage road. My guess is they cut over more southerly."

He pushed his horse down the rather steep slope and presently was threading a tortuous trail that undulated from draw to ridge and down into draw again. Rather roughly he paralleled the stage road, curving as it curved, and all the while watching the soft ground beneath. At every mark of travel he stopped to study and reject it, and so pressed on until the waning light warned him. Thereupon he abandoned the patient method and made a swift guess. "If I was leadin' that bunch and on my way to the Wells I'd use the alley of Sweet Creek — providin' I was bashful about bein' seen."

Sweet Creek was on another tangent. He ran down a draw, crossed the succeeding ridge via a meadow-like notch, and veered his course. The tendrils of dusk were curling rapidly through the trees and the ravines were awash with cobalt shadows. The breeze stiffened; far up on the stage road he heard the groaning of brake blocks; then he was confronted with fresh tracks in the yielding earth. He reined in.

The tracks were made by a solitary beef followed by a lone rider; they led out of the west — out of the Wells direction — and seemed headed toward the east. This he considered slowly. His own range was just over the stage road, and from all indications one of his own riders had found a stray and was pushing it back to proper territory. "But who would that be?" Denver asked himself. "All the boys are workin' the Copperhead side today."

He changed his mind about reaching Sweet Creek and pursued the tracks as they went upward, crossed the road, and kept on. A freighter's lantern winked from a hairpin turn of the road above him; a creek purled and gurgled down the hillside. It was dark then, and he had lost all clear sight of the spoor he was tracing, but he kept going and never hesitated until there came a place in the ravine where the trail forked. Dismounting, he struck a match and cupped it to the earth. Rider and cow had turned north; and north was the way to his own D Slash quarters.

"Must be one of the boys," he decided. "But who the devil's been straying away off here? If it ain't that —"

Pungent odors told him he was not far behind the preceding rider. Another mile, and he caught a faint sound in the thickening fog. Reaching a high point, he had the wide mouth of Starlight Canyon looming beside him; and at the head of that long sweeping space were the blinking lights of his house. The sound of advance travel was more distinct; in fact, it seemed to approach him rather than follow ahead. Puzzled, he kept a steady pace, not wishing to draw too swiftly upon one of his own riders. In the darkness D Slash men were apt to be ticklish; he had taught them to be so.

The rider seemed to be having trouble with his stray. The lash of a quirt arrived distinctly, followed by a grunt of anger. Brush cracked; quite without warning, cow and rider were dead ahead. A horse whinnied.

"Who's that?" drawled Denver.

"What the hell — !"

A warning chill pricked at Denver's scalp. He announced his name abruptly and pulled off the trail, then called again: "Who are you?"

CHAPTER VII
"THE SKY IS THE LIMIT"

For answer he had the smash of a gunshot and the flicker of muzzle light. The stray cow plunged deeper into the brush. A second shot cracked his ears; and the weaving outline of the unknown man came against him, striking him flank and flank. An arm reached out and slashed at his coat, and for a moment there was nothing but an aimless snarl of two horses bucking free of each other and two men coming to grips. Denver's gun was out; the unknown man pulled free and fired as Denver opened up. The man screamed, and Denver saw his form sprawl out of the saddle and strike ground, horse's feet plunging over him.

Denver jumped down and approached, hearing a mighty suction of breath. After that silence fell; when he lit a match he saw a dead man's face glaring up from the earth.

"Redmain rider," grunted Denver tonelessly. The trail quivered with men racing out from home quarters. He stepped back and waited until they were within hailing distance.

Then called, "Hold on, boys."

"What's up?"

"Ran into a snag. One of the wild bunch is on the ground here. Look around the brush. He was driving a beef up the trail, and I overtook him. I want to look at that beef."

They rounded the stray from the underbrush. Somebody closed in and dropped a loop about the brute's neck. Denver went over and lit a match, looking for the brand. When the light went out he was swearing disgustedly at himself. "Why in the devil didn't I take a tumble to that half an hour ago? It's a plant. They've took one of Fee's critters and blotched my mark on it."

"Mighty awkward job," opined one of the men. "Too poor a switch to fool anybody. Who is that fella?"

"Some stranger," said Denver. "Redmain's got a whole bunch of new hands in his string this year. Pick him up and bring him to the house."

"Then what, Dave?"

Denver was racing for quarters, the power of speech lost to him. All that cool control which had carried him like a machine through the encounter was gone. The black devils of his temper clutched at his throat, poured fury through his veins, and made of him a mad conscienceless killer. It stripped him of every

133

last kindly instinct, it tore away his sense of safety, it made the muscles of his body tremble as in a spasm of pain. So he flung himself off his horse and ran up the porch, not the David Denver of normal life, not the responsible ranchman, nor the drawling figure welcomed by men and loved by women. Not any of these now. To-night the dominant, long repressed instincts rode him unmercifully. To-night he was Black Dave Denver.

The blurred face of a hand appeared in his pathway. He swept the man aside, he ripped out an order — "Get my saddle on the gray gelding" — and tramped across the living room to where a rack of guns stood. He unbuckled his belt and threw it aside; and from a high peg he took down another belt and another gun. This he hooked around him, lifting the weapon from its seat, throwing out the cylinder and spinning it beneath the flare of those flame flecked violet eyes.

There was a spell in that smoothly whirling metal that checked the restlessness in him. For a long period of time he held the gun in his hand, absorbed by the sinister beauty of it, eyes running the barrel and touching the worn wood that had felt the grip of his father before him as well as his own. It was an instrument of last resort, that gun, and its muzzle had spoken sentence in more than one trial of wills.

This night Black Dave Denver meant it to so speak again. With that thought he thumbed in six cartridges, snapped the cylinder home, and dropped the weapon lightly in its seat. Once or twice he lifted and settled it, then turned the belt somewhat farther around. After that he turned for the door. His foreman stood in the way, cautiously yet stubbornly.

"We'll ride too," said Lyle Bonnet.

"You will get out of my road and stay out of it," snapped Denver.

"Well, we'll foller."

"Stay behind."

"Listen, Dave —"

"I told you what to do," said Denver. The foreman dropped his glance and retreated. Denver strode to his horse, spurred up the slope and down the trail he had just used, dipping into the canyon and skirting the melody-making creek. At the road he swung up the grade, gelding bunching beneath him; somewhere beyond the summit of that particular ridge and in the utter darkness of the night he entered a dismal side path and tipped downward. This went west, clinging secretively to the pines and the remote holes. Sweet Creek curved out of the unfathomed mystery, paralleled Denver a mile, and then fell off, declining the upthrust of another ridge that seemed to cast a more impenetrable shadow into the world.

As he rode, going ever deeper into this wild land, he began to collect himself. The first wild burst of passion wore away, the fog of the night cut through and released his over-whelmed critical faculties. Thus in a measure he lost some of that savage desire to trample down and smash whoever was responsible for the attempt to plant a switched brand on him. Not that his desire to settle the matter was in anywise abated; but some of the urgency of that desire fell away. Rather critically he surveyed his course.

All roads led to the Wells, and all this night activity emanated from the mind of one man — Lou Redmain's. Yet it was conceivable that some other outlaw, working under the shadow of Redmain's reputation, might have tried to plant the cow. It was also conceivable that some far greater and hitherto unsuspected authority lay behind the act. Denver had noth-ing to substantiate the latter belief, but it had been working in his mind since the inception of the vigilantes. Impalpable, without a shadow of fact or incriminating deed, it was but another of those whispering hints running abreast the wind.

"Somebody, disliking me and knowing my temper," he reflected, "might have planted the cow. Figuring that if the vigilantes found it I'd be hooked, or figuring that if I discovered it first I'd make a play right square into Redmain. And that's what I'm about to do."

The factor upsetting this idea was that one of Redmain's men had been with the cow. Yet even Redmain could not count on the utter loyalty of all his followers. Intrigue undermined every faction, honest and dishonest.

Contradictory impressions came from all sides. There was no clear path out of the tangled web; and Denver, understanding this in his more logical state of mind, came to a decision.

"Whoever is behind it, Redmain or another, I reckon I won't be fool enough to bust into a set play. Better to unravel this business before swallowin' bait. That cow is just one small item in some damned sight bigger plan of things."

The trail reached a crest and a blank wall of trees. At right angles to it ran a broader alley through the forest — the north and south Henry trail. Denver halted and put an ear against the wind. After several moments he left the saddle and ran his hands across the earth, feeling innumerable churned indentations of travel. Not yet satisfied, he retreated a distance on the Sweet Creek trace, got a match, and knelt close to the earth; the exploding flare of light broke the pall but a brief instant and was whipped out, yet in that length of time he had seen cattle and pony tracks mixed together.

Crouched there he made his judgment. "They went toward Copperhead the other night, took a bunch of stock and brought it back here. They're up yonder in some lonesome and godforsaken hole right now. Lorn Rue got too close to that spot, was killed, and packed off. Now if I could poke my way into that mess —"

He threw the inclination aside and resumed his saddle, striking north on the Henry trail. Forty-five minutes later he came down a slashed hillside and was met by a few dull lights shining out of grotesquely huddled buildings. Presently he had arrived at the end of a curving street along which eight or nine forlorn and shaken structures faced each other, each seeming about to slide off the steep slope. This was the Wells, once a flush mining camp but now the nest of malcontents. A dreary, evil spot with a pervading gloom hanging over it. Denver's eyes roamed the street, seeing shadows detach themselves from odd apertures and slide off. Pressing his lips together, he aimed in, arrived at a breast-high porch and stepped over to it. Out of cracked and grimy windows flickered dim lights, and through a set of swinging doors floated a mixture of harsh sounds and unlovely smells. The sounds began to fall off, chairs scraped, and somebody ran across a squeaking floor. When he pushed the doors aside a still, quiet scene was before him.

He never previously had paid the Wells a visit; nor was he prepared for the drab, lackluster sullenness of this saloon. All lights were pitched low, and the flutter of untrimmed wicks gave to the fetid, smoke-ridden atmosphere a palpitating uneasiness. A long bar ran across one end of the room; the rest of it held a stove, many chairs, and a few decrepit tables. In this space Denver's swift observation noted about thirty people, a half dozen of which were women. And behind the bar stood a coal-black giant whose palms pressed the weight of his torso downward on the mahogany while he blinked at Denver. One of the women laughed, the sound like a slap in Denver's face. He stepped aside and spoke to the barkeep.

"Send for Redmain."

The barkeep held his answer for a long, insolent minute. "He ain't here."

"You lie," said Denver evenly. "His horse stands outside. Send for him."

"If you know so much, go get him y'self, mister."

"Tell him Dave Denver is down here and

proposes to see him."

The barkeep held his tongue. A girl slipped quietly out of a door, and such was the silence that the noise of her heels going up some invisible stairway echoed blankly back. The thick, miasmatic breath of hostility rose all around him; he saw their eyes glittering on him, he saw the predatory hunger of their desire. Yet they said nothing and he stood posted against the wall until another door opened and Lou Redmain came quietly in.

"Glad to see you, Dave," said the man, triangular face blurred in the haze.

"I reckon this is the chief's palace and these gentlemen and ladies his principal people," observed Denver.

Redmain let the bite of that sarcasm go by unnoticed. "For my purpose," said he softly, "they do me very well."

"One of 'em didn't," stated Denver, an increasing chill in his words. "One of them ran a misbranded Fee cow onto my range and made a bad job of it. He's of no further use to you."

The room began to rustle with repressed talk. "Bury the fool, and I'll do you a return favor some day," said Redmain, still unmoved.

Some of the heedless, reckless anger rose again in Denver. "Am I to understand you're

140

accepting the responsibility for that act, Redmain?"

Redmain moved across the room. "Listen, Dave," he answered: "there are considerable people who'd like to see either one of us out of the road. Be pretty easy, wouldn't it, for any such person to rig a thing like this?"

"He was your man."

"And if he was alive I'd kill him!" exclaimed Redmain, letting go. The slim body swayed. "I gave you my word in Sundown I'd stay clear of you! I meant that!"

"It was a Fee cow," added Denver.

Redmain's face shifted expression rapidly. "Don't miss much, do you? Well, what if I have got some Fee cows? I ain't got all of them. That critter could have come from any other direction as well as from my territory."

"Could but didn't," was Denver's terse reply. "It came out of this country."

Redmain stood silent, studying Denver closely. Presently he shook his head. "That too is possible. I won't say I can trust every man I've got. You know and I know that none of us can see everything going on around here. From now on neither you nor I can prevent cross plays. It won't get any better. It'll get worse. Men are after me. And whether you know it or not, men are after you. I have never been on your trail, and I repeat I never will be on it."

"I'm not sure I know your limit," said Denver thoughtfully.

"I've got no limit. The sky's my limit."

"When a man talks like that," Denver shot back, "he draws the line nowhere. And he'll respect nothing."

Redmain's face darkened. "You've got my word," he repeated. "I recall you drank with me when no other cattleman in this county would be seen in the same saloon with me."

"Let it be so," agreed Denver. "I came here to tell you, however, that I am fully prepared to take care of myself and my interests. If the time comes when your interests run counter to mine then I can no longer stand aside."

"We will never fight over that," interposed Redmain quickly.

But Denver broke bluntly through. "At your rate of speed it's entirely possible we may lock horns."

"I should hate to see that day come."

"Maybe, maybe not. Men change; times change. I came here to let you know exactly how I stand on the subject. One more thing, Lou. If Leverage goes down and you are back of it, neither heaven nor hell will be big enough for both of us."

"I doubt if heaven will see either of us. Hell is big enough for all."

Their talk dropped suddenly off and tension of their meeting began to oppress all others in the room to the point of restlessness. Moments dragged by, the rugged and powerful Denver looking down at Redmain's slighter figure with a driving intentness the outlaw had never before experienced. Then Denver moved toward the door.

"If you disclaim responsibility for that business," was his final word, "I'll accept it. I'm not joinin' the pack against you because there's something tellin' me most of the time that but for a turn of the card I might be in your shoes and you in mine. However, when a man flies high, he covers considerable territory — sometimes other people's. Consider it, Lou."

Redmain stood at the swinging doors, watching Denver pass out and ride from the street. A pallor crept around his mouth and nostrils and some dreadful storm of feeling shook him terrifically. He turned on his heels, half ran across the room, ripped open an inner door, and paused only to lift one hand at a loitering henchman. The man came quickly into the half dark hall.

"Go after him!" breathed Redmain.

"Get him, yuh mean."

"No, damn you, follow him! See where he goes!"

"Why not get him, chief?"

"Because I told you not to! Because I am not ready! Because I don't want him killed around my territory! Get out of here!" And, still shaken, he passed up the stairs to his room and tramped around it endlessly while the rising clamor from the saloon came brokenly to him.

CHAPTER VIII
JUDICIAL MEASURES

"If yuh want to see somethin' rich, ripe, and rare," proclaimed Steve Steers, bursting into Grogan's, "come over to the courthouse."

This being on a Saturday afternoon, Grogan's was crowded and lively. The gentlemen to whom Steve addressed his remarks — Denver, Steele, and the Englishman — were considering the state of the nation at one corner of the bar, a bottle conveniently disposed at their elbows.

"Nothing less than murder could interest anybody in Yellow Hill these days," replied Cal Steele amiably. "Have a drink and forget your sorrows."

"It's Fleabite Wilgus and his hoss," said Steve.

"Why didn't you say so in the first place?" drawled Denver. By common consent the four of them grouped together and left the saloon. Just outside all stepped aside and lifted their hats. Lola Monterey walked past with a red parasol bobbing over her jet hair; and her eyes, smiling impartially on them, came to temporary rest on Dave.

"Supper at five, David."

He grinned. "I'll be there, Lola."

She passed on, and the men cut over to the courthouse, Cal Steele grumbling. "How do you rate that, Mister Denver? Seems to me the wicked have all the fun. Going to the dance?"

"Never heard about it."

"You will," prophesied Cal Steele. "It's next week at the Copperhead school. Figure out which woman you're takin' so I can ask the other."

They walked through the courthouse door and turned into the judge's chamber, half filled with spectators. Crowding against the wall, they saw Fleabite Wilgus leap to his feet and interrupt a line of legal palaver. "I'm dummed if I make head er tail to this. The true facts is, that's my horse and I mean to have it."

"Keep your pants on," admonished John Coke, judge of Sundown's justice court. "You're paying attorney fees to Langdell, so let him do the talking. Now, Tuggs. . . ."

Tuggs was an unhappy and impoverished appearing little man past the prime of life. He moved his warped and calloused hands rather helplessly around. "Well, they ain't

146

much more to it, Judge. I come to town and let my rig stand. When I walked outa the New York Store Wilgus had unhitched my hoss and was leadin' him away."

"My horse," said Wilgus in a subterranean mutter.

Tuggs swallowed and said nothing. Niland, who was representing him, said, "All right, Tuggs. Go on. What then?"

"Well, I walks up to Wilgus and I says, 'Fleabite, you got no call to monkey with other people's proputty that away. Gimme my hoss.' I took holt of the headstall. Fleabite says, 'Git away, it's my hoss!' Fleabite then belts me in the face and takes the hoss away. So I had him arrested."

"A pretty pass," fumed Fleabite Wilgus, "when a skinny, no-account runt like him can arrest a man able to buy him out ten thousand times over. Ain't there no decent respeck fer social standin' in this here community?"

Langdell frowned at his client and said, "Shush, you ain't helpin' yourself." Facing the judge, he added, "Why carry it on? Wilgus will admit he struck Tuggs and take the fine. In so far as the horse is concerned, that's another case. If Tuggs will not admit the animal to be Wilgus's horse, then we will start replevin proceedings."

The judge leaned forward and nodded at

Wilgus. "What makes you think this to be your horse?"

Wilgus got up, a shambling, ragged man for all his wealth in land and cattle. All about him was the air of narrow sharpness. He spoke in a falsetto whine. "Well, they ain't nothin' to it. I missed that horse four years ago and never heard of him since till this mornin' when I saw Tuggs come to town. I spoke to Tuggs about it, but he wouldn't give me no satisfaction. I will admit bein' a little hasty, but it's my horse."

"Wait a minute," interposed Niland. "You missed that horse four years ago? Now you run a pretty big horse ranch. How many of the brutes have passed through your hands in those four years?"

"Couldn't say," mumbled Wilgus evasively. "Mebbe three-four thousand."

"And you maintain you recognized this particular horse out of four thousand, over an interval of four years?"

"Sure," said Wilgus. "I never forgot a horse's face. Anyhow, that was a particular horse. Sentiment attached to it. I nourished that horse, I loved him like a pet."

Denver leaned near the Englishman, chuckling. "He'd sell his grandmother down the river. Sentiment — shucks."

"What's all this got to do with an assault

148

and battery case?" protested Langdell. "Let's have the fine. We'll go into the other matter later."

"I'm interested," said his honor. "I know Wilgus, I know Tuggs, and I have recollections of the horse. This being a court of first resort I consider it no less than my duty to go so far afield as necessary in any case to prevent subsequent litigation. Why should we embrace the thought of replevin when a simple face-to-face parley might do away with such action? Tuggs, you maintain it is your horse. Where did you get it?"

"I bought it from a trader," said Tuggs. "He ain't in the country any more. That was two years ago. Maybe he's got a Wilgus brand. Most hosses around here have. But he's got other brands likewise. I paid money for the beast. He's mine."

"Hm," said the judge. "Sheriff, bring in the horse."

"Oh, now," protested Langdell, "he'll kick hell out of the furniture."

The judge considered the objection briefly and ruled it out. "Speaking from personal recollection of Tuggs's horse I would say that if the beast is able to kick hell out of this court's furniture, then he is not the horse I think he is. Bring him in, Ortez."

Ortez, the sheriff, departed. In a little while

the courtroom heard a hollow, stumbling clatter, followed by the sheriff's pleading voice. "Come on, boy, this ain't goin' to be hard. Listen, you condemned lost soul, hold up yore head! Yeah, now lift yore foot. Quit leanin' on me — yore supposed to be the horse, not me! Well, I know yore tired, but what the hell am I to do about it? Henry — Henry, for God's sake come over here and get this damned brute off my chest!"

Presently Ortez came perspiring into the chamber, dragging a long rope. Next in order was Henry, also hauling on the rope. And finally Tuggs's horse limped through the door. Undoubtedly he was a tired horse. Planting his feet wide apart he rolled his jaded eyes and fetched a dismal groan. He was a wrinkled horse, a sway-backed horse, a horse that embodied every disgraceful thing a horse should not be. His ears flopped limply, his knees interfered, and his lips quivered as if he were about to burst out crying. Practically the only sign of life he displayed to the incredulous courtroom was to sway toward the wall with the presumable intent of leaning against it. Ortez warned the court glumly.

"If you want any testimony from this horse yuh better take it quick. I got to git him out of here afore he dies on me."

"That brings up a debatable point of fact,"

150

reflected Niland. "Is he a horse?"

"Well," grunted Ortez, "they's horses and they's horses. This is still another kind of horse."

"He must have been born old," added Niland. "Makes me tired to look at him."

"If he were able to sit," said the court, "I'd offer him a chair. Tuggs, is this the animal you use as a beast of burden?"

"Well, he's all right," muttered Tuggs. "When I got him hitched to a load on a level stretch I can ride in the wagon too. Of course, I have to favor him a little. When we hit a mite of a grade I walk. If the grade gets steep I push. I got to have a horse, don't I?"

"What seems to be the record as to brands?" inquired the court.

Ortez shook his head. "If there's any outfit which ain't put their brand on this horse durin' the past thirty years I fail to detect the absence. He's a walkin' directory."

Denver walked to the beast and ran his hand over one scarred side. Cattleland brands its beef stock freely and without regard for appearances, but a horse is marked as little as possible. Starting just above the stifle, the customary branding spot, Denver began to unravel the story of this jaded charger's peregrinations. He had been a Fee horse, he had stayed awhile with Gallant at Flying G.

Thence he had moved — all this registered in burns that wandered up from stifle to hip and thence outward along the flank — through Three Pines, Hogpen, Double Ought, Thirty Ranch, Bar Y, Broken Jug, XL, Lazy UT, and the Gate brand of Wilgus. Nor was there any order in the arrangement of brands. They crowded together, overlapped, doubled up — proving anything or nothing.

"Denver," called the court, "I'll designate you as expert witness. What's your impression?"

"Wait a minute," interposed Ortez. "There's two sides to a horse. You ain't seen nothin' yet. Come over and read some more."

Denver walked around the animal and chuckled. "My first impression is that if there's any more branding to be done on this horse you'll have to get another horse. All I can say now in regard to the specimen before me is that he's better than sixteen years old."

"Now, now," cut in Wilgus, "he ain't a day over twelve. He just looks a little tired, that's all."

"Beg to differ. They quit using the Lazy UT brand sixteen seasons ago. This horse has been places and seen things. In fact, he's practically an original passenger of the Ark."

The horse leered at Denver's coat buttons, nibbled on one in a spasmodic burst of energy,

152

and sneezed. Ortez evidenced alarm.

"Y'honor, this horse ain't himself at all —"

"Was he ever?" interrupted Niland.

"— the crowd excites him. The air is bad. I got to get this horse outa here. Henry, lend a hand."

Niland rose. "Considering the fact that ownership is going to be difficult to determine, why not settle reasonably? Let Wilgus make an offer for the horse. Tuggs would accept rather than go through a long suit. If we could establish a fair price —"

"This has got nothing to do with assault and battery," repeated Langdell.

"The mills of the gods grind exceedingly small," said the judge. "If you're determined to get the assault and battery end of it over with I'll oblige. Wilgus is fined twenty-five dollars. Now let's see about this offer of sale. Wilgus wants the horse. Tuggs will sell. Niland has suggested a price."

"Including rope and halter?" asked Langdell.

"Certainly not," said Niland. "A rope and halter represents around six dollars. Are you buying hardware or horse? I offer the horse as is, without gear, delivered on the streets of Sundown."

"He might run away," objected Langdell.

The court frowned heavily on the attorney.

"Mr. Langdell, don't let your wild fancy get the best of you. Did you ever hear of the horse running? Can you produce any living being who saw or thought he saw in the aforementioned horse any inkling of a desire to run away, either impulsively or after due deliberation? Just what evidence can you adduce to prove that this horse is even familiar with the act of running?"

Out of the crowd came a hollow assent. "True, brother."

"Well," considered Langdell, "we might go so far as to make an offer — if you agree to deliver the horse at the Wilgus ranch."

"Now, now," scoffed Niland. "It's eleven miles to that ranch. I refuse to embark on any such hazardous experiment. The horse is in delicate health."

"Gentlemen, get together," adjured the court. "I think you ought to make an attempt to strike an equitable balance."

Langdell whispered to Wilgus and came to a sudden decision. "Very well. Give us five dollars, Niland, and we'll take the horse off your hands."

Niland threw up his arms in disgust. "Have you forgotten the horse is valuable?"

"For what?" jeered Langdell.

"Your client says so."

Wilgus half rose. "Sentimentally, understand. I wouldn't go so fur as to say it was anything else."

Niland conferred with Tuggs. "Tuggs," he announced, "is ready to let Wilgus give him twenty dollars cash or another sound horse such as this one."

Langdell raised an unbelieving eyebrow; and even the court seemed rather dashed. Rumors of difficulty drifted into the hall of justice. The sheriff had piloted the horse as far as those difficult steps and now was audibly preparing for the worst. "Henry, don't stand down there thataway. If he starts a-goin' too fast he'll crush yuh."

"Let's take him down rump first," suggested Henry.

"No — no! He'll break his back."

"All right. Head first she is."

"That ain't so good either. He's apt to bust his neck."

This defeated Henry; he grew sarcastic. "Hell's afire, how many ways yuh think a horse can come downstairs? Listen, I'll get a pint of oats and hold it here. That'll move him."

"No — no! You want this horse to faint right here?"

"Aw," exploded Henry, "give him a push and see what happens!" The courtroom gathered that Henry was walking away, for the sheriff's plaintive remonstrance rose to heaven.

"Now, Henry, don't leave me like this. I'm holdin' him up, and I ain't able to let go!"

Wilgus rose from his seat. "You fellows are makin' a lot of monkey business out of this deal. That's my horse, and I mean to have him."

"You won't consider settlin' it?" queried Niland.

"I ain't a-goin' to pay a penny for what's already mine," stated Wilgus. "I'll allow he ain't pretty and couldn't drag a feather, but it's the principle of the thing. If I got to sue to get him, that's what I'm a-goin' to do."

"The province of the court is to see justice done," said the judge, eyeing Wilgus. "Arbitration having failed, we shall now see whose pound of flesh is whose. This is your legal right. Do you intend to bring action?"

Wilgus muttered to Langdell, and the lawyer spoke for him. "We do."

Ortez limped into the courtroom.

"I leaned him against Grover's stable and left him," was the sheriff's weary reply.

"How did you get him down the steps?"

"He fell down. And I hope I never lay eyes on him again."

The judge frowned. "It won't do, Sheriff. The court now orders you to take charge of the horse, pending determination of ownership. Take him to Grover's stable. See that he lacks for absolutely nothing in the way of food, attention, whatever medical services as may be deemed necessary. In short, watch over him with charity and compassion. Plaintiff Wilgus will post the necessary bond. Next case."

Niland came up to Denver with Tuggs ambling forlornly behind. "That means I ain't goin' to get use of my horse?" he wanted to know. "But I got to have a horse."

"Never mind," soothed Niland. "Strictly speaking, Tuggs, you never had a horse. You had an aged companion. Things will come out all right."

But Tuggs was miserably downcast. "What'm I goin' to do for a horse? Here's my rig in the middle of the street."

They had left the courtroom and were standing on the steps. Niland looked sympathetically at his client and lifted his eyes to Denver. Denver suddenly beckoned to a passing citizen. "Grover, step here a minute, will you?"

Grover, the owner of Sundown's stable, walked over. Denver explained the situation. "Everybody's got a horse but Tuggs, and you've got this for the time bein'. Just you haul out a good twelve-hundred-pound gelding and back it into Tuggs's rig. I'll have one of my men bring in another for you."

"Done," said Grover and walked away. Tuggs sputtered ineffectually.

"It's yours," cut in Denver, "and say no more about it."

The crowd eddied around them, and Tuggs was carried away. Fleabite Wilgus came out, muttering to himself. Steve Steers walked toward the hotel with a harried glance. Al Niland was chuckling. "Oh, this is going to be some case, Dave. It will go down in history. I ain't even started yet."

"What the devil are you driving at, Al?"

Al pointed at the departing Wilgus. "As an attorney I aim to get a square deal for Tuggs. As a human being I aim to give that miserable man the biggest kick in the pants he ever never got and should have had."

Cal Steele walked out with Langdell and beckoned the two. "Come along with us, will you? I want some witnesses to a deal."

The four proceeded past the Palace to the street's end, circled the last building, and climbed to Langdell's office. Langdell pulled down the shades against a beating sun, and reached for the inevitable bottle and glasses.

"I am of the belief," he told Niland, "this is going to be a drawn-out case."

"It is big with possibilities," Niland gravely assured him, "and fraught with consequences that may echo down the corridors of time."

"It is my suspicion you're going to leave no stone unturned," proceeded Langdell.

"If I find any stone unturned," Niland assured him, "I'll fire the stone turner."

"Justice must be done," stated Langdell, lifting his glass.

"We shall do justice and others," cheerfully acquiesced Niland, and they drank. Langdell settled in his chair, very slightly smiling.

"As attorney for my client, a most worthy man," he drawled dryly, "I shall check you at every turn, match you witness for witness, dollar for dollar."

"By George, that's fine!" exclaimed Niland. "You know damned well I don't like you, and you don't like me. But, reserving that state of mind for the present, I'll say you're sometimes halfways human."

Langdell flushed. "I suppose we must all have our fun before we die, Niland. As for disliking you, I seldom let anybody become so large in my mind as to spend time wasting emotion on him."

"Hah!" grunted Niland, sarcasm creeping into his words. "Now you're mounting the ivory pedestal again. You ought to let your humor out for air more often."

159

Denver sat back and studied these men through half-lidded eyes. Niland never minced his words and never failed to sting Fear Langdell with those short jabs of reckless, cynical truth. Langdell stared back at his opponent, mouth pressed grimly together, stiffly resentful. These were two absolutely opposite kinds of men. Denver understood the open-handed Niland very well; understood and sympathized with his friend's impulsive kindliness and sharp brain. But he had never yet penetrated that well guarded mask Colonel Fear Langdell threw in front of his mind. There was, he felt, always some remote thought, some deep feeling moving secretively in Langdell's body.

"Well," broke in Cal Steele, "you fellows are out of court, so why fight? All I wanted you two for was to witness an agreement Langdell and I have drawn up. I'm selling him three hundred and fifty head of stock."

"Sign here," said Langdell, shoving the conveyance over the table and indicating the appropriate place. Niland dashed off his name hurriedly. Dave followed suit.

"Why don't you market your own beef?" he asked Steele.

"Langdell ships five times as much as I do," replied Steele, lazily accepting Langdell's check. "So I find it easier to take a profit this

160

way than to do my own shipping. As a matter of fact, I'm going to go over to a feeder business one of these days. Buy, feed, and sell to a shipper like the Colonel here. Good business."

"Good for you, good for me," agreed Langdell. "Any time you want to dicker again let me know."

"I'll be around in maybe two months," said Cal Steele and got up. Leaving Langdell in his office, the three went back to the street. At Grogan's Steele tipped his head suggestively. "Let's damp down the dust, boys."

"Leave me out of it," drawled Denver. "I've got further business. And by the way of a parting benediction I will gently suggest this is no time to drink."

"Go with God," murmured Cal Steele indolently. "Any time's time to drink. Make up your mind about this girl proposition, Dave. I'm second best man, either way, understand. Come on, Al. You haven't got religion yet."

Niland followed Steele into the saloon, and they took their familiar corner at the bar, broaching a bottle. Niland studied his friend critically. "You," he announced, "are a fool. Why stand aside in favor of Dave? You know he hasn't got his mind set on Lola."

"How do I know it? How do you know it?" Steele's face settled to unusual sober-

161

ness. "Tell me that."

"I know it because I know Dave," replied Niland emphatically. "Maybe he hasn't got his mind made up. Maybe he's thinkin' back to the time when he and Lola were a little younger, a little wilder and more headstrong. Maybe he's wondering. But I know what the answer will be. He'll swing to his own kind. Lola's one thing. Dave's another. At heart, Cal, you're more her style than Dave is."

Steele looked shrewdly at Niland. "That's not a bad guess. How much do you know about me, anyhow?"

Niland said quickly, "I never pry into a man's life. You know that. I take you for granted."

"Hm," muttered Steele. For quite an interval the two men stood still. Then Steele spoke, rather abruptly, rather sadly. "Nevertheless, a man can't keep himself hidden, even if he sealed his mouth. Every act exposes him. As far as Dave is concerned, I'd rather cut off my neck than hurt him. So I stay away. You heard me tell him I was a second-choice man, didn't you? Well, I am. As far as he's involved. I'll be that as long as I live — gladly."

He had touched some deep vein of thought. Downing his glass, he went on. "Some men have the power of drawing others. Not very many. Dave has. Look at us. I've got more education than he has. You've got a mind that cuts deeper and farther into truth than he has. But what of it? Dave is a better man than both of us put together. Why? Because he never varies from that burning light of conscience. He never strays from himself, never seems to falter. Time and again I've seen him come against some tough problem and decide one way or the other without flinching. He thinks he's a skeptic, as we are; that's one reason he likes us so well. But he could no more be the sort of purposeless fool that I am than fly to Mars. There's an enormous force driving him straight ahead."

"Which brings us to another item," grunted Niland, favoring the bottle. "He's bound to drive straight into opposition at the rate things are balling up in Yellow Hill. His neutral stand leaves him high and dry — right out in the daylight to be shot at."

Steele's fine face was tremendously sober and oddly set. "Listen, the most damnable visions keep coming to me, night after night. Faces staring at me from behind a bloody film. Sounds nutty, doesn't it? I have risen from a solid sleep with the horrible thing right in my eyes. I have heard shots, and men groaning. Sometimes the film thins out, and I think I see one of those faces and recognize it as my own. Sometimes I think I see Dave. Sometimes Lou Redmain. But when I reach out and am just on the point of identifying them, the bloody haze falls down."

"Cut that out," admonished Niland, "or I'll get the willies."

Steele's eyes were blackly brooding. "I've always been a fellow to take things as they came along. Never worrying much. Life's always been pretty easy, pretty full of sunshine. But for two months, night and day, I have felt as if I were drifting along toward darkness. I keep looking around me, and the sun's there, and the stars are there — the world's just the same as it always was. But still that ungodly black curtain keeps coming nearer and I'm heading for it. What's behind it — who knows?"

"Stop that," said Niland sharply. "You know what you need? You need to go over to the Palace, get one of the girls to sit beside you, and then drink hard."

"It's been tried before," said Steele and pulled himself out of his stark mood with visible effort. "The kind of forgetfulness one buys at the Palace only lasts so long. Well, I was born with a silver spoon in my mouth, and fair pastures were mine by heritage. But my star is a restless one and sometimes dark in the sky. The brightest spot in this little flicker of existence that is me comes from knowing I am a friend of Dave's. What's the matter with that bottle — leakin'?"

"The Palace is across the street and three doors down," said Niland.

CHAPTER IX
DARK HUNGERS

A familiar horse stood by Durbin's hardware store. Denver, stopping on the instant, ran his glance along the street and discovered Lou Redmain. The outlaw was posted in the mouth of an alley, his attention riveted on the hotel porch. Denver drew aside from the eddy of the crowd and found what held Redmain's interest. Eve Leverage sat in a porch rocker with Debbie Lunt and Steve Steers beside her.

Even with fifty feet intervening, Denver caught a change in Redmain's dark and pointed face. The formal indifference was gone and in its stead was an utter absorption. Unaccountably it reminded Denver of a time in early boyhood when he had left his father's house, climbed a distant ridge, and saw for the first time the sweeping vastness of the prairie. It came back to him even now, that shock of surprise upon finding a world he had never known about, never dreamed of. All of an afternoon he had lain on his stomach, swelling with vague desires. And it seemed to him that Lou Redmain, staring across the street,

166

might be going through a like turmoil of spirit.

Denver shook his head and felt a pity for the man. All that Redmain stood for was repulsive and hateful to Eve Leverage. That dusty street might as well be a thousand miles wide, so great was the gulf separating the minds of these two. Redmain could never cross it. And Denver knew that Redmain recognized the fact; he also knew that to Redmain this was bitter knowledge.

"Poor devil," grunted Denver. "Here he is, built like the rest of us, with the same stuff in him — and still he never will belong. And what makes the hurt still worse is to realize that but for his own folly he might have been the kind of a fellow Eve would like."

Thinking this, Denver was considerably jarred to see Redmain suddenly square himself in the alley and walk straight for the porch. He got to the steps and whipped off his hat before Eve saw him. Steve Steers rose. Then Eve nodded her head, neither friendly nor unfriendly. Denver caught himself from going forward.

"Here, here, this is no better than eavesdroppin'. None of my business." Turning, he went to the bank.

To Eve the meeting came with sharp unexpectedness. It was impossible for her to like Lou Redmain. She abhorred outlawry as only a woman can whose menfolk are exposed to the dangers of outlaw violence. The black hints surrounding Redmain made her shudder. Yet she met the situation with cool detachment, inclining her head at this strange visitor whose eyes seemed to burn into her. The wind ruffled his hair as he stood soldierlike on the steps. Steve Steers cleared his throat impatiently, but Redmain never noticed Steve.

"A pleasant day," said he, and Eve was surprised at the supple melody of his voice.

"It has been nice," she replied.

He seemed to listen to her words rather than to the meaning of them; and she felt the almost hungry impact of his glance. It made her flush a little. Steve was quite still. Debbie held herself scornfully back.

"I have been looking for your father," went on Lou Redmain. "Will you tell him I have seen some of his strays away up behind Sharon Springs?"

"I will," said Eve. "And I know he'd want me to thank you for mentioning it."

"I already have my reward, Miss Eve."

"How is that?"

"Talking to you," he answered, inclining his head.

"It seems a slim reward to me," she reflected.

He shook his head. "It is not possible for you to know what things a lonely man finds pleasure in."

She let the silence pile up. Redmain shifted. "Doubtless you will be going to the dance."

"I think so."

He appeared to brace himself, to take a deeper breath. "If I came, I wonder if you might find it possible out of the kindness of your heart to give me a dance."

She met the question squarely, holding his eyes. "I'm sorry, Mr. Redmain, but I wouldn't want to. And I don't mean to hurt your feelings."

He took the rejection impassively. "A man should never ask too much of a world that gives very little." Then rather gently he added, "You have not hurt my feelings. I quite understand." Raising his hat, he turned quickly and walked away toward the east end of town.

"Why," exclaimed Debbie, "I should have slapped his face!"

"Don't say that," rebuked Eve, looking troubled. But the trouble left her the next moment when Denver swung up to the steps and took a chair. She wrinkled her nose at him. "I have been advertising myself on this porch for one hour, David. What's wrong with my charm?"

He chuckled. "Would have come earlier, but I saw somebody else answerin' the ad, so I waited."

"Then why didn't you come and break into it?" Debbie asked.

"Like to give every man a chance," drawled Denver.

"Do you think he had much chance?" demanded Eve.

"No-o, but the poor fellow needs a little sunshine now and then."

"Sometimes," said Debbie, "I think the men of this county are scared to death of Lou Redmain."

Eve grew impatient. "Debbie, you can say more foolish, unwise things!"

"Well," retorted Debbie, "everybody knows he's an outlaw, and yet he walks into town like he owned it. Why isn't he arrested?"

"Lack of proof," murmured Denver. "One of the funny things about justice is you've got to establish guilt before you can punish. On that score, Redmain's as free as the birds of passage."

"Everybody knows he's guilty," said Debbie. "That's enough."

"So you've joined the vigilantes," grinned Denver. But he sobered quickly. "I doubt if he is ever arrested. I doubt if Sundown jail ever sees him. He'll go like all outlaws go —

170

rough and sudden, out in the hills."

"Something ought to be done," insisted Debbie, not to be shaken.

"Something will be done," Denver reassured her. "And the result may surprise you as well as shock you."

"A large round fact and no mistake," chimed in Steve.

Debbie suppressed him with a single glance and rose. "Steve, I'm going shopping. Come help me carry bundles." Denver watched them depart with doubt on his face.

"She sure treats him rough, Eve."

"I think it's shameful. He stands everything from her."

"Yeah," agreed Denver casually. "But there's just one thing she doesn't know about Mister Stephen Burt Steers. When he finally puts his foot down he does it firm enough to make the welkin ring."

The two of them settled into comfortable silence, side by side, while the sun slid to the west.

"Sunshine's nice," said he.

"But soon gone."

"Not while you're around, Eve."

"Sounds fishy," said Eve skeptically, "but I like it."

Lou Redmain went away from the hotel

171

with clouded eyes. He maintained a set face until, beyond the end of the street, he swung to the north and climbed a wooded trail. And at that point, no longer under inspection, he let the accumulated resentment pour out of him.

"A pariah, an outcast! Not fit to be touched, not good enough to be danced with! That is me — Lou Redmain! I could stand hatred from her better than the pity she showed! Good God, am I not a man like the rest? Haven't I got some decency in me she could see and make allowances for? No, never! I took my trail, and now I've got to travel it alone. I'm branded, and there is no hope of change. Damn them all!"

Even then, swayed by fury, he looked cautiously about him and ducked into a stand of pines. At the head of the trail stood a small house, and he crept beside it guardedly until he saw Lola Monterey standing in the kitchen. The door was open, and through it came the soft, throaty hum of a song. He emerged from shelter and swiftly crossed over. She heard him and turned to the door; but the light in her eyes faded at sight of the man. And a jealous, protective rage swept over his body.

"You were expectin' somebody. Who was it, Lola?"

She shook her head. "Not you, Lou."

"No? What are you doing up here — what kind of a place are you runnin'? By God, the last thing I'll let —"

"Stop it! It is not your right to carry on so."

He choked down his bitterness. "I suppose not. But I took good care of you once. I kept an eye on you. Seems like I'm still tryin' to."

"Have I forgotten it?" she asked him. "What is the matter with you? Here you come storming down as if you were mad."

"I reckon we're all mad," he muttered. "Anybody's mad to take life seriously. Mad as hell."

"You have done something," she observed.

"So. I walked in front of Sundown and asked Eve Leverage for a dance next week. What did I get? Pity!"

"Did you think she would dance with you, Lou?"

He stared at her. "Well, why not? What have you been hearin' about me, Lola?"

"Many, many things. None of them good."

"And you believe them?"

"Look at me," said she softly, "and tell me none of these stories are true."

He accepted the challenge, but of a sudden she was a blur before his eyes, and he dropped his head, groaning. "Why should I? Lola, you were one of the two people in the world I feared to have know about me."

"So I must think of you as a man who once was gay and impulsive and kind — and now is only a memory of that man. Lou — what a fool you have been to throw away all that you might have been!"

"What difference does it make?" he muttered defiantly. "I wasn't born to follow the herd. I was born to go the other way — what is wrong in that? Who has the power of telling me what is wrong? Nobody! The pack makes right — the pack makes wrong! That's all. If I don't run with the pack I'm not ashamed. I am my own law. I am as good as any!"

"You are trying to put glory on your weaknesses. I hate that kind of a thing!"

"Who are you to talk?" he retorted.

He had struck her hard. She drew back, answering slowly, sadly, "Whatever my faults may have been, Lou, they have hurt only me. Never another soul in this world."

The drum of a woodpecker sounded sharp and clear in the late afternoon. Redmain raised his hand with a queer gesture of finality. "I saw it coming. Nothing could keep it from you — about me. There isn't anybody left now who's got any illusions as to the kind of a man I am."

"I remember the kind of a man you once were, Lou," she reminded him.

"Three years ago," he broke in gruffly. "People don't stand still. They go on. They're pushed on. I couldn't be that kind of a fellow any more if I wanted. But the big thing is — I don't want to."

"I am sorry for you."

"I'm not!" he snapped. "The pack can't catch me, can't squeeze me into its ideas and morals. It never will. Before I'm through I'll show them all what a man can do of his free will."

"Lou, you must not say that."

He pursued his thought heedlessly. "I'll see you no more, Lola. I'll never come to Sundown again. This is the last time my welcome's any good here. Well, I'm sorry you know about me. But I'm glad to remember there was a time —"

He saw the gleam of a tear in her eyes as she faced him. Down the trail was the sound of someone. Redmain retreated to the edge of the trees. David Denver was approaching the house.

"Your man's comin', Lola," said he grimly. "Better take good care of him. He thinks he's neutral, but he ain't. He couldn't be if he wanted. I won't let him! It won't be long before we meet, and then you'll have somethin' to cry about. Before God you will!"

He ducked from sight. On a dead run he

175

descended through the trees, avoiding the trail, and aimed for Sundown's west end.

"I'll do no dancin' next week," he panted, "I won't be there! But it is a dance none of 'em will ever forget. I'll see to that. From now on I play this game for all it's worth. From now on let them take care of themselves!"

CHAPTER X
MURDER AND MUSIC

The Copperhead school was to-night the rendezvous for every able-bodied man, woman, and child within forty miles. Sounds of revelry emerged from every opening and floated across frosty air; lights gleamed through every opening, and the brisk melody of guitar and fiddle made lively rhythm. Men whooped cheerfully, women laughed; and the movement of the crowd never stopped, for Yellow Hill believed in playing with energy.

Copperhead school itself never could have held them all, but there was no need of that. The school was only a minor appendage built on to Casper Flood's enormous hay barn. To-night the floor was cleared, cleaned, and waxed, and if the footing was sometimes rough nobody cared. All around the walls sat the matrons who no longer found comfort in the actual struggle, the patriarchs who secretly cherished a desire to shine as dancers and were restrained by family opinion, and the children — many of whom were sound asleep on improvised beds.

Midnight long since had passed, yet the dance went buoyantly on. Carriages departed, riders came in. Out under a tree men foregathered between dances to partake of cheer; and just inside the door a clump of punchers formed the inevitable stag line. In another corner of the barn stretched a mammoth table which earlier in the evening had groaned under vast mounds of sandwiches, fat hams, haunches of beef and cakes by the dozen. At present it resembled the devastated field of a great battle. Yet the folks still trooped to it, the hot coffee still steamed out of the enormous blackened pots, and from somewhere food still was fetched. And the music went on, and the dancers swirled under the gleaming lights.

"The best dance," sighed Mrs. Casper Flood, "I ever remember. Don't Dave and the Monterey girl look well? Seems like they fit."

"Ha," said Mrs. Jim Coldfoot, who had been eyeing a dark corner of the barn. "They had ought to fit. Been chasin' together long enough. Who's he goin' to marry, I want to know? I notice he pays his attention pretty evenly between the Monterey woman and Eve. Why didn't he bring Eve to this dance 'stead of Lola Monterey?"

"Why don't you ask Dave?" inquired Mrs.

Casper Flood ironically.

"Would if I thought he'd tell," said Mrs. Jim, in no manner abashed. "All I got to say is if Eve Leverage likes him and is put out by his goin' with that other girl, then she keeps it well hid, the little devil."

The music stopped with a flourish and couples began circling for seats. By degrees intimate friends collected in small knots. Presently Denver and Steele and Steers, with their partners, gathered at the table. Niland came up and joined; and lastly the Englishman arrived with one of the Fee girls. The Englishman, alone of all that assemblage, was dressed in full evening habit. His ruddy face was a burnished crimson above the utter whiteness of a stiff shirt. He bowed and he bent with a scrupulous nicety. He was urbanity and polish personified.

It was a tribute to Almaric St. Jennifer Crevecœur Nightingale that the circle at the table opened readily to admit him; and it was a still greater tribute that this circle began to cast humorous comment on his get-up. For when cattleland abandons formality toward a man, that man is accepted.

"What I wish to know," demanded Niland, indicating the full dress, "is do you pin it on or buckle it on?"

"Let's widen the inquiry," added Denver.

"Do you step into it, climb into it, or roll into it?"

"One acquires the knowledge by degrees," said Nightingale gravely. "It takes ten years to learn the proper angle at which to wear a top hat. Why, dear fellas, every curve and cut is prescribed by tradition, hallowed by memory. What you see before you is the cumulative sartorial wisdom of ten gen'rations of Nightingales, most painfully acquired. Why, my great-great-great-grandfather on the Jennifer side earned the Garter for no less a service than showing His Majesty how to be seated in a chair without wrinkling his tails. At Culloden, where one of my ancestors commanded, the battle order was delayed ten hours till swift couriers could find a daisy for this said revered ancestor to wear in his buttonhole durin' the battle. And, mind you, the enemy was so versed in etiquette it refused to attack us until my sire had found the daisy."

"Ah!" sniffed Steve Steers suspiciously.

"Upon my word," stated the Englishman, grave as a hanging judge.

"Don't let them kid you, Nighty," broke in Steele. "I sported one of those in the bygone years. It was a pleasure — as most things were to me, then."

"I reckon you acquire a taste for it," reflected Denver, "like olives or eggplant."

Mrs. Jim Coldfoot was discovered on the edge of the circle, aimlessly stabbing at food. It was apparent she meant to miss no word exchanged by these people.

"I like to see men in dress suits," said Lola.

"I could think of nothing more charming," added Eve.

"Now, there!" exploded Niland. "Right there's the insidious influence of the get-up. Nighty wears it, the women fall for it, and pretty soon we'll all have to follow in line. I consider this grave enough for the vigilantes."

"Supposing," suggested Denver, "we excuse ourselves for a smoke and consider the state of affairs at mature length?"

"Is it just a smoke you want?" was Debbie Lunt's malicious question. She looked at Steve, and he joined the departing men uneasily, while the rest of the women laughed.

Out in the yard they assembled. There was a slight gurgle. "What was that the Governor of South Ca'lina said to the Governor of North Ca'lina?" asked Steve. "Personally I despise strong drink, but my feet's hurtin' me awful."

"Don't see why they should," retorted Denver. "You been ridin' around all evenin' on somebody else's feet."

"I'd kill any other man for that," growled Steve, and began to cough. "Whoosh! Somebody hit me on the back 'afore I strangle. Who

181

kicked me in the stummick?"

The Englishman, not yet quite up to the group, was suddenly plucked on the sleeve. A pair of shadows said "Shush!" in unison and drew him away. "It's us, Meems and Wango. Yore a stranger in the country and had ought to be introduced to somethin' nice. Come right over here. By this wagon. Lean agin it while I get the bottle. Don't want nobody else to see or they'd jest swamp us."

"But —" began Nightingale and was pushed against the wagon's side with cordial insistence.

"That's all right. Don't let yore gen'rosity get the best of you. Wango and me believe we owe it to a stranger once, anyhow. Here it is, the finest whisky money can buy. Take a drink. Take a big drink. Hell, take two-three drinks and see if we ain't got the best —"

"Oh, very well," agreed Nightingale and accepted the bottle. The partners crowded beside him, patted him on the back. Nightingale lowered the bottle. "Is this what you are proud of?"

"Ain't it the doggonedest, bestest —"

The Englishman belched magnificently. "I think your trust in nature is jolly well misplaced. Thanks for the disinfectant, and excuse me while I join my friends."

Meems and Wango waited until Nightingale had crossed the yard, then turned toward their horses. "After that," said Meems, "I think we better take our leave. Never know what a furriner will do."

"Yeah," agreed Wango. Together they swung to saddle and aimed for the maw of Copperhead bridge. Wango spoke doubtfully. "Say, Buck, do yuh think that was really funny?"

"Sure it was funny," insisted Meems. "I thought I'd die of laughin' —"

"That's a long jump and run from any proof it's funny," gloomed Wango. "Supposin' he takes exception?"

"Ah, shucks, Englishmen don't get mad. They just look pained."

"Well, mebbe it was funny."

"Sure it was funny. Haw, haw!"

"Damned if it wuzn't funny! Haw, haw, haw!"

The echo of this blank and hollow laughter ran back through the covered bridge and dismally died. A rider came out of the Sky Peak region, flailing down the sloping road. Meems and Wango, chary birds, moved off the highway without comment and halted. The rider ran past but drew to a walk at the bridge and went quietly across. Meems and Wango proceeded onward.

"Make him out?" whispered Wango.

"Yeah. I saw."

"Now, I wonder —"

"Shut your face. Yuh didn't see him atall, get me? You and me don't know nothin'. And is happy as such."

"Gosh, we're ign'runt ain't we, Buck?"

"You bet. I misdoubt they's two fellas in the world that knows as much as we do and is so plumb ign'runt."

Denver and his friends returned casually to the dance hall. It was Steve Steers who, stepping around Nightingale, first saw what had happened. Compressing his lips, he began to wigwag at the others. The Englishman walked forward to his lady and bowed ceremoniously; and by this time there were twenty people grinning at him. The Englishman began to feel something wrong and swung about, thus exposing his back to the length of the hall. Somebody whooped joyously. Whereat Nightingale twisted his neck, and looked among his friends.

"Do I," he demanded, "look odd?"

"Who've you been associatin' with lately?" Denver asked.

"Hm," breathed Nightingale. "Did those extr'ord'n'ary fellas, Meems and Wango, have an ulterior motive?" He bowed again at his lady and with a calmness that was iron-like shucked his coat to expose all the bracing and lacing and scaffolding of his shirt. He held up the back of the coat critically. Upon it clung a square sheet of paper, damp with paste, and across the paper was inscribed:

FOR RENT OR HIRE
SEE JAKE EPSTEIN
NOBBY CLOTHIER.

"So they took me," observed Nightingale, ripping off the sign. And though he maintained the utmost gravity, something like a beam of laughter sparkled in his azure eyes.

The women were outraged. But Denver chuckled broadly. "Well, we've got one point cleared up about that rig. He doesn't pin it on; he buckles it on."

Cal Steele, smiling languidly, let his glance play around the hall. His head jerked, and on the moment darkness came to his face. Rather forcibly he recovered his smile and murmured to Eve, "Just excuse me a minute." He strode out of the barn.

"Folks," said Eve, "in two or three hours it will be daylight. Most of our men have a day's work ahead. Supposing we go home."

"I think I do more work than anybody

here," put in Nightingale. "Keepin' out of my foreman's way."

Steve Steers flushed and appeared uncomfortable, as indeed he had appeared most of the evening.

"Always was an officious rascal," drawled Denver. "The trouble is to keep him on the job. Temperamental I mean."

"Ain't I among friends?" was Steve's plaintive groan.

Debbie started to defend him with tartness, but Cal Steele returned and drew the circle's attention. Worry stamped his cheeks. He spoke without the customary ease, almost jerking the words out.

"This is bad. I've got to go home. Now. David, could I appeal to you to see that Eve is taken care of? Eve, my dear, I'll make up for this —"

"It's all right," Eve assured him quickly.

Denver was watching his friend with sharp attention. "Want help, Cal?"

"No. Not at all. But I've got to go."

It was Steve who had to crown his evening's misery by one supremely inopportune remark.

"Well, yuh got two girls now, Dave. What you goin' to do with 'em?"

In itself the statement was harmless; but it brought to the minds of all the long-standing question in Yellow Hill concerning Dave and

Lola and Eve. In the moment of dead silence Steve saw his mistake and was practically paralyzed. He turned a dull red. It was Eve, herself flushed, who bridged the strained scene.

"That's soon settled," said she coolly. "Let Lola come home with me tonight."

"I would like that," replied Lola, dark eyes shining across at Eve.

Cal Steele gave the group a short flickering smile. "Good-night to you all. I have had the evening of my life. And until we meet again — bless you, my children."

Denver was plainly worried, and he started after Steele. "Sure you don't want help, Cal?"

But Cal Steele shook his head. "Dave, old man, if I did I'd come to you first of all." The inner strain of his thoughts aged him; he stared at Denver like a man racked and wrung. "Just remember that. I'd always come to you first — and last. So long."

He disappeared, leaving behind the hint of trouble. Some of the sparkle went from the party, and by common consent they slowly paid their farewells and walked from the hall. Denver put Eve and Lola in his rig and went over to intercept Steve. "Listen, when you leave Debbie home, why not cut around by the rock road to the ranch? Just to see if anything's on the wing?"

"Can do," grunted Steve.

Dave hurried back and found his foreman, Lyle Bonnet, loitering in the stag line. "Pick up what boys you find from the outfit," he told Bonnet, "and take the straight tail to Starlight. If you hear anything, have a look. Now, hustle."

He returned to the buggy, spread the robes around Lola and Eve, and silently aimed for the Leverage ranch. In the course of the ride he hardly spoke a dozen words, wrapped as he was in uneasy thought. At the Leverage house he helped them down and turned the buggy about. They stood on the porch a moment, the fair, clear-minded, and boyish Eve beside Lola, who seemed to him so often all fire and flame. It struck him queerly that these two, opposites in character, should tonight be sharing the same house. Eve's drowsy, practical, "Good-night, Dave, go home and get some sleep," made a pleasant melody in the night. Lola only said, "Good-night," in a slow whisper, but somehow it was in Dave's ear all the way across the yard. In the main road he put the horse to an urgent pace, the thought of Cal Steele's drawn face troubling him.

Eve lighted a lamp and showed Lola to the guest room. "Sleep as late as you please. I'll take you to town in the morning. We've had a splendid evening, haven't we?"

Lola's dark eyes glowed. "Tonight you smoothed over the hard truth, and I admired you more than ever I thought I would." She threw back her head and acted out Steve's unfortunate sentence. " 'Well, you've got two girls now, Dave. What are you going to do with them?' But David could not answer it if he wanted. He doesn't know. Neither do you, nor I."

Eve seemed a little pale and tired. "I have been wanting to ask you something for a long while. Did you find the three years' absence to help any? With David?"

"Why?"

Eve answered slowly. "If I thought my leaving for a time would make any difference I'd go to-morrow."

"And come back on the next train for fear of losing," said Lola. "I know."

"What would you do to please him?" asked Eve.

"You see me standing here. I could be a thousand pleasanter places. There is your answer. I would go any place for him, do anything. Do you understand that?"

Eve's body stiffened. The message in Lola's eyes, the blaze of feeling repelled her. Lola laughed softly. "You wouldn't, would you? You want to be discreet. You are afraid. You

189

want things without paying for them."

"That is not love," said Eve quickly.

"Not your kind. But it is my kind. Love is everything. Like fire, like torture, like thirst. You must be half a savage to know it. I'm half a savage. You're not."

"But it isn't love," repeated Eve, biting her lip.

"Not your kind," said Lola, a trace of scorn in her words. "Let me tell you. David Denver is too strong a man to be held completely by any one woman. He is kind, yet when the black mood is on him he could double up his fist and destroy. He speaks softly, yet always with a fire burning deep down in him. He will never be happy, he will never find all that he wants in any one woman. Yet my kind can hold him — for a little while. What I must do to have him — that I'll do. But never, never will it be enough. I throw myself away gladly. And in the end he will destroy me. That is love. You know nothing about it. Go East, where you won't be hurt."

"You don't know him at all," said Eve.

Lola's mood changed on the instant. "Of course I don't. If I knew him — I could have him! You — what do you know that I don't? Tell me that!"

"Isn't it a little late for us to be talking so?" asked Eve.

"You are very calm and very wise, aren't you? You are one thing — I am another. Perhaps if both of our natures were in one woman Dave would puzzle himself no longer."

"Sometimes," said Eve with a shadow on her face, "I think I am two women — and one of them is like you, but never able to come out and be seen. Good-night."

Denver drove the buggy across his yard and unhitched, throwing the horse into a corral. Lyle Bonnet came off the main house porch.

"No developments?" asked Dave.

"Nothin'," said Bonnet, sleepy-voiced. "There was a few shots beyond Starlight about an hour ago. But I'd say it was some galoot comin' home from the dance."

"I suppose," agreed Dave. "You better turn in."

As for himself, he crossed through the main room and settled down on the south porch of the house. From this vantage point he could, on a clear day, look down the sweep of Starlight canyon and on into the open prairie for thirty miles or more. He liked to sit here and feel that he was for a while above the heat of the world. It gave him a sense of peace. But tonight he could not summon back that peace. Cal Steele's face, strangely

191

distorted, kept rising before him. Yellow Hill was going to war, no doubt of it. Riders were in the night and man's hand was set against man's hand. Jake Leverage had not been at the dance, nor had Lou Redmain. These men were busy elsewhere. And behind them were many riders on the hunt.

"So it will be," he muttered. "And how long will I be able to stay up here and mind my affairs? God knows. I despise posses about as much as I despise outlaws. Who is to say whether the hunted is so much blacker than the man hunting? Let every man stand responsible for his acts, and let every man fight his own fights. Yet that is something soon enough impossible to do. Then what?"

Starlight throbbed with weaving, swirling shadows; the sky was hidden behind the fog mist. The country seemed to lie uneasy. Denver, who responded quickly to the primitive moods of the earth, felt the shift and change as if the temperature had dropped twenty degrees.

"I will fight my own fights," he said to himself. "No matter whom it puts me against. I don't want to go against Redmain, but if it must be then it shall be. All I ask —"

He stiffened and turned his head slightly to the wind. Above the slow rustle of the night emerged a foreign disturbance. It came from the upper trail — a tentative, cautious advance of a horse. Denver slid his feet quietly beneath him, rose, and slipped into the house. He dimmed the lamp and went out to the yard, going on to the vague bulk of a pine trunk. There was a rider just above the place; and that rider seemed to be turning with considerable hesitation from one angle of the slope to another. Denver waited patiently.

Then the horse stopped, but from the shadows came a weird sobbing noise that shot a chill along Denver's nerves. He left the tree and challenged. "Who's there?"

A trembling reply came back. "Dave — oh, Dave — !"

"Cal!" shouted Denver, racing forward.

"Dave, my God, I'm shot to ribbons!"

Denver reached the horse as his friend started slipping from the saddle. He caught Steele in his arms, feeling the warm blood all along the man's clothes. "Cal, by all that's — ! Hang onto yourself! I'll have you layin' easy in a minute. Doc Williamson will get here right away. Cal!"

Denver stumbled across the yard. The bunkhouse door sprang open, and men ran out. Somebody dashed for the house and turned up the lamp. Denver marched in, laid Steele on a couch, ripping at the crimson wet shirt. But Steele rolled his head in negation and opened his eyes, staring up at Denver.

"No use — doin' that. I'm — shot — to — pieces."

Denver cursed bitterly. "Who did it, Cal? By the livin' Christ, I'll rip the throat out of the man!"

Steele's lips began twitching. "I said I'd — come to you — first or last, didn't I?" he murmured. "Tried to do you a favor, old boy. Like you'd do me. Listen to me —"

But there was no more from Cal Steele then, nor ever would be. His head slid forward, and the invisible hand of death reached down to place the everlasting seal upon that fine face.

CHAPTER XI

TRAILS

Dave Denver made his preparations in the dark hour preceding dawn. He ordered the best horses saddled and brought to the porch. He opened his gun locker and distributed the rifles resting there, at the same time dividing his outfit into three parts, one to patrol his range, one to return to work, and one to ride under him. From the patrolling party he dispatched a man to Sundown for Dr. Williamson and another to Steele's ranch. The rest of that particular group he detailed to various points in the hills. All ate a hurried breakfast. The work party went off discontentedly; and when the first gray light of morning broke through the fog he gathered his chosen riders, mounted, and swung up the side of the ridge to trace the hoofprints of Cal Steele's horse. Lyle Bonnet, traveling directly behind, offered a brief suggestion.

"Better send somebody to tell Leverage. It's a matter for the vigilantes."

Denver shook his head. "I'll never ask anybody else to do a dirty chore I ought to do myself. And don't get it in your head, Lyle, that I want anybody else to settle this. I'll find the party who killed Cal — and I'll smile when I see him dead."

The yielding earth bore the print of Steele's last ride for better than two miles straight down the trail. At that point the tracks swung into the slope of Starlight, crossed the bottom of the canyon, and angled along the far side. Once Denver halted and got down. Steele had fallen from the saddle. A carpet of leaves was marked with the man's blood.

"He had a bad time gettin' back on," muttered Denver. "Don't see how he ever made it. It's clear as day his strength was about gone."

Beyond Starlight the trail went zigzagging through timber. Denver advanced slowly. His friend seemed to have got lost and in sheer despair given his horse free head. All through the timber were places where the pony had circled, doubled on its own course, and straightened again for the canyon. As the day broadened Denver pushed deeper into the secretive glens and pine reaches guarding the Copperhead watershed. Cal Steele's trail began to straighten.

"Not far from the place now," said Denver. "See, he had control of himself for a little while and managed to make a true course."

196

Thirty minutes later Denver halted in an upland meadow and pointed at the broken surface of the soil. Hoofmarks overran the meadow and muddied it as if to blot out some sinister story that had been there. Into this confused area ran the pony tracks — and there were lost to distinct view.

"Here's where it happened," announced Denver, eyes flaring. "Now let's see where all these night birds went afterward. Cut back into the trees and circle. Keep out of the meadow or you'll make the ground worse than it is."

Lyle Bonnet, already on the quest, jumped from his saddle and bent over. "Here's a hat, Dave."

Denver rode over and took it. He looked briefly at the sweatband. "Cal's," he said. And while the crew scouted off he went back to the center of the meadow and tried to construct some sort of a story. "Cal had warnin'," he reflected. "Somebody came to the dance and tipped him off. Then he came here, smashed into trouble, and made his last stand. Those shots Bonnet heard must have been the ones that riddled him. They came from this direction about a half hour or so after he left the dance. That means he lost no time. Didn't hunt around but rode right into it. In other words he knew where this bunch was — or the messenger knew. And who was that messenger?"

Lyle Bonnet returned. "Must have been twenty men in the party. They pulled the old Apache trick. Shot him to ribbons and then scattered. There's a dozen or more tracks leadin' away to every point of the compass."

"So," reflected Denver. "But before they could go away they had to come. Must be some tracks pointing in."

"Yeah. They rode up from the Copperhead together, accordin' to my judgment."

Denver studied Steele's hat. "Blood on it. Blood all over the trail. A good man's blood waterin' this damned dark country. Come on, we'll start trackin'. No use wastin' time here."

With the crew behind him, he swept across the meadow and struck the inbound trail of the night party. It took him downhill to the southeast. From the clots of mud spattering the brush he knew that the group had come along at a fast clip. Come from where? Presumably from the river. But there was extraordinarily rough country along the river at this point, which brought him to the possibility that the outlaws had dashed out of the Sky Peak country and crossed the bridge. That as well seemed unlikely. The dance hall was too close to the bridge to permit unobserved passage of any large party during the evening.

Lyle Bonnet's shrewd mind had been going along much the same line of reasoning. "They musta spurred out of the south, Dave, and circled the schoolhouse at a distance."

"Maybe," agreed Denver. "But maybe they didn't. Maybe they were on Steele's range, or Nightingale's range, and looped around to the meadow. They were near enough this country at midnight for some friend of Steele's to see them and give Cal a warning. That meadow is on my range but close to Cal's. Maybe he got warning they were rustling his stuff and rode off to take a hand. And found them on my soil instead."

"Sounds unlikely," observed Bonnet. "It was awful dark last night. Either he knew right where they were, or else they made a powerful lot of noise. No trail he might have took to get home would bring him near the meadow. What defeats me is why he didn't let somebody know about it instead of ridin' off alone."

Denver shook his head, saying nothing. Cal Steele was a man of moods and never quite fathomable. Mystery surrounded his last hours, a part of the brooding mystery that of late hovered over Yellow Hill County.

He drew in, having reached the gravel road connecting Sundown Valley with the ranches along the Coperhead. At this point the outlaw trail left the soft ground of the ridge and fell

199

into the road, merging with all the other prints of travel along it.

"They come from Steele's or Nightingale's all right," stated Bonnet after a long inspection. "But that ain't what we want to know. Our question is where they went afterward. How about sendin' two-three boys back to the meadow and trackin' down some of those departin' buzzards? Sooner or later we'd find where the bunch come together again."

Denver rolled a cigarette. "No, there's an easier way, Lyle. If it was just one man or two men we'd have to scout from the beginnin' and unravel what we found. But when it's a mess of twenty or more there ain't much doubt in my mind as to who we're looking for. There ain't but one gang in Yellow Hill that big."

"Meaning Lou Redmain," mused Bonnet. "If you consider doin' what I think yuh are, then I'd say send somebody back for the rest of the crew. Eight of us ain't enough."

For a still longer time Denver sat in the saddle, staring down the road. He was arrived at last at that crisis to which he long had hoped he never would come. To live and let live — such was the very foundation of all his thoughts and acts. He wished to have no part in judging what was good and what was bad. Yet for all that he could not escape from the clear call of his conscience. He would fight his own battles, he would justify his friends. No matter if it meant the end of all peace, no matter if it meant Yellow Hill was to be torn asunder and left aswirl with powder smoke.

And so it would be when he turned the crew around and started west on that road. He was too wise to believe differently. Inevitably the force he represented would collide with the force that Lou Redmain stood for; and in that conflict nobody could say what result would arise. It was grim irony that he trembled on the very margin of an act he had condemned at the Association meeting. He had rejected the quasi-legal opportunity to strike at Redmain and now was about to strike without the shadow of any formal sanction. This was war, this was violence but one degree above Redmain's own outlawry. No matter what background there might be of rough-handed justice, that staring fact remained, and David Denver was too candid with himself to avoid it.

Yet he had no wish to avoid it. Through many months he had seen violence smoking up to some enormous culmination. Quite clear-sightedly he had seen it and made known the fact that he was not to be counted as a partisan unless the one and only one proviso arose. Well, it had arisen. Cal Steele was dead. And somewhere Lou Redmain was preparing to strike again. For with a man who declares the sky to be his limit there could be no halfway point, no line of decency. Redmain would go on, from one piece of violence and banditry to another, with increasing contempt of law. He would never stop — until he died. So the problem lay clear and simple in David Denver's mind. He tossed away his cigarette, turning to the crew.

"I reckon I'm responsible for whatever happens and whoever gets hurt. You know what's ahead. I won't ask anybody to ride with me that feels different. Sing out now before we start."

A short constrained silence followed. Lyle Bonnet raked the men with sober eye and spoke for them. "Now that you've got that ceremony off yore chest, let's waste no more time."

"All right —"

The sound of a cavalcade came drumming around the bend. It was Steele's crew with Hominy Hogg leading. The party halted.

"We was a-comin' around to meet yuh by Starlight," explained Hominy. "What's the ticket?"

"We're crossing over Sundown Valley," said Denver.

"The sooner the better," grunted Hominy. "I thought you'd do it. That's why we come loaded, all of us."

"Didn't you know about what happened before I sent a man over?" queried Denver.

"Nope. Steele left around eight last night, alone. Said he'd probably be home considerable late. That's the last we saw or heard, till Ben come along with yore note."

"Didn't one of you fellows ride to the dance and give him a message?" persisted Denver.

Hominy Hogg looked blank. "Nobody as I know about. Fact is, none of our outfit went to the dance. Steele seemed to sorter have trouble on his mind and told us to stick close to quarters."

"I'd give a great deal to know who the man was," was Denver's slow answer. "He led Cal to the slaughter — and disappeared. You understand, boys, that we're starting something, and it may be a long pull before we're finished. If anybody's got an idea this is just a holiday he'd better drop out."

"Whud yuh suppose we come for?" countered Hominy. "This business leads back to one gent. Go ahead. You do the thinkin' and we'll do the shootin'. As long as it takes."

Denver reined his horse about and set off, the men pairing behind. Around and down and up the twisting gravel road they galloped, thirty-odd riders heavily armed and single minded. They passed the mouth of Starlight and came into the Sundown-Ysabel Junction stage road. They traversed the plank bridge at Sweet Creek and labored along the hairpin turns, and so came at last to the level stretch across which Shoshone Dome threw its shadow. Here Denver turned over the soft meadows of Sundown Valley and entered the dark land bordering the Wells.

All along this route Denver's mind kept plucking away at the puzzle of Cal Steele's unknown informant. Who, other than one of his own crew, would come hasting out of the night to warn him? And, having done that, vanish from the picture? If this man had known of the outlaws and had considered it important enough to reach Cal Steele, why then did he not go back with Steele and engage in the same fight? Perhaps he had done so. And escaped when Steele fell. Then why was it that the man had not gone to tell others instead of dropping from view? Had he been wounded and crawled into some thicket to die? Or was the fellow some traitorous friend of Steele's who had knowingly led the latter to destruction? This was possible, though it seemed queer to Denver that Steele would let himself easily into a trap. Steele had lived in the country long enough to understand all the tricks.

But over and above all these speculations one unexplainable fact kept jarring every probable hypothesis. Steele had gone off without help, without confiding in another. And he had gone off in a seriously upset frame of mind. Only a disturbance of major import could have placed that pallor and those lines on the easy-going man's cheeks. Each time Denver reverted to that final scene at the dance he was conscious of a strange chill, a premonition of evil. His mind beat against the black curtain of uncertainty. For a brief instant that curtain slipped aside, and Denver caught sight of something that repelled and hardened him. He ripped out an oath. Lyle Bonnet forged beside him swiftly.

"See somethin'?"

But Denver shook his head and set his jaws. He pulled himself away from his painful thinking and with visible effort concentrated his senses on the tangible world about him. He experienced a sudden dread at allowing himself to tamper with that concealing curtain again.

Lyle Bonnet was once more beside him. "You goin' to smash right down, Dave? Or put a ring around 'em?"

Only then did Denver realize the full absorption of his thoughts. He had covered five rugged miles almost sightlessly. They were in a widening bay of the pines, a bay that entered a scarred hillside clearing. And over there, slumbering under the full sun, were the unlovely buildings of the Wells. Nothing moved in the street, By common consent the party halted.

"Looks a little fishy to me," observed Bonnet. "Too damned deserted. I'd hate to run into a pour of lead."

"Not even no smoke from the chimbleys," observed Hominy Hogg.

Denver's nerves tightened, an acute clarity came to all his senses. In that lull of time every detail of the sagging buildings, the frowzy street, the scarred hillside registered indelibly on his brain. He actually felt the quality of suspended, breathless silence emanating from the place and the almost animate glare of the windows facing him.

Denver made his disposition of forces quickly. "You take half your men, Hominy, and circle for the top of that hillside. Then walk out of the trees and straight down. Lyle and six others will go to the right, curve clear around, and get set to come into the street from that end. I'll wait here. Hominy's got the longest trip. When he rides to view, the rest of us start accordingly."

Hominy wanted to be absolutely sure of Denver's intent. "In case they don't quite make up their minds to fight or be peaceable, what's our cue?"

"If Redmain's yonder," said Denver, "there can be no question what he'll do. He's burned his bridges and cut himself off. Nothing left for him but fight it out."

"But in case —"

"There ain't any other answer, for him or for us," broke in Denver with sudden impatience. "Get going!"

The two parties filed through the trees; Denver waited with cold patience. He had come to the Wells once before, ready to cast up accounts. Lou Redmain had spoken softly, calling upon his given word as a mark of friendship, yet all the while meaning not a syllable of it. This day there would be none of that. The outlaw chief had forfeited the right to make a promise. There remained no solitary rule of human conduct by which he might establish his faith. He had nothing left but his jungle instincts, plus that lusting spark of domination that at once made him far more dangerous than any other beast of prey. For, while the lower animals obeyed the inevitable cycle of their kind, a renegade man obeyed only his own impulses, and it was impossible to tell what these impulses might be from hour to hour.

The stark barrenness of the town challenged Denver's watchful eyes. Methodically he swept every corner, every rubbish pile, every shaded crevice. Some doors were shut, some swung ajar. The street seemed cleared for ambush, yet if Redmain were hidden there, no sign or portent rose to warn Denver. As he considered this he looked aside and found Hominy's men advancing from the high trees. At once he gathered his reins and walked into the clearing, the following men spreading fanwise to either side of him. Hominy accelerated the pace and deployed his party to command the Wells from behind. Lyle Bonnet, having less room to maneuver on the far side of town, elected to speed up and so reached the street in advance of the others. Denver spurred by the first building and jumped to the high porch of the saloon. Watchfulness gave way. He yelled suddenly. "Spread out! Smash down the doors! Don't bunch up!" And he plunged into the saloon one pace ahead of Lyle Bonnet, gun lifted to debate his entry. The oncoming riders carried him a dozen feet before he hauled short, surprised at what he found.

There was no opposition, no renegades ranked along the walls. Behind the bar the black giant lolled, saying nothing. A dozen oldish men and six or seven women clustered sullenly at the far end of the place and stared back with apathetic hatred. Half expecting trickery, he turned about. But he could hear the others of his party running from building to building, calling down their signals. Hominy roared a savage challenge. "Where is that skunk-stinkin' pirate? Knock hell out o' the joint!" A woman laughed, shrill and scornful.

"You better get up earlier in the mornin' to find anybody here, Mister Denver!"

He swung on the drab group. "Well, where are they?"

"You'd like to know, wouldn't you?" retorted the woman. "Go and find out!"

He aimed for a rear door, went through it at a stride, and found himself in a hall. A stairway climbed to dim upper regions. Bonnet and a few others pursued him.

"Careful," muttered Bonnet; "this is a damned fine slaughterin' pen!"

Denver struck the banister with his gun barrel and listened to the echo run blankly through upper emptiness. That seemed to convince him. He sprang along the stairs three at a time, arrived at the second-floor landing, and saw more doors yawning into a hall. His men filed in either direction covering these dingy rooms One room at the end seemed larger than the rest, and Denver went in. The bed was made, and a trunk and some personal effects indicated occupancy, but from the open bureau drawers and the scattered tills of the trunk he guessed what Redmain had done.

"They've scattered," he told the incoming Bonnet. "Took their travelin' gear and departed. Redmain knows he never would be safe a minute with this for headquarters."

He dropped the top of the trunk and stared at the "L. R." burned in the wood ribs. Bonnet found grim amusement in that. "The high card's own private roost, uh? By golly, he'll sleep in harder places than this from now on."

Denver only heard part of his foreman's comment. He had found half of a book page tacked to the wall with this fragment of verse on it:

"Into this Universe, and Why *Not Knowing Nor* Whence, *like Water willy-nilly flowing; And out of it, as Wind along the Waste, I know not* Whither, *willy-nilly blowing."*

Denver ripped the page from the wall and crushed it in his blackened fist. "The poor condemned fool! What couldn't a man like that do with a drop of honest blood in his veins? Don't tell me he can't tell what's right and what's wrong. He knows the difference. He'll travel the crooked trail with fire in his heart just because he knows the difference too

210

damned well! And there's the fellow who's going to be hunted like a rat, shot at, starved, brought to stand, and knocked over! He knows better!"

A woman came, breathless and defiant, to the door; the same one who had scorned him. There was still a trace of prettiness about her. "Can't you keep your dirty hands off his things?" she cried. "Get out of here! You'll never catch Lou Redmain by prowling through his trunk! Leave it alone."

"It's your room, too, ma'm?" asked Denver.

"Well, what if it is?"

"My apologies," said Denver gravely. "I don't make it a habit of enterin' a lady's room. Not even if it's about to be destroyed." He passed her and went down the stairs.

She followed him. "What's the meaning of that?"

He crossed the saloon hall again and found Hominy waiting, morose and restless. "Well, they ain't here, that's plumb clear. What about these guineas left behind? Why not pack 'em to Sundown and let the county treat 'em for awhile? Otherwise they'll get word to Redmain and tattle. When he comes back —"

"He won't come back," broke in Denver softly.

"I ain't sure about that."

"No. He'll have nothing to come back to. We're putting him on the country for good."

"What're you driving at?" insisted the woman.

Denver raised his voice to the uneasy camp followers of the outlaw bunch. "You've got five minutes to pull your belongings out of doors. I am burning the town."

"Not a bad idee," grunted Bonnet. "I never did burn a town afore. Be somethin' new in a short but sweet life."

"Lou will kill you!" cried the woman.

"That's one of the two possibilities," said Denver. "The other is that I may kill him. I reckon you'll only have about four minutes left. It ain't my desire to burn any of your possibles, so I'd suggest you hurry."

The rest of the riders followed him to the street. "Set fire to four or five places at the same time," said Denver. "This joint is dry as pitch, and it'll go in one quick roar."

"Ready?" inquired Bonnet.

"Give these poor devils their chance, Lyle."

The black barkeep walked from the saloon barehanded. "I come here without nothin' and I'll leave without nothin'. Ain't takin' no favors from you, Mister Denver."

"That's too bad," drawled Denver. "But maybe you'll do me one. Maybe you'll take a message to Redmain for me."

"I do nothin' for you, Mister Denver. Never."

"Just as well. You'd be too slow. Now I see horses in that barn yonder and a wagon. Hitch up the wagon and turn out the rest of the animals."

The denizens of this condemned town straggled from the buildings. Denver moved down to the end of the street and sat quite still in the saddle. His attention reverted to the stable, and he spoke casually to the nearest hand. "The big boy takes too long to hitch a wagon. Go down there and let him smell the end of your loop." Instead of one, three men galloped off to carry out the chore. Denver felt the restlessness of his party, and he knew they wanted to do the job and be away. But he tarried until he thought all of the people had retrieved their possessions. They came toward him, a shabby, disreputable set that stirred him to faint pity. Aimlessly they milled at the street's end. Out of the stable came the wagon and team, the giant lashing the beasts into a dead run. He had three loops around his neck and three riders spurring ahead, threatening momentarily to haul him out of the vehicle. Denver raised his arm and the ropes slacked away. The giant halted the wagon and rolled his eyes at Denver.

213

" 'Fore God, you'll suffer fer this!"

"Somebody suffers," was Denver's laconic answer. He raised his gun to the sky and fired a single shot in warning to whoever might have loitered in the buildings. Then he called out to those men waiting to apply the match. "Let her burn."

The woman who had enough spirit to defy him ran against his horse. "You — you'll find a day to regret this!" she cried. Of a sudden Denver bent down, one arm sweeping her aside. There was the flat, startling report of a gun. The woman's right hand was wrenched up, revealing the weapon. Denver seized it and threw it far aside; and even then the tight calm remained on him.

"Can't say I blame you," he muttered. "Was I in your place I reckon I'd do the same."

The smell of smoke drifted down the street. A sinuous tongue of fire licked up a porch rail. The woman screamed at him.

"Now I know why they call you Black Dave! You call yourself a man — and do this?"

"What's your name?" demanded Denver.

"May!" said the woman, spitting it at him.

"A pretty name. The sort of a name that fitted the girl your mother figured you'd be. There's pride still in you. You'd like to kill me, wouldn't you? What for? For a man —

214

a man not worth an inch of your finger. You've lived in this ratty hole a long spell, haven't you? No comforts, no safety, nothin' cheerful. And all you've got to show for the bargain is that bundle of clothes in your arm. You've been pretty badly cheated."

"Who are you to talk?" she cried. "You're gloating because you've hurt a few poor fools that can't hurt you back! You ought to have the hide whipped off you!"

"I reckon the shoe begins to pinch," he replied. "You never felt that way when your men folk rode back from killin' a man, did you? You knew Lou Redmain was a killer, didn't you?"

"What of it? You're one yourself, you dog!"

"That's right," said Denver slowly. "As black and dirty-handed as any other. When a man starts on this business he swallows his conscience and closes his mind. And before I'm finished you and your kind, as well as a lot of other people, will consider me worse than you ever considered another human bein'. This is war, girl. And I'm deliberately forgettin' there ever was such a thing as a white man in your tribe of cutthroats. Get in that wagon, you people, and clear out of here. I don't care which way."

High flames shot from the pitch-dry buildings. The men who had set the blaze dodged

215

through the street, shielding themselves from the increasing heat. Denver looked grimly at the black giant.

"I said you'd be too slow. Redmain, wherever he is, will see my message in a few minutes. Come on, boys."

He gathered his party and spurred up into timber. Lyle Bonnet quartered down from a remote angle of the trees, where he had been drawn by his ferreting curiosity.

"I think that outfit hit for the country back of Leverage's place. Tracks indicate it."

"Well," snapped Hominy, "we've burned the rat out, anyhow. That's one detail."

"Just one place we won't have to look for him," agreed Denver. "But it's a long hunt yet. Redmain's got a talent for this business. Close in here and listen to me careful. I want these things done exactly like I tell you."

He looked behind. As they ran along the pine-cramped trail he talked to Hominy and Bonnet in subdued phrases.

CHAPTER XII
FIRES AT NIGHT

Denver cantered down Prairie Street and racked his horse before Grogan's around the middle of the afternoon. Dismounting, he slipped the cinch of his saddle a trifle and proceeded toward the saloon; but he was arrested on the threshold by sound of his name. He swung to find Fear Langdell leaning out of a second-story window.

"Dave, would you mind dropping up to my office a minute?"

Denver crossed the street and circled the last building on that side. When he climbed the stairs and entered the hot little cubicle he found Langdell pacing the floor. Without preliminaries he broke into a kind of nervous talk entirely at variance with his usual self-control.

"Good God, man, I haven't had a decent minute since your rider came in with word that Steele was done up! Why, I talked to him in this very room less than twenty-four hours ago. We discussed our plans for the next few months. Now he's gone — like that. Who killed him, Dave?"

"The ground was full of tracks," said Denver. "A big party. Use your own judgment."

"You've made up your mind as to the killer, ain't you?" insisted Langdell, stopping in the center of the room.

"Yeah."

"Always a close-mouthed man, Dave," grunted Langdell. "You got no call to be cagy with me. You know what I stand for. You know my shoulder's to the wheel with Leverage."

"I'd still like you to use your own judgment," said Denver. "My guess might be wrong."

"So?" retorted Langdell. "I observe you consider it a good enough guess to act on it."

"Who told you?"

"That mess of no-accounts come in from the Wells. They'll be kicked out of town before sun sets if I've anything to say."

"Let 'em alone, Fear. We're not fighting them. We're shootin' for big game, not sparrows."

"So you fired the Wells?"

"Yeah," said Denver impassively.

Langdell threw his cigar out the window. "Ain't that a sort of sweepin' thing to do?"

"If so," replied Denver, "I'm prepared to stand the consequences. My way of doin' business is to make up my mind and then move.

I don't call a meetin' of the county and try to pass the buck. If these big ranchers had stopped belly-achin' and done their dirty chores long ago, Cal Steele would be alive today."

Langdell's face turned sour. "For some queer reason," he blurted out, "you set yourself against every idea I bring up. I'm free to say I don't like it. I expect more of you, Dave."

"You expected me to lead the vigilantes once," pointed out Denver. "But now that I do the logical thing, which is hit at Redmain wherever I can, you back water. What do you want, anyway?"

"I know, I know. But this is different. You're laying yourself open to a charge of lawlessness."

"I don't see any particular legality in the acts of the vigilantes," was Denver's cynical rejoinder.

"It's got the approval of every important rancher in Yellow Hill," argued Langdell. "It's got the weight of the Association behind it."

"Then my acts ought to have the same approval. I'm doing neither less nor more than the vigilantes would do."

"Different altogether," insisted Langdell. "You're actin' as an individual. If there was somebody mean enough to stand on due form he could hook you bad at law."

"Was I you," drawled Denver, "I'd forget about law for awhile. It's been pretty feeble around here lately."

"Oh, hell," exclaimed Langdell, "I was just trying to point out something for your own protection. Now it looks like I'm crawfishing on my published sentiments, which I'm not. But since you intend to go after Redmain you ought to throw in with Leverage."

"Disagree."

"Why?"

"I know what I'm doing and why I'm doing it. More than that, I know the kind of men riding with me. That's more than I can say for the vigilantes. I still maintain some party or parties unknown are grindin' axes with the vigilantes. I don't propose to help 'em. I fight my own way."

"Of all the cursed nonsense!" broke in Langdell, shaking his arm violently. "You ought to know better, Denver! You're the same as questioning my honesty. Good Judas!"

A wagon and a group of riders came clattering down Prairie Street. Denver rose and went to the window. Leverage, with a dozen or more men, made a sort of escort to the wagon, which was driven by Doc Williamson.

In the bed of it lay a figure covered with blankets. Denver turned sharply away.

"Never mind how I go about this business," he said. "The point is, I'm after Redmain. And I'll get him if I go down in ruin. Never think I won't!"

"Have it your own way," grunted Langdell. "Now that you've burned out his quarters, what comes next?"

"I don't know," muttered Denver.

"You mean you're not telling," corrected Langdell.

"Leave it like that if you want."

Langdell's cold, hard formality returned to him. Denver lifted his shoulders and turned to leave, halting at the sound of somebody coming rapidly up the stairs. Leverage walked into the room. Seeing Denver, he nodded his head vigorously. "Good boy, Dave. I hear you burned the Wells. Now we can work together. Here, let me give you this confounded job of mine. I'm too old. I think I've aged ten years in the last two weeks."

"You waste your breath," interrupted Langdell. "Dave wishes to be the big toad in his own small puddle. He doubts the virtue of everybody but himself."

"Maybe," was Denver's laconic reply. "Or maybe I ain't built to dangle on the end of somebody's string. I'll leave the Christian charity to you, Fear. You seem to be drippin' with it."

Leverage caught the strained situation immediately. He had entered the office expectantly, but when he saw Denver still to be unchanged of opinion, that expectancy died. However, he made haste to ease off the tension.

"Well, I believe I've got wind of Redmain now. I've been ridin' fifteen and sixteen hours at a stretch. So's some of my men. And we've got a smell."

"Where?" asked Langdell with swift interest.

"Up behind my place. Across the Henry trail in the high meadows. I got a rumor he's makin' a run for the valley to-night with part of his bunch. I aim to ambush him, cut him off."

"Do it," snapped Langdell and pressed his lips together.

"Don't want to join me, Dave?" asked Leverage.

"I'm workin' it a little different," replied Denver. "Better for us to go separate. But for your own sake, trust no rumor and don't walk into any traps. Redmain's an Indian for that sort of hocus-pocus."

"I guess I can take care of myself," answered Leverage, with a trace of resentment.

"Sorry," said Dave. "I won't presume to advise you again. May see you tonight and may not. In either case, I'll be somewhere around your territory."

"Don't let's ram into each other by mistake," warned Leverage.

On the threshold of the door Denver paused and turned to catch Fear Langdell's frosty, intent glance and so received the definite knowledge of the man's personal antagonism to him. Going back to the street he reflected on this. "Queer combination of righteousness and bigotry. He despises anybody who don't track with him."

They were taking Steele's body into Doc Williamson's place. Denver veered off to Grogan's. A part of Leverage's men trailed to the bar with him. It was quite apparent to him that they knew about his recent activities and that they were anxious to find out if he meant to throw in with the vigilantes. Range etiquette forbade the open question, but it stood in their eyes, nevertheless. And so, drinking and turning away, he answered it in a roundabout fashion.

"Good luck to you boys," said he, and walked out of Grogan's. Presently he was cantering from town.

He left dissatisfaction behind him. "What the hell's the matter with that fella?" one of

223

the vigilantes wanted to know. "Too proud to talk to us?"

Another of the bunch was quick to defend Denver. "Keep yore shirt on, Breed. He's got sense enough to keep his idees to himself. If we'd quit publishin' our intentions to the world mebbe we'd ketch a fish now and then. Don't worry about Dave Denver. He's up to somethin', you bet."

Grogan lounged up to them. By and by he grunted. "Funny thing. He comes right in, stays five minutes, and walks right out again. Now, does that make sense?"

"If he didn't have a purpose," maintained Denver's defendant, "he wouldn't 'a' been here. I know Dave."

"Well, what was his idee?" demanded Grogan.

"Yore guess is as good as mine," was the other man's abrupt answer.

A slim, olive-colored little man emerged from the Palace, climbed on a calico pony, and quietly left Sundown. He circled the town, crossed the stage road a half mile behind the vanishing Denver, and fell into a lesser trail. Twenty minutes later when Denver was running along the flat stretch beyond Shoshone Dome this fellow stood on a ridge and watched, and a little later began a solitary game of distant stalking.

224

★ ★ ★

Denver, meanwhile, was engaged in a mysterious game of his own. A few miles beyond Shoshone Dome he drew beside the road, dismounted, and went to a stump. He capsized a loose rock, and found a piece of paper. There was a scribble of words on it. With a pencil he added a line of his own, signed his initials and put the paper back. After that he raced up and down the hairpin curves until he arrived at the Sweet Creek bridge. Here again he imitated his first performance under the timbers of the bridge; and again travelled with the highway as it swooped into the valley of Sundown. Presently he was at the mouth of Starlight. But instead of turning for home he tarried to study the distant reaches of the road. Cattle and men filled it yonder, emerging from a hill trail. He advanced at a set pace and found a half-dozen men from Fear Langdell's ranch driving approximately two hundred head of stock to the south. Langdell's foreman came up — a long, lean man with a cheerful drawl.

"We crossed yore territory, Dave," said the foreman. "Want to cut this bunch for strays?"

"I'll just take a stand down the road a bit and watch 'em pass," replied Denver. He went on a distance, drew aside, and rolled a cigarette. The foreman followed him.

"Got goin' awful late. We won't make the

railroad today. Nice critters for the market, ain't they?"

Denver's glance went expertly through the passing line of cattle, reading brands. Most of the stuff was in Langdell's own original brand; but at odd intervals he saw steers Cal Steele had sold to Langdell for shipping; recognizable as such by the vent — a small replica of the owner's brand — each carried on its hip. Denver suddenly dropped his cigarette and crowded his pony into the stream of stock, coming abreast an enormous brute with sweeping horns and a red blaze on an otherwise cream head. He leaned down, passed his palm across the brand, and looked carefully at the earmarks. When he withdrew from the procession Langdell's foreman was once more beside him.

"What's the caper, Dave? That's a Steele steer we bought last week to ship."

"Ahuh. Just wanted to look closer at the ugly critter. Well, I find nothing here belonging to me. See you later."

The outfit went by, the bawling and the shouting diminished downgrade. As long as man or beast remained in sight Denver kept his position, scarcely moving a muscle. But the cast of his face slowly changed, lines deepening, lips compressing. Through his mind raced an unpleasant truth. That steer

226

had worn a Fee brand last year. He was certain because he remembered finding the animal strayed into his own stock. And he had driven it back across the Copperhead bridge to Fee territory. No mistake about that. Undeniably the same Fee beef now going to market with Cal Steele's brand.

Of course such things honestly happened now and then. Cattlemen sold to other cattlemen; or in adjusting occasional cases of misbranding at roundup time they swapped beef to rectify these errors. But what overthrew either of these possible explanations was the fact that this particular steer had lost his Fee brand. Steele's brand proclaimed to the wide world that the steer had originated as a Steele beef. There was only one answer — a switching of marks, a careful and expert doctoring. His eyes had picked up no suspicious blurring; but his inspecting palm had felt the slight roughness and variance of the outer ridges. Even so, had he not known that steer by sight, he would have passed it as a genuine Steele product. And since both Steele and Fee used the same small underhack on the ears of their cattle, the switch would pass any casual observer's inspection.

He drew a deep breath, wishing he had never seen the steer. There were other explanations, he told himself. Yet common sense kept insisting that no matter what explanation he might conjure up to protect the memory of his friend, somebody's treachery was at the bottom of this change. The black mystery of the country had cast its shadow even over the man he loved above all others.

He stiffened in the saddle. Brush swirled beside him. A body shifted, out of sight, and a soft voice spoke to him. He caught himself after the first sidewise glance and stared impassively down the road.

"Joe Hollis saw riders passin' across the Henry trail from where he was hid, Dave. He passed the word along the line. And Lyle Bonnet placed Redmain's bunch in one of the high pockets about seven miles west of Leverage's place. Seemed like they was takin' it easy. Saddles off."

Denver spoke from the side of his mouth. "Go back. Collect the boys where the Leverage back trail runs into the Henry. I'll be along a couple hours after dark. But tell Lyle not to let 'em out of his sight. If they move, follow. In such a case, leave one man at the junction spot to meet me, and another one or two along the line so I'll know where to come. Get going, and be careful. There's somebody scouting me."

He spurred along the road to Starlight and went rapidly up. Two miles in from the highway he saw a fresh track across the soft earth and cut down the side of the canyon. The sun was dipping over the western range when he cantered across the D Slash yard and dismounted. He threw his horse into the corral and joined the remnant of his crew at the supper table.

They had nothing to report, these restless home guards. They had worked the lower corner of D Slash range and found everything proper. Steve Steers had come along during the middle of the afternoon with a small bunch of D Slash strays. They had told him of Steele's death.

"And I thought he was a-goin' to shoot me when I spilled the news," said Dan Russell. "Never saw a fella stiffen up thataway. He wanted to know where you was, and I said I figgered mebbe yuh'd be home to eat supper. He rode off like a bat outa hell. Didn't bother to take four cows and beavertails we had fer him."

Denver nodded. "Comes hard on him. He'd bunch any other job in the world to join this chase. But he can't walk out on Nightingale. I bet he's stampin' the earth."

"Well, now," put in Russell, "ain't it about time us fellas got into this jam? Shucks, we're entitled to some fun. What's the percentage —"

"Tonight," replied Denver, "you boys stick right here. Burn all the lights on the place. Make lots of noise. Somebody stay in the main house — as if it was me. Baldy, rope out the gelding for me. Also, three-four of you get into the kitchen and help Si slap up a mess of sandwiches. I'll be carryin' 'em back to the bunch in the hills."

"How about knittin' some mufflers?" grunted Russell, full of discontent. "If this ain't the damnedest —"

Steve Steers and Al Niland appeared at the dining-room door. Denver got up from the table and walked back into the living room with them, carefully closing the door.

"Missed you by ten minutes in Sundown," said Steve tersely. "I never stopped ridin', once I got the news."

"Go back to your business, Steve."

"Is that all the advice you got for me?" challenged Steers. "You ridin' tonight? Then so am I. And so is Al."

"Listen to reason. You can't leave Nightingale in the lurch. Do you think this is just a one-night affair? It ain't. Nobody knows when the last of it will come. You've got no business slashin' around the hills, leavin' Nightingale's range wide open to Redmain. You know it."

"So that's the way I stand by my friends,

is it?" was Steve's bitter retort.

"I guess I've got to hit from the shoulder," stated Denver. "You've always been a wild-eyed buzzard. There never was a job you wouldn't quit in a minute. Well, here's one time when you've got to measure up to your job. It ain't a question of what you want to do. It's a question of what comes first. You're foreman of a ranch — and it's up to you to see it ain't robbed poor."

"Go ahead, slap the spurs into me," grunted Steve petulantly. "What's one Englishman's cows to me stacked up beside Cal Steele? Oh, damnation, I reckon yore right!"

"Yeah, he is," broke in Niland. "There's more angles to this Redmain business than just foggin' him. Maybe he wants everybody to go on a wild-goose chase after him. Never any way of tellin' what that quick mind of his is hatchin'."

"Just so," agreed Denver. "And that lets you out of any ridin' for a while, too. I've got something I want you to do."

"Me?"

"I want you to nose around Sundown and find out how long Steele had been sellin' stock to Fear Langdell."

The other two stared at Denver in an almost startled manner. Steve Steers was puzzled; Al Niland's much sharper mind cut right through to Denver's unspoken reason. But in spite of that and in spite of the fact Denver was one of his closest friends, he parried. "Why? What do you know about those transactions that don't please you?"

Denver drew a long breath. "What do *you* know about them, Al?"

Niland shook his head. "I never pried into Steele's affairs. If you got anything on your mind, let's know it."

"Get away from bein' a lawyer for a minute," muttered Denver. "I saw somethin' different on your face."

"I'd never judge a man by unsubstantiated thoughts," was Niland's very slow answer. "Cal had a habit of goin' into fits of depression sometimes. And he'd say a few flimsy things. But that ain't anything to speak about."

Steve finally caught up with the train of thought. "Here, here, you fellas, what you tryin' to cook up?"

"What I say must never be repeated," said Denver. "It must die right here, understand? Never to be spoken again — even if it takes perjury to cover it."

"That's unnecessary for you to say," Niland reminded him.

Denver came to a stand in front of them. "I found a steer in Langdell's shipment this afternoon. It was one Steele had sold him last week. It had Steele's original brand and Steele's vent mark. No other brand. But last year it was a Fee cow. I recognized it. No chance for mistake."

To a man in cattle country this needed no explanation at all. Niland and Steers were dumbly silent. It was natural that Steers, being absolutely loyal, should mirror shocked belief; and it was equally natural that Niland, with his knowledge of human error, should slowly nod his head. Through the open doors came a soft wind. The crew strolled along the yard. The bell-like clarity of an owl's hoot floated in. Denver went on: "I have figured this thing backward and forward, and I continually come to a conclusion I despise. There's other ways of explainin' it. There might be a crook in Steele's crew who is plasterin' other critters with the Steele brand for his own profit. But how would such a fellow cash in? I don't see that. It's also possible Redmain might have done the job in the hope it would be discovered and so discredit Steele. Yet I doubt it. That switch from Fee to Steele was absolutely an expert job. I wouldn't have noticed it unless I'd personally hazed the cow last year."

"Well, then," broke in Niland, "what's the answer?"

"Whatever the answer," said Denver quickly, "we keep it to ourselves. Forever.

233

Cal Steele is dead, and he's entitled to his clear reputation. He'll have it, if I've got to turn Yellow Hill upside down. But somehow or other Redmain's in this. And I'd like to know more about Fear Langdell's connection. Did he buy from Cal Steele knowing about the blotting or not?"

Niland's face began to lighten up. "If I could nail that man to the cross after all he's done in the name of justice I'd give my seat in heaven! I wonder if that's why he filed his request with the judge to act as executor to Steele's estate? To cover up —"

"Never say it," warned Denver. "But you've got to get in there and find out, somehow."

One of the hands ambled through the front door. "Hawss is ready for yuh, Dave." The owl's sentinel signal echoed again. Denver lifted his head, becoming aware of the sound. "So you've both got your work cut out," he went on. "We won't ever get the whole story straight. Steele will never tell his part. Redmain's beyond the talking stage. There's nothing left but to go after him, never give him peace. That's what I propose to do. As —"

He broke off and moved for the door. The hoot of the owl had become too insistent. Crossing the porch he descended into the darkness of the yard. The call came again, along the ridge. Advancing toward it, he reached the grade. A question came through the blanket of shadows. "Denver?"

"Who's that?"

"It's us — Meems and Wango. We want to see yuh."

"Then come down here like white men. What's all this hocus-pocus for?"

"Well," came Meems's solemn answer, "we got a decent respeck fer our hides. We're comin' — but not into the lights. What we got to say is private, is that a go?"

"All right."

The two shuffled forward. "You'll keep the source o' this inf'mation to y'self?" insisted Meems.

"I said I would."

"Yore word's enough with us. It ain't none of our business, y'unnerstan'? But yore in this fight and it jest didn't seem right holdin' back. Only, don't give us away, and don't ask us to testify. When we're through talkin' we drift. See?"

"Get it out of your system," grunted Denver.

"We was just a-leavin' the dance last night when a fella come ridin' outa the dark. We seen him go acrost the bridge and as fur as the schoolhouse. He didn't come back thataway. But when we heard about Steele we jest put one and one together. Mebbe it makes two. Mebbe it was the gent that drawed Steele away from the dance."

"Who was it?"

Meems sighed and let the silence stretch out. "I'll speak the name," said he finally, "and yore free to act on it. But yore the only man in God's green footstool I'd do such a thing for. And forget who told yuh."

"Agreed," said Denver.

"It was Stinger Dann," muttered Meems; and as soon as the name was spoken both men backed off and were lost to sight. Denver heard them ride rapidly away.

As for himself, he strode to the house at half a run. Niland and Steers both caught the blaze of light on his face and came nearer.

"I have found the man who pulled Steele away from the dance. It was Dann. Whatever Cal's connection with Redmain, I think he started away from that schoolhouse with the idea of protecting my stock. Remember, he was shot on my range — and Redmain's men were there. Trying to protect me from that bunch of killers."

"I don't believe he'd have no truck with Dann or —" Steve started to say, half-heartedly. But Niland broke in.

"There's part of the story. No matter how far into Redmain's scheme he might have been, he'd still stick up for you or the rest of us. Dammit, Dave, Redmain must have hooked him into this dirty mess!"

"If I didn't think so," was Denver's sober reply, "I wouldn't be riding now."

"Be doggone careful," grunted Steve Steers. "I hate this business of me laggin' behind."

Denver was already on the gelding. He ran up the hillside to the trail, went a few hundred yards along its familiar course, and abruptly switched to a dim side trace. The ground buckled up from ravine to ravine, and the dim stars gave him no sight. Nevertheless, he pressed the gelding on, suddenly fell into the Sundown-Ysabel Junction road, and settled to a long run. Down the hairpin turns with steel flashing on gravel; over the Sweet Creek bridge, on along the level stretch that led around to Starlight and thence to the open prairie. Short of Starlight a mile he veered to the right and went with equal rapidity through massed pines. Then the gloom was broken by the wink of a ranch light, and he rode up to Leverage's gate. The wheeze of the hinges was like an alarm. Nearing the porch, he was challenged by an invisible guard.

"Who's that?"

"Denver. Where is Jake?"

"You tell me and I'll tell you."

237

"Can you reach him?"

"Sorry."

The front door of the house opened. Eve stood framed in the glowing yellow rectangle. "That you, David? Come in."

Denver stepped to the porch. "I reckon I haven't time. I'm tryin' to find your dad."

He heard the intake of her breath. "Is it important?"

"Eve," called the unseen guard gruffly, "you shouldn't stand in the light."

Dave drew her out, shut the door. "I consider it important."

She dropped her voice. "He left here before supper — alone. I think he's riding beyond the Henry trail with the vigilantes. That's all I know."

Once more the guard's cautioning words cut in. "Yuh shouldn't peddle no inf'mation to nobody, Eve. How do we know?"

But Eve had a temper of her own. "Clyde, will you hush! You're covering too much territory."

"Maybe I'll pick up his tracks," said Denver. "I'm headin' that way."

"David — there's something in the wind tonight?"

"Maybe," said Denver.

Her hand rested light as thistledown on his shoulder. "Oh, David, if I were only a man!

Not to shoot and destroy, but just to be along. Anything is better than this uncertainty."

"Don't worry. Your dad's got a big bunch with him."

"Do you think he is the only one I worry about?" asked the girl softly.

"Bless you for that," muttered Denver. "I've always been a hand to think I did very well ridin' the single trail. But when you say somethin' real comfortin' like that to me it's mighty pleasant. It sticks with me a long time. I guess a man never realizes what loneliness is —"

He bit off the rest of it and turned away. "No time to lose now. Don't worry."

"You should never ride by yourself after dark," said Eve.

He was in the saddle. "If your dad comes back very soon tell him Redmain's been located in a high meadow due east of here about seven miles. Tell him to watch out for a trap. Redmain never strikes direct. He's too tricky for that."

"And yourself, Dave?"

"I was told today," he said morosely, "that I was as much of a savage as Redmain. I reckon I'll be all right. So-long till I see you."

"So-long, David."

He cut around the house, and fell in with the western trail. A few rods from Leverage's it began to warp with the rising slope. The cleared meadows fell off, and he was riding once again in the abysmal shades of the forest. And around ten o'clock of the night he reached the Henry trail, feeling the presence of a man about him. Quietly he let a phrase fall into the utter silence.

"All right."

"Denver?" questioned a husky voice.

"Yeah. Who is it?"

"Hank Munn."

"Which way?"

"Still up yonder to the west. We better drift."

"Lead off."

Munn came out of the trees, rode across the Henry trail and proceeded due west, Denver following. The path was narrow, extremely crooked, and overhung by branches that swooped down to rake them as they passed. Munn put up with the tedious vagaries of the path until a small clearing appeared. At that point he swapped directions, hurried over the open space, and with another sudden shift went down a glen soaked in fog. Water guttered across stones. The horses splashed through a creek and attacked a stiff bank with bunched muscles. Presently Munn halted in black nowhere and cleared his throat.

There was no answer. Munn forged on a

few hundred yards. Again he coughed. Out of the brush rode a sentry.

"Munn?"

"Yeah. What made yuh drag yore picket?"

No answer. Munn dropped back to second place as this new outpost led them on. More turns, more offset alleys through the pines, yet always climbing toward some high point; a high point they abruptly came upon after a hundred yards of end-over-end ascent. There was a murmured challenge ahead. Men closed in. Lyle Bonnet spoke from a short distance. "Dave?"

"What've you got, Lyle?"

"Come over here. Here. Look off down yonder."

Denver crowded his horse beside Bonnet and saw, far below, a point of flame shimmering through the rolling fog; rising and falling and trembling with a queer, shutter-like effect.

"Redmain's camp," said Bonnet. "I been watchin' it better'n four hours. Saw 'em movin' around until the fog came in. Can't make out nothin' but the fire now. All the boys is here. And it's up to you."

CHAPTER XIII
SURROUNDED

"Done any exploring down there?" Denver asked.

"I got boys posted along the ridge here, but nobody's scouted that bowl. I was afraid of losin' 'em, and I didn't want to bring on no premature fightin'. They prob'ly got the brush speckled with gents."

"Good enough. Munn, where are you? Drift along and collect the bunch right here. I'm going down. Need another man."

"Right beside yuh," announced Bonnet.

Denver paused long enough to issue his orders. "If you fellows hear one shot, come along. If you hear more than one shot, also come along, but don't waste any time. Otherwise wait for us."

He turned from the ridge. Bonnet muttered. "A little to yore left — there's a good way of gettin' below." Accordingly, Denver slipped away from the main party, let himself down what appeared to be a convenient alley, and immediately was plunged into a black and solitary world. The avenue of approach shot one way and another, drifting from high levels to water holes and back again. Perceptibly the outlaw camp fire brightened and the fog thinned. Bonnet breathed in his ear. "This is one of the two-three entries to the bowl. They'd be apt to have it guarded." Denver accepted the warning and abandoned the easy travel. Curling around the trees, he circled the beacon fire until he judged he had completed an approximate quarter turn. Bonnet's wind rose and fell asthmatically; then Denver plunged forward in long and staggered spurts. A thick rampart of trees shut out the gleam of the fire. He halted once more, waiting for Bonnet to catch up. Bonnet murmured, "Not far now," and Denver cut straight through the trees to find himself on the smooth rim of the bowl. Fifty yards off the camp blaze shot up with a brilliant cascade of sparks. A man threw an armful of wood on it and quickly retreated to outer darkness.

That move evoked a sudden suspicion in Denver's head. Where were the horses and the men of Redmain's outfit? Certainly not anywhere along this particular angle of the bowl. He touched Bonnet's arm and began a swift march around the rim. He saw a man crouching beside a horse. By degrees he came nearer. The man's cigarette tip made a fitful glow; the horse stirred. For a long time Denver kept his place, trying to penetrate the gloom behind that man. But he saw nothing. To all intents and purposes that fellow was a solitary watcher. And as the dragging minutes passed Denver definitely accepted the belief. Redmain had posted a decoy and fled.

There was but one conclusion to draw. Redmain somehow had caught wind of the forces moving against him and was now playing his own particular game under the black cloak of the night. Denver stared at the fire guard. He touched Bonnet on the knee and whispered, "Stay here." Curving with the tree line, he arrived in the rear of the outlaw. A hundred feet intervened. Stepping ahead in long, springing strides he reached the horse at the moment it jerked up. The man sprang to his feet and grunted. "Who's that?" Denver's gun leveled against him.

"Snap your elbows."

The outlaw swayed as if calling on his nerve. But the fighting moment went winging by. He was lost, and he knew it. His hands rose.

"Step this way," grunted Denver. "Turn around. Stand fast." His free hand shot out and ripped the man's gun from its holster. He tucked it behind his own belt. The outlaw jeered him with a sudden revival of spirit.

"A hell of a lot of good this'll do yuh."

"You're lucky to be out of what's comin'. Anybody else around here?"

"Think I'd tell if they was?" growled the outlaw.

"Just a catamount of wheels, ain't you," reflected Denver. "Walk over to the fire where I can see you."

The outlaw obeyed. He had a strange face, and Denver commented on it. "Another slick-eared gun fanner from other parts. Redmain must have a young army."

"Big enough to whip the tar outa you, once ever yuh tackle it," stated the outlaw coolly.

"We'll have a chance to find out soon enough," said Denver. "But you'll have no part in the fun."

"The Sundown jail won't hold me," challenged the outlaw.

"Your ticket don't read that far," was Denver's laconic answer. This stopped the outlaw dead. His teeth clicked together, and the bones of his face sprang against the tightening skin.

"So that's yore style, uh?" he muttered.

"You seem to like the life. So don't bellyache over your pay. Come on, Lyle. He's alone."

Bonnet came swiftly around the fire. "We better get organized, Dave. How about shakin' this specimen down?"

245

"Where'd Redmain go?" demanded Denver, shooting the question at the outlaw.

"I ain't sayin'."

"You've got a bare chance of escapin' the rope," Denver warned him. "Talk up. Where'd he go?"

"I'll take my funeral and be damned to you! I don't squawk in the first place, and in the second place I'd never expect no mercy from Black Dave Denver even if I did tell. You take a long run and jump for yoreself."

"My-my," said Bonnet. "How would you like a belt in the mug? It might loosen your thoughts some."

The outlaw stood sullenly defiant. Denver brooded over him. "Who told Redmain that Leverage came across the Henry trail tonight lookin' for him?"

The outlaw flung up his head and laughed ironically. "Mebbe you'd like to know what Redmain knows. I'll say —" Out of the south came a sputter of shots. Denver cursed and raised his gun to the sky, letting go a single bullet. Again the night wind bore down echoes of trouble. This time the firing rose strongly sustained. The outlaw wrenched himself backward, yelling.

"There's yore answer, damn yuh! We'll do what we please in this country afore we're through!"

"What the devil!" snapped Bonnet, staring at Denver.

"Leverage," said the latter with an electric bitterness, "has run into a trap." He fired again, threw out the weapon's cylinder, and replaced the spent cartridges. Going to the outlaw's horse, he untied the rope, and shook the loop over the man. The outlaw protested. "Good God, don't tear me apart with that string!"

Denver's men swarmed over the clearing. Hank Munn charged up to the fire, leading the horses of Bonnet and Denver. Denver beckoned the man. "You — take this buzzard we've caught and herd him back to my ranch. Tell the boys to keep him."

"Why bother —"

"You've got your walkin' papers," said Denver, stepping into his saddle. Without warning he spurred into the timber. He fell upon a trail and righted himself; the horse labored mightily. He came to the summit and for a moment groped his way clumsily through brushy underfooting. The horse saved him the necessity of search, kicked clear, and reached a broader pathway. So he lined out to the southward with his men strung behind; Bonnet's urgent call to close up was echoed still farther back by Hominy Hogg.

This was not the side of Yellow Hill with

which he was very familiar. He knew the terrain only in the sense that every rider of cattleland has a rough contour map in his head of whatever lies within fifty or a hundred miles of home range. His sense of direction told him he traveled in a parallel line with the Henry trail, which ran somewhere off in the eastern blackness; his ears told him he was headed into the drawn-out fight yonder to the south.

The firing came clearer, swelling to a pitched volume and dying off to scattered volleys. From the changing tempo Denver almost was able to see the fight — the sudden locking of forces, the milling and the swirling, the abrupt buckling into shelter, and the stealthy groping for advantage in the pitch-black night. Redmain had timed his maneuvers perfectly. He could only have done so through clear information as to the parties moving against him. The fact that he had left a fire burning and rode away to begin a pitched engagement was proof of it. Plainly Leverage had moved into a trap and was now fighting for his life. Leverage was an honest man, a plugger. But never for a minute could he match the tricky touch-and-go brilliance of Lou Redmain. It wasn't in the cards.

He was coursing down a long and straight grade. Lyle Bonnet drew up, neck and tail, and shouted, "It ain't far now! I think they're scrappin' near Peachey's Burn! If we keep on like this we'll smack right into a crossfire! How about drawin' up just before we hit it?"

Denver stiffened in his seat. All the while his straining ears had been fastened to the sharp echoes; it came to him with a shock that he was listening into a queer lull. The firing had ceased. The gloom of the trail widened into a gray circle. Bonnet called again. "This is that old hermit's clearin'. We're only a half mile —"

The little clearing spilled over with sound. Horsemen smashed out from yonder side. Denver cried, "Pull up!" and was surrounded by his own men as they drove out of the trail. A gun's shattering blast beat into his group. Denver shouted. "Leverage — stop shootin'!" And from the growing mass of riders emerged a challenge. "To hell with Leverage!" Followed by a pour of lead.

"Redmain!" yelled Denver and spurred his horse. "Spread out — let 'em have it!"

"Come and get it, Denver!"

It was mad, riotous confusion. He was jammed elbow and elbow with his own men; Redmain's riders plunged on. He saw them shifting rapidly across the cleared area; he opened a point-blank fire, crying a warning. "Spread out — spread out!" Outlaw and posse raced around the fringes of the meadow. Every man was on his own, and in the center a dozen of them had met in a wicked hand-to-hand encounter. He thought he heard Redmain, but wasn't sure. Dann's bellow was too barbaric to be missed. He hauled his pony out of the whirl and cut across.

"Come on, D Slash! Follow me!"

Right on the heels of the challenge a rider shot from the massed and weaving figures and drove into him. The belch of powder covered his face. He veered aside, firing at the bobbing target. There was a yell, a terrible guttering of breath; rider and horseman alike disappeared into the mêlée. Denver plunged on, feeling his men behind. But the target he aimed for had shifted. Shifted and given ground. Dann bellowed again, deeper in the woods; and like phantoms Redmain's men slipped away through the trees. Hominy Hogg spurred past Denver.

"I know this trail!" he bawled. "Come on!"

Denver heard Dann again, a few yards to the left; he galloped between the clustered pine trunks and rammed a turning rider. An arm reached out, slashed down, missed his head by an inch and struck into his thigh with the barrel of a gun. He clamped the gun in his left hand, beat back with his own weapon, and heard a bone snap. His antagonist gasped and tried to fight clear. Both horses pitched.

Denver crooked his right elbow about a sagging head and dragged the man bodily from the saddle; his left hand ripped the fellow's weapon clear, and at that point he let the man fall and spurred away.

The encounter had taken no more than two or three minutes, but in that space of time both the pursued and the pursuers were far ahead. Denver fought through the brush, ran into a fresh deadfall whose branches would not let him pass over, and swung to skirt it. Still he found no trail. An occasional shot drummed back. Riders were drifting all over the country. Presently the horse seemed to find a clear pathway and went along it. Denver considered himself being pulled too far northward and attempted to angle in the other direction. Each attempt brought him sooner or later to some sort of a barrier. Back on the trail he decided to return to the clearing and make a fresh start. He hauled about and heard a rustling dead ahead. Another rider darkly barred his path.

"Who's that?" said the man huskily.

Denver had the feeling a gun was trained on him. "You tell me and I'll tell you," was his grim retort.

"I don't make yore voice."

"Maybe I've got a cold," muttered Denver, feeling his way along. Any D Slash man would

know his voice, though some of the Steele outfit might not. The reverse was also true. It
was possible that this might be a Steele hand.

"Well, well," grunted the man, "we can't
stay here all night. Let's get it over with. You
sing out and so will I. We done spent enough
time in these god-forsaken trees."

"Sounds to me," observed Denver, "that
you don't like this part of the country."

"Mebbe so — mebbe not. Depends. It's
good for some people and not so good for
others."

"Come far?" asked Denver.

"In one way, yes. In another way, no."

"Had a square meal, lately?"

The man thought that one over carefully.
"Brother, you got a ketch in that. I eat now
and then."

"Just what part of the country are we in?"
pressed Denver.

"You want to know, or do you want to know
if I know?" parried the other.

"Let it ride. Your turn now, fella. If you
got any ideas how to break the ice let's hear
'em."

"How about you and me lightin' matches
at the same time?"

"A good item," agreed Denver. "We'll
count to ten and strike."

"I'm damned if we will," said the man, suddenly changing his mind. "You fell too quick. Must have somethin' up yore sleeve. No, it's out. I tell you — supposin' we just natcherlly turn about and ride in opposite directions?"

"You sure we want to go in them directions?"

"What directions?" said the man cautiously.

"What directions have you got?" drawled Denver.

"Good God, am I goin' nuts?"

"I'd have to know you better to tell." Denver shifted in his saddle. He heard a creaking of leather, and finally an irritable mumble. "What you doin' over there?"

"Nothing, brother, nothing at all."

"That's what I'm doin', and I don't like it."

"Got your gun leveled on me?"

"No."

"You lie like a horse," said Denver.

"Let it ride, then," said the other and began to swear. "Supposin' I have? If I thought you was what I got an idea yuh are, I'd knock yuh outa the saddle and no regrets. Yellow Clay County —"

Denver let his arm drift down. It touched, gripped, and drew the gun clear. He broke in softly. "You're one of Redmain's imported gun slingers, mister."

"How do you know? Who are you?"

253

"The name of this county's Yellow Hill!" The explanation all but cost him his life. A bullet bit at the brim of his hat before his first shot blasted into the eddying echo of the other. The shadow in front became but half a shadow, the upper part melting down. He heard a stifled moan; the man's horse bucked away and stopped. Denver advanced five yards, swung down, and lit a match. The first flare of light was enough. And there was a cropped sweat on his own face.

"High stakes for that gamble," he muttered, pinching out the match. That was all. He turned his pony and started along the trail. Every vestige of pursuit had died in the distance. Somewhere Redmain's men were slipping through the trees, collecting again, and somewhere his own riders were groping as blindly as he was. At the end of five minutes he detected a fork of the trail, and he took the one going south. It was a bad guess; after some three hundred yards it stopped and jumped aside like a jackrabbit. He accepted the offshoot wearily. So he drifted, feeling himself sliding more to the northwest. After a time he ceased to keep count with the changing trails; and when he did that he automatically lost himself. Somewhere around one or two in the morning he cast up his accounts mentally, drew into the secretive brush, tied his horse short, and unsaddled. He wrapped himself in the saddle blanket, gouged a channel to fit his hips, and was soundly asleep.

The training of the range man will not let him sleep beyond dawn; and his vitality springs freshly up after a few short hours of rest, no matter how much physical punishment has gone before. This is his birthright, and never does he lose it until the day he forsakes the queer combination of sweaty drudgery and wild freedom of cattleland and tries another trade. The regularity, the comforts, and the pleasures of the city man may come to him. But never again will he wake as Dave Denver did on this morning, alive, buoyant, energy driving through him; and never will he see through the same vision the first bright shafts of dawn transfix the gray mists. For a thousand such mornings the outcast range man may have cursed himself from his blankets; but looking back upon that time he will wistfully know the best of himself was left there.

Saddling, Denver took the trail again. To the south it was still dark. But ahead and northward the country lightened up rapidly. The trail widened, climbed considerably, and at last left the trees altogether; and he found himself standing on the rim of one of the innumerable small holes framed within the hills. The trail dropped down without much ceremony to the floor of the hole. A half mile onward the hole narrowed to a rocky throat. He thought he saw a trail shooting up the ridge to the right of this throat, but the fog, though diminishing, was still thick enough to blur his view.

"Tom's Hole," he grunted. "Great guns, I've dragged my picket halfway to the Moguls. Now, what to do? Straight back, or across the hole?"

To retreat meant bucking a lot of rugged terrain that he knew little enough about. But he was clear enough in his geography to reflect that beyond the north end of the hole was an east-west road which would carry him into Sundown Valley. His men also knew the road, and it stood to reason that those who had lost contact with the main party would probably drift that way as soon as they oriented themselves. It was no use considering a scout through the timber for them.

He knew some of his party had been hit, and it worried him. Those who had been knocked out in the meadow would be taken care of by now, for he remembered that, in the heat of the chase, he had told somebody to stay behind. And Leverage would be coming up. But he wanted to assemble the outfit

256

and count noses. Possibly he would have to scout the timber for a few missing men.

Where Redmain was he had not the slightest idea. All his work in establishing isolated pickets to check the trails had been swept away and would have to be done over again. The first thing was to get organized; and with that in mind he dipped down into the hole as the tendrils of mist began to steam up from the earth like smoke from volcanic fumaroles.

"The first trick belongs to Redmain," he reflected dourly. "He juggled Leverage and me neat as you please, struck twice and got away. There's a leak a mile wide somewhere on our side of the fence. He knew all about Leverage's moves; and apparently he knew about mine, or guessed well. None of my riders would go bad; some of the Steele men might. I'll have to do some weeding. And I'll have to play fox better."

He cantered across the bottom of the hole, aiming for the now distinct trail at the far end. High on one rim he saw a doe emerge from the trees; and the next minute he halted, correcting his mistake. It was a small pony. From another angle a man stepped out and lifted a rifle. The peace of the morning was shattered by a rolling report. A jet of earth kicked up five yards short of him.

He reached for his own rifle in the boot

and jumped from the saddle. The man lowered his gun. Another gun crack broke over the hole. Flat on his belly Denver swept the circling rim, unable to locate the second ambusher. Methodically he laid a line on the first man and fired; but his target had dropped from view. Another shot landed directly beneath his horse. Denver jumped into the saddle and whirled to run back up the grade. Immediately he saw it was blocked by three or four riders. He swung again and sank his spurs, racing for the northern mouth of the hole. He was a fair target, and the high rim seemed suddenly to sprout marksmen. They opened at will, wasting lead all around him. Lying flat in the saddle he flung his pony on toward protection of the rocks and was within a hundred yards of them when he saw this exit to be blocked as well.

A hat and gun popped into sight. Denver swerved, accepting the only other course open, which was the trail that climbed steeply beside the rocks. He let the horse have its head and pumped a brace of bullets at the fellow. Twenty feet on up he commanded the man's shelter and fired again. The gelding trembled with the effort he put into the climb; Denver quit worrying about the other guns trained on him from the rear. The man below, having no means of security from the overhead

Denver, began to scurry blindly. The trail clung to the very edge of the cliff as it ascended. A matter of fifty rods higher it leveled into the ridge's summit. Denver grunted, "Go along, my boy, this is another thing we just squeezed through," and looked behind him. A small body of men were galloping in pursuit, sliding down the trail he had shortly before taken. "How in the devil did I pass through that mess of —"

The gelding faltered. Denver squared himself and found the game lost. The top of the trail was blocked by waiting outlaws. Distinctly he saw Dann's sullen, savage face glaring at him. In such a place, with neither safe retreat nor safe advance possible, Denver reverted to the elemental instincts that ruled him. He raked the gelding cruelly, threw up his rifle and pumped his remaining shells at them. Their horses pitched, a man capsized — and that was all he ever saw of the scene. A bullet struck the gelding; it stumbled, and Denver went vaulting over the rim. He struck first on his shoulder and felt the cold stream of pain shudder through his veins. Then, still conscious, he went careening down the stiff slope, loose rock rattling beside him. He heard one more shot. Then sound and light and feeling departed altogether. He was at the bottom of the slope, blood gouting from his head.

CHAPTER XIV
STEVE

About a dozen of the Bucket punchers came riding into Sundown during the middle of the morning, squired by Nightingale himself and Steve Steers. Al Niland walked out of the courthouse, lines of anxiety on his face.

"Well, heard anything yet?"

Steve shook his head. "We came by D Slash. There wasn't only a few boys there. Denver ain't come back so far, nor any of the bunch under him. Nobody's heard a thing."

"You know about Leverage?" queried Niland.

"Why, we met a fella on the road that told us somethin'. He rammed into Redmain, as I got it, and didn't make out so well. And took a little lead himself."

"Worse than that," interposed Niland. "He's halfway dead. Old Jake thought he was sneakin' up on Redmain's wild ones when Redmain smashed him just where Jake wasn't entertaining any suspicions. The vigilantes buckled up for a minute, but Jake rode right at Redmain's party, yelling for the rest to come along. He took it plenty. May live and may not."

"Yeah, but that ain't what gets me so much. What in the name o' Judas was the matter with these aforesaid vigilantes? Redmain hit and run, didn't he? And they heard more firin' up above a ways, didn't they? They mighta known it was Denver loopin' into action. Why didn't they folla?"

"They stopped to pick up the pieces, I hear," said Niland. "When they finally did follow there wasn't anything to be seen of anybody except one D Slash fellow some cut up."

"Agh," snorted Steve disgustedly. "First time I lay eyes on one of these vigilantes I'm going to tell him somethin' to make his ears ring."

"Well, we ought to hear pretty soon," said Niland and jerked his thumb at Grogan's. Steve looked to the Englishman questioningly.

"Do as you please," said Nightingale. "I'll be over at the Association meeting for a while. If by then we have no word about Denver, we'll ride back to his ranch. And if there is still no news, I wouldn't be surprised but what we took a little jog into the country he disappeared through."

Steers and Niland watched him amble across the street. "He's furrin," observed Steers, "but blamed if he ain't a human duck. Been a-frettin' about this business all mornin'. I spend half my time unroppin' him from the rope he essays to throw and the other half tryin' to figure if his jokes is sad or funny. He actually don't know enough about a cow to figure whether yuh carve out beefsteak on the hoof and turn the critter loose again or what. But he shore knows horses."

"How about that drink?" suggested Niland.

"You bet I will," agreed Steve, and turned around. In so doing his eyes fell upon a feminine figure standing by the hotel porch. Instantly something stabbed Steve Steers in the middle of the back; or such was the impression Niland gathered from the look that froze on the puncher's face. He swallowed hard, and mumbled. "That is, no thanks. Got to see Debbie." And he trotted toward the porch like a hound that had been whistled for. Niland sighed and went into Grogan's alone.

Sundown quivered with tension. The news of Leverage's ill fortune had reached town early, and shortly after a call went out for a meeting of the Association. So now men rode in and walked the streets uneasily; drifted together to exchange news. A man had ridden down Prairie Street to scout the road. Earlier in the morning a Leverage puncher had galloped in to summon Doc Williamson, refusing to talk. And Doc had gone off with the man hurriedly.

The practical defeat of the vigilantes shocked Sundown out of its lazy calm. Lou Redmain ceased to be a minor factor in the country; in one brief evening he had achieved notoriety, and when the gathering men spoke of him it was with a lurking doubt mixed with their profane anger. If he had whipped Leverage, if he had so recruited the wild bunch that he could stand off an organized force, who ruled Yellow Hill then? What was to prevent him from instituting a guerrilla warfare from one isolated ranch to another? The timid felt this immediately and began to fall silent, lest the red mark of destruction be placed against them and their habitations; and Sundown witnessed the drying up of casual talk, the coming of an alien reserve. For always in a land where the law goes to pieces the first rule is the rule of self-preservation.

Al Niland was in Grogan's, brooding over this, turning other matters as well darkly around his mind. Steele's death had made a gap in the ranks of friendship that never would be filled. If anything happened to Denver — Niland rejected the thought. He simply could not tolerate the premise that disaster would ever overtake Dave Denver. Other men might weaken or blunder, other men might go crashing down to ruin and death. This was mortality. But, logical as Niland was, he somehow could never bring himself to accept Denver as ordinary. Denver always came crawling out from the bottom of the wreckage, grinning cheerfully. In short, Denver's career had created a legend of personal power that was hard to shake off. Niland was analytical enough to realize this; he knew also that nobody could look at Denver impartially. Men either hated him or trusted and followed him with a kind of fanatical zeal.

"Good God!" grunted Niland. "I'm conductin' a post mortem. All I got to say is this'll be a sorry place if he's gone down the chute. Which the Lord forbid!"

He turned from the bar and saw Steve Steers coming in. Steve looked harried. Niland thought, "Debbie's pushed him just an inch too far, and I'm sort of glad." Steve made straight for the bar and slapped his palm resoundingly on the mahogany.

"Trot out the hog wash," he called.

Grogan, who never liked any such reference to his product, pushed bottle and glass toward the puncher. "No law compellin' you to drink my liquor, Steers."

Steve straightened. Honeyed softness caressed his words. "Grogan, my lad, I have observed your lordly manner some frequent, and I'm reminded of the horse that put on a shirt and tried to eat off the parlor table. I pay for your booze, and I'm entitled to pass judgment on it. If you got anything definite to say to me, let's hear it."

Grogan stared, the rims of his eyes reddening. There was cruelty in the man, plenty of it, and he never hesitated to cuff a trouble maker out of his place. Yet he backed water in front of Steve Steers. "Somebody must've stepped on yore foot, Mister Steers."

"Be that as it may, I feel like steppin' on somebody else's foot. Al, you drinkin' with me? I despise drinkin' alone."

"Sure," said Niland. "But I thought you was temperamentally opposed to liquor."

"Ha!" snorted Steve and took his jot without a quiver. "That's the trouble with me. I ain't got a mind of my own any more. I can't do nothin' without lookin' on the chart to see if it's proper. Debbie issues orders. Her old lady tells me where to head in. The old gent bites me off short. Even the eleven-year-old mutt of a Lunt kid roots me on the shins. I'd like to haul off four feet behind my breeches and spank him into next leap year. But no. I'm just the swivel-eyed ape which hangs around the Lunt house and gets pushed outa the road. Ha! Grogan, bring me a glass that ain't half plugged up with scum. I want a drink."

"I don't know if I better leave you alone," reflected Niland. "You'll foam any minute now."

"Hear anything new?" demanded Steers, drawing the bottle to him.

"No. Don't even see any of the vigilantes in town."

Steers turned to face the room. "Vigilantes? Ain't that somethin' to make yuh die laughin'? Hey, is there any of you vigilantes in these premises? I'd shore like to see what great big scrappin' hellions yuh are!"

There was no answer. Without question he was on the warpath. One of the Nightingale riders, seeing the foreman of the outfit hell-bent for trouble, slipped quickly from the hall. Steers raked the assembled citizens with a bright eye. "None present, uh? Well, I reckon they must all be home in bed, nursin' their busted arches. If I'd run as fast as they did to get away from Lou Redmain I'd have busted arches, too. And what is more, I wouldn't have nerve enough to come back to Sundown!"

Niland thoughtfully called Steve's attention to the empty glass. "After a large statement like that you must be dry. There was heat in the remarks. Presuming on the perquisites

266

of friendship I would suggest you have covered a scope of ground somewhat wider than the spread of your elbows. Think it over."

"Think? All I been doin' lately is thinkin' — about my duty, about my responsibilities, about bein' a gentleman. What's it brought me? Nothin' but grief. I wasn't made to think. I was made to bust forth and do the first thing that came in my head. What're all you dudes sittin' around for? Somebody run out and see if they's news of Denver. You — over there. Git goin'."

"Pretty soon you're going to need an armored battleship to get out of this town whole," prophesied Niland.

"Oh, no," said Steve, dripping in sarcasm. "Ev'body's all tuckered out from runnin'. Tie that, will yuh? Runnin' from Lou Redmain, the kinky little belly-slashin' rat! Runnin' away from him and leavin' a man in the lurch which none of 'em is good enough to lick his shoes!"

Niland let out a small sigh of relief. Nightingale men were slipping unobtrusively into the saloon. Steve had his bodyguard, though he failed to realize it. He lowered his voice to Niland.

"She said she'd turn me off like a crummy shirt if I ever got drunk, Al. Yeah, Debbie said that. Now you just watch me. She's a thousand times too good for a shif'less egg like me. I'm unregenerate. She thinks she can straighten a crooked nail. Dammit, I don't want to be improved. Just stay around and drink now and then with me while I get drunk. Grogan, trot out another bottle of that doctored dishwater."

"I've got no more time to drink, Steve. Something on tap."

"Any time's time to drink," said Steve, falling upon Cal Steele's well remembered phrase. The two men stared at each other as if the ghost of their friend stood lazy and smiling between them. Steve's face was suddenly lined and heavy. "I know. You go on. You're in no position to wallow in the mud with me. I'll get somebody." He shoved himself away from the bar and concentrated on the room. His finger stabbed out, and it may have been wholly by accident that it fairly tagged two rather willing characters — Meems and Wango. Possibly it was accident, though the gentlemen in question seldom missed a free meal and never had been known to refuse a drink.

"Come here!" bellowed Steers. "You two! Stand right beside me. When I drink, you match me. See?"

"It ain't as hard as it sounds," said Buck Meems. "Mebbe you'd better let us get evened up afore we start off."

Steers seemed to recognize them for the first time. "Huh — the human sponges. Well it's all right. I'll know I'm drunk when I see you road runners start wabblin'. Al — Al. When you hear anything come right back and let me know."

Niland nodded, spoke quietly to one of the Nightingale punchers, and walked out. What he said was, "Don't any of you fellows cramp his style. He could just about lick the contents of the saloon alone in his present state. Don't encourage him by interfering."

Niland paused to scan the street for new arrivals and found none. He crossed to Doc Williamson's office, but it was empty. Lola Monterey came quickly from the New York grocery and wheeled in front of him, whereat he lifted his hat and answered her question before she asked it. "Not a word, Lola."

He saw her fists double up around a package. It made him offer the old and well worn assurance. "No news is good news. There never was the hole Dave couldn't wiggle through."

"If you knew Lou Redmain as I do —" said she, and never finished the sentence. He watched her walk away, and an odd flash of thought came to him about the Biblical Mary and Martha. The opera house doors were closed, and a puncher guarded them; on impulse he used his right as an Association member and went in. Fear Langdell slouched in a stage chair. A small rancher held the floor, talking in a half-hearted sort of way.

". . . I want you-all to realize we've got no militia to call on, no rangers to drag in. Here we are, the biggest, roughest county in the state, cut off from down country. We always have had to fight our own battles, and we will now. Some of you smoke eaters forget that these hills make perfect shelter for the wild bunch. Just try and run 'em all down. If we'd gone about this with a less heavy hand and a hell of a lot of less advertisement we wouldn't of pushed the bad ones into a single herd where they can do us the most damage. We are lookin' right square into no-law country. Lou Redmain's got nothin' less than another Hole-in-the-Wall bunch. And if you had lived in Wyoming like me you'd flinch every time you thought about it. I figured Leverage would anyhow keep things quiet by a show of force. But I had hopes Denver would smash 'em once he made up his mind. There ain't anybody else that could. If he's gone, I just don't know how I can face the prospect of livin' on my place with the wife and kids. I just don't . . ."

Niland left the hall in need of air. "So they're singin' Dave's swan song. Well, they don't know the man!" But, going along the courthouse corridor and back to his office he remembered an odd thing Denver once had told him. It was about how fast bad news swept over Yellow Hill County. Denver had pointed to the sky and said, "It's one of those things I don't try to explain. Call it the invisible telegraph, if you want. But it comes through the air. I know it. I've felt it. The Indians knew it too. The news of Custer's being wiped out traveled to tribes three hundred miles south before a messenger could even ride thirty miles. It's just another part of the mystery of this country. Whispering Range — there never was a truer name. Some days there's a pressure all around me that's like a smotherin' blanket. I know better than to take chances on those days. Somewhere there's an old medicine drum beating, and the echo of it passes along."

Niland closed his office door, locked it, and threw the dark reveries from his head with conscious effort. Impatiently he lit his pipe, unlocked a drawer, and took therefrom a long leather folder. Out of it he drew a broken sheet of paper, smoothed it on the table, and bent his slim, rebellious face in scrutiny, as he had done a dozen times in the last eight hours.

He had found it in an odd corner of Cal Steele's desk which he had inspected after being appointed executor of the dead man's estate. He would have set it aside as of no importance except that in the back of his mind was the question Dave Denver had planted there. He had been musing ever since over the figures penned upon it. On the left margin apparently Steele had indicated dates. In the center the figures obviously stood for sums of money, and each one following its date. Niland had concluded that these represented proceeds from cattle sales. But what defied his logic was that to the right of each sum had been set a figure 3 as a divisor, and still to the right of this divisor was put down the exact third of the original sum. There were a dozen such individual transactions over a period of about a year.

Nothing in his subsequent searches quite satisfied him. There were instruments of sale of stock between Steele and Fear Langdell registered in the courthouse. Some of them closely followed the dates on this sheet of paper. Others seemed not to. Casual questioning had revealed no sale of cattle from Steele to any other rancher in the district; but the cattleman had made four moderate shipments to the Salt Lake yards during the year. And that was all Niland had discovered.

Niland settled back and blew the smoke heavily across his table. That figure 3 kept working through his head. Cal Steele had no partners. He had no relatives in the country. Nothing in his papers indicated kin or birthplace. Behind his arrival in Yellow Hill were only silence and mystery; nor had Steele ever broken it by spoken confidence. So then, why this three-part division of money?

He put away his pipe with a quick gesture, placed the sheet of paper in his pocket and rose. "Lord forgive me!" he muttered. "I may be sorry for what I find." He went through the business of unlocking and locking, passed to the street, and aimed for the bank. A quick survey told him no news had arrived so far in Sundown. And carrying his oppressive, foreboding fears with him, he entered the bank and met Ed Storm, a blocky middle-aged man who had inherited the institution from earlier members of the family. Storm's assistant was also in the place. Niland nodded briefly to the inner office and entered it. Storm came afterward.

"You look," he observed, "like you were standing on the peak of Ararat two days after the flood, with no grub in sight."

"Well, I feel like I'd been sent for and was only half present. Ed, you know me pretty well, don't you? There ain't a whole lot you don't fathom about me."

"This has all the earmarks of a touch," grinned Storm. "I've seen you throw back five-inch trout and refuse to shoot a doe. Nothing wrong with your moral integrity."

Niland failed to respond to the humor. He talked in jerky phrases, seemingly far afield. "Ethics. We've all got our professional ethics. They're fine things to start life with. Yet I doubt if there's a professional man living who hasn't violated his creed time and again. For admirable purposes, too. Man builds up a pretty schedule of ideals — and life knocks it flatter than a pancake. When I'm old and shot and look back down the crooked trail I hacked out, I think I'll be kind of sad at the fine thoughts I threw overboard. But I think I'll also hope to hear somebody in the hereafter say, 'Well done, good and faithful servant.' "

"Now that you're all wound up, toss the loop," said Ed Storm.

"I'm going to ask you some questions," went on Niland with a rise of energy. "They're questions you could only properly answer in court, but this is something that never will get to court. It dies outside of sight. You understand, Ed? You know, too that I have never blackmailed a man, never clubbed him down with any information I've had against him."

"Fire away — and we'll see what we see, Al."

"All right. I'm not going to explain anything. If you get any ideas on the subject from the way I bore in — that's under your hat. First, did Lou Redmain ever have an account in this bank?"

"That's easy. No."

"Did he ever cash any checks here — within the last year?"

"Yes."

"Were any of those checks from Cal Steele?"

Storm arched his eyebrows. "No."

"From Fear Langdell?"

"Nope."

Niland paused, stared thoughtfully at the ceiling. "You've cleared checks through the bank from Langdell to Steele for sale of beef. I know that. But have you cleared any checks from Steele to Langdell?"

"No-o," said Storm with a slight drag in the answer. Niland studied the banker. Unconsciously he was exercising his habit as an attorney of reading the qualifications and reservations behind witnesses' answers.

"Listen — was Cal Steele in the habit of drawing out large sums of money at a time?"

"Cash — yes."

Niland plunged into the opening swiftly.

"Right after receiving these checks from Langdell?"

Storm stopped to think. "Not necessarily on the same day or week. But he was a hand to draw heavy whenever his balance got substantially large. My one observation is that on the occasions when he drew considerable cash he'd take a trip south to the capital."

Niland's thoughts went off on this tangent. He was aware that Cal Steele often went away for a few days. On the heels of this reflection he tried to place Langdell's whereabouts at those times and found himself doubtful.

"Does Langdell have a bank account at the capital, Ed?"

"Oh, yes. That'd be necessary for him, considering all the investments he's got scattered around."

"Well, after Steele made his trips to the capital, did you ever observe Langdell switching money from the bank there to your bank?"

"Couldn't answer that without looking into the records," said Storm. He leaned forward in his chair, watching Niland. The lawyer decided to test the meaning of Storm's attention.

"Anything you'd care to say to me, Ed, that might bear on the subject?"

But Storm shook his head. "I'm just giving you straight yes or no answers, Al."

Niland leaned back. "I'd give a great deal to see the written record of Fear Langdell's check account durin' the last six months. And it's criminal as hell to suggest it."

Storm rose without a word and left the room. A few minutes later he came back with a sheaf of papers in his hand. He placed them casually on his desk. "No, Al, I couldn't hand you Langdell's records. That would open me up to all sorts of grief. I'd never want to be placed on the witness stand and have to confess that I verbally gave you any such dope. By the way, I've got to go out front for about ten minutes. Just make yourself at home, Al. I won't be back for ten minutes."

The two men swapped glances. Storm went out and closed the door. Niland leaned forward. Those papers Storm had left on the desk, he saw, were the ledger sheets and transit check records concerning Langdell's account. He drew the crumpled slip from his pocket. Occasionally his pencil touched and checked a figure; but when, an exact ten minutes later, Storm returned, he found Niland slouched idly in the chair. "Sorry I had to run out on you. Anything else you want to know?"

"No," said Niland.

"Whatever has passed between us is confidential."

"I'd like the privilege of tellin' one man, Ed."

"Hell!" grunted Storm, frowning. "Who is it?"

"Denver," replied Niland, and added, "if he's alive."

"I trust you — I trust him. Now I'm going to wash my face and hands."

"I've tried it at times," reflected Niland, getting up. "But what's the use? Nobody can live a useful life without gettin' dirty. What do you expect of Sundown? See you later, Ed."

On the street he found the scene changed somewhat. A great many men were standing just outside Grogan's. Nobody was going in and nobody coming out, but those by the doors seemed intently interested at the sounds emerging. Thinking that Steve Steers had developed a fight, he elbowed through the crowd and entered. Steve was lecturing the room morosely.

"When I tell you buzzards to play cards, then yuh can do it, and not a minute before. This always was a lousy joint, full of petty ante grafters and run by a sticky-fingered mug who's got a spine made o' yella soap. Meems, quit crawlin' against the bar."

Niland came forward, and Steve stopped talking. Both of his elbows were hooked against the bar; he swayed like a tree in a

278

heavy wind. The alcoholic stupor blurred his vision; he failed to recognize Niland until the latter approached to arm's length. Then Steve stiffened — and remembered.

"Any news?"

"None."

"I had ought to of gone along," muttered Steve. "Ruther be dead than wait like this. Have a drink, Al."

Niland shook his head. "How drunk do you have to be, Steve? You're about paralyzed now."

"It ain't enough," sighed Steve. "Grogan, this bug-killer of yores is either rotten poison or else yore miserable mug is double. Always did know yuh to be two-faced."

Grogan leaned against the bottle shelf, breathing hard. One palm lay against a black-jack on the shelf. "I had about enough from you, Steers. My face is good enough for you, and my liquor is straight."

"Both of which is neither," jeered Steve. "Layin' for me, ain't yuh? Try it and I'll break yore back, you ox."

Meems and Wango went off in a sputtering argument. All Grogan's free lunch platters were on the bar in front of them, fearsomely raped. The litter of chicken bones and half bitten sandwiches strewed the floor at their feet.

"Don't yuh eat nothin' but white meat?" demanded Wango. "I been nibblin' on wings and necks till I c'd crow an' fly away. Gimme a chanst."

"Thasso? Ev'time I reach I run into yore cussed arm. Git yore fool head outa the platter. It ain't no bed."

"I'm tellin' yuh once an' all — quit throwin' yore bones anunder my feet!"

"I allus — uck — throw scraps to the dawg, Wango."

"Don't throw no more bones anunder my feet!"

"He calls 'em feet!" cackled Meems.

Steve reached for the bottle. "Hit this, you sod busters. Ain't there nothin' that'll stop yuh but arsenic?"

Meems shook with palsy as he drank. Wango paled and began to shudder enormously. Both of his feet were inside the brass rail; attempting to maneuver around, he began to wilt. His feet slid, his knees buckled, his hind quarters struck the rail, bounced, and settled to the floor. Meems, bereft of moral support, laid his head on the bar. "I reckon — I done got ample," he moaned. "My Gawd, what a night!"

Steve stared at the partners. "They never was no good and never will be. But if they look like I think they look, then I shore must be hog drunk." With a jerk of his arm he swallowed what remained in his glass. "Now I got to take my punishment. Stay here, Al, till I come back."

He batted the doors before him, glowered at the crowd, passed through. Toward the hotel he rolled. There was sweat on his face and a film over his eyes. Once he thought he would never make it and slouched against a hitching rack; but a horse backed away from him, and that roused sufficient anger to propel him to the hotel porch. He couldn't see Debbie and he knew he never would be able to master the stairs. So he dropped his anchor and called.

"Debbie — oh, Debbie."

Then she was standing above him, silent and still. She held her chin steady, but in a sudden passion of self-disgust he saw that he had hurt her as no other soul had ever done. The deep blue of her eyes was covered by a cloud. He had shamed her, soiled her by coming out in the street and calling her name. The damage was done, and for the rest of his life he would regret it. Even so, he clung to his purpose.

"Debbie," said he, "I'm drunk."

Something else appeared in her eyes. She spoke softly and not with the tart impatience to which he was accustomed. "I see that, Steve. Maybe we have waited too long. On the first of the month we'll be married. And you'll never drink again."

"What's that? Debbie — but, Debbie, yuh said —"

She was gone. Steve turned and plowed back to the saloon, on through the crowd, on across the hall to the bar. And in front of Al Niland he exploded.

"My God, Al, why don't wimmen make up their minds and stick to it? Here I went and spent thirty dollars to get this way — and it went for nothin'! Wimmen — why — !"

A running, rising murmur swept the saloon. "Here's somebody! Clear that door — !"

"Doc —"

"Denver —"

That last name was repeated again with a dying inflection. The talk fell off. Steve turned slowly. The first face he saw was that of Al Niland, set and pallid. Then he discovered a figure framed in the doors, a tall, spare figure. Doc Williamson. Doc passed a hand across his forehead and broke the hush.

"I guess you boys had better know it. Dave Denver is dead."

All men are touched with queerness. Steve Steers pivoted on his heels and faced Grogan behind the bar. He called Grogan a name, a name than which there can be none worse when spoken as Steve spoke it. Grogan leaped

282

for his blackjack. Steve smashed the man's head with a whisky bottle and flung the broken neck after Grogan's sinking bulk. He saw nothing but red streaks of fire, and it was an act of Providence that guided him through the door. Fifteen minutes later one of the Nightingale men found him stretched on the ground back of the Palace, stone sober. Crying like a child.

CHAPTER XV
WHEN THE DARK GODS CALL

A long gray column slid sinuously through the green thicket and shot across the Sundown-Ysabel Junction road. The last man in the column dismounted, erased the hoofmarks in the dust with his coat, and caught up with the procession. Then the column vanished through the ranking trees of the high ridge near Starlight Canyon. Some minutes later it reached a commanding summit, halted, and took rest. Lou Redmain rode off by himself to where the road, the lower end of Sundown Valley, and the Leverage home meadows were spread out before him. He tipped back his hat, fingers tapering down a cigarette. Having lighted it and swung one knee over the saddlehorn, he began a slow survey of the country from north to south.

For all his apparent ease of posture, there was a wariness about him, an animal restlessness. His clothes were streaked with dirt; a dark stubble of beard ran from temple to jaw. Normally Lou Redmain was almost like a woman in neatness and choice of clothes.

Now, unkempt and sullen for lack of sleep, his features betrayed him. The willfulness, the faithlessness, the unbridled appetites — these faults any man could see at a glance. Redmain had never been anything else, nor anything better than he was now.

Yet he had changed. Through the years he had been denied a full fellowship with the range people. Hating these people because of that, and hating himself because he understood better than any living soul the rotten streaks in him, he had lived in solitary rebellion, cursing a society he could not enter and could not destroy. He had drifted to the Wells, despising the brutally degraded human beings he necessarily was forced to call his friends. The Wells became his town, the outlaws in it his henchmen. So inevitably the passions guiding Lou Redmain led him step by step into organized thievery. Now he stood on the summit of the ridge, inflamed with the knowledge he had met the best force society could launch against him and tricked it to defeat; hardened and made desperately dangerous by knowing that in the black night just gone he had forfeited every right to mercy and publicly branded himself with the one brand no human being can ever erase — murder.

His gaze traveled as far as the mouth of Starlight. A rider emerged from Starlight, turning west; whoever it was, he went slowly and seemed to sway in the saddle. Redmain whipped a pair of glasses from his coat and bent them on the road for a long interval. Perceptibly the corners of his mouth tightened. Then obeying a cagy impulse, he ran the glasses along the trees fringing Starlight's mouth and on ahead of the rider to where dark angles of the hill country abutted upon the road. He replaced the glasses, and went down to the resting men.

"Up and ride," said he, and spurred ahead without waiting. He threaded the pines, swung to avoid an open meadow, and fell upon a narrow trail. His men strung out, murmuring. He turned and spoke with stinging calm. "Choke off that noise and quit straggling."

Dann drew nearer. "Stage comin'?"

"Never mind," grunted Redmain. He departed from the trail so unexpectedly that Dann shot past him and had to swing back. Some hundred yards down a rocky glen Redmain paused and motioned the party to collect. In front lay a screen of trees; just beyond was the road. He had judged his distance well, for the sound of the rider came around a point of rocks. Redmain tightened his grip on the reins, motioned his men to stand fast, and suddenly shot out of the pines. Eve Leverage, traveling slowly and slackly, saw him. She roused herself to defensive action. The horse sprang forward, her quirt flashed down. Redmain laughed, ran beside her, and got a grip on her pony's bridle cheek piece. Never uttering a sound, she slashed him desperately across the face with the quirt, leaving her mark definitely on him before he jerked it out of her hands. A queer, glittering grin stamped his features.

"Like to cut me, don't you? Words or quirt, it's all the same to you."

"If I had a gun I'd kill you!"

"Considerin' the condition of the country," was his even rejoinder, "you ought to carry one."

She was dead white. She had been crying. Her eyes were blurred, her fists clenched, and she seemed to be fighting for breath.

"You creeping, savage beast! Get away from me — I don't want to touch you!"

"The good, nice people of Yellow Hill," said Redmain, coldly bitter, "have taught you the proper lessons, I see."

"Keep your tongue off folks you're not fit to cringe in front of! I pray God will strike you dead!"

"When your men folk go out to kill it's right and proper. When I use my gun in self-protection I'm nothin' more to you than a savage. Think straight. When the pack is out to destroy it's just as crazy and inhuman as anything on earth. I'm fightin' to live as I want to live! To be let alone — to keep from bein' broke in the damned treadmill! What's wrong with that? I'm a man, and I'm darin' to do what a lot of other men would like to do but ain't got the courage! Because I don't want to follow the pack and think as it thinks — because of that the pack outlaws me. Makes me a target! I'm an animal — but they don't even give me the benefit of a closed season like they would other animals. No, I've got to be destroyed. And you condemn me for wantin' to live!"

"I believe nothing you say!" cried Eve. "You slink in the dark, stealing what belongs to other people! You shot my father, never remembering that years ago he defended you and gave you another chance after you had stolen some of his cows! And you have killed a man who broke with all the ranchers in this country because he wanted you to have every chance a human being could have! A man who publicly said he believed in you — long after you had lost the right to be believed! Stay away from me — you're — you're unclean!"

He was still. But the words ripped him apart, destroyed the sham glory he had built around his bloody acts. Fury leaped in his eyes. "I thought you'd be comin' from Denver's. Been up there to grieve over the hero of the hills, uh? He will never wear a tin crown again!"

She lowered her head, turned it away from him. Redmain laughed harshly at the agony he saw.

"Thought you was mighty kind in giving me your pity that day in Sundown. I'll show you what I think of pity."

He wrapped her reins in his free arm. She struggled for them, but Redmain slapped her hands away. "Stay still — or I'll make you wish you never'd been born."

She slumped in the saddle. "Nothing can hurt me more than I've been hurt," said she dully.

"Pretty talk," jeered Redmain and started west on the road. A gesture of his arm brought the rest of the party from the trees. Gathering speed, Redmain followed the road for a quarter mile and then swept into the trees once more, this time on the south side. Twenty minutes through the forest he paused and rode alone to a break in the greenery. Leverage's ranch quarters drowsed in the sunshine, here and there a puncher idling at chores. Redmain beckoned the party to him and led it along a circle — approaching the ranch from another quarter and closing quietly in. Redmain took

Eve's reins and muttered at the waiting riders.

"No shooting unless it's necessary. Circle the house. Get all hands out in the yard and strip 'em. Dann, you're in charge of that. I'll be going inside. Torper, you watch the road for anything coming this way. Let's go."

He shot into the clearing and bore down on the main house with Eve beside him. A Leverage hand discovered the raid and yelled at the top of his lungs. "Redmain!" Men sprang from all directions. Dann boomed stridently.

"Cut that out or yuh'll shoot the girl! Pitch up, you galoots, and do it quick!"

Redmain was sure enough of his strength to ride straight to the porch, jump down, and haul Eve from her saddle. Mrs. Leverage appeared in the doorway and screamed. She ran for her daughter, striking at Redmain. The outlaw laughed and let the girl go. "Oh, she's not hurt, woman. Where's Leverage?"

Mrs. Leverage backed away, spreading her arms across the door. "Stay out of here! You've done enough harm!"

He pushed her aside. Knowing the arrangement of the house very well, he went directly to Leverage's bedroom. The rancher lay between the sheets, body battened up with pillows. When he saw Redmain he turned his head very slightly, and his lids narrowed. Mrs.

Leverage ran over and put herself by the bed.

Redmain had a thin grin. "Got curious, Jake. Wanted to see what I'd done to you. Next time you'll probably know enough to mind yore own business. In the first place, you're too old to take chances. Also, you ain't quite bright enough to get me. I've known every move you made for two weeks."

"You wet-faced little rat!" snapped Mrs. Leverage. "Let Jake alone! Get out of here and go away. I always did know you were treacherous, but I thought you drew the line somewheres. What did you come here for, anyhow?"

"To let the Leverage family know I ride when and where I please," droned Redmain. "Nothing's going to stop me."

"Well, you've made your brag. Now clear out."

"You don't get off that easy," said Redmain, showing his vicious pleasure. "Jake was big-hearted enough to take the lead in wipin' me out. Now I'm going to set an example for Yellow Hill and show folks just what happens to men that try to hurt me."

He turned back to the porch. His men had collected the Leverage hands and herded them against the corral bars. Dann came out of the bunkhouse with an armful of plunder. Redmain stopped him.

"Dann, drop that junk. I want everything moved from the bunkhouse and piled in the yard. Pull all the machinery and wagons out of the sheds. Get it together. Start a fire under it, burn it to cinders. Toss on anything you see layin' about that's worth a cent."

He paused and cocked his head aside, as if expecting to hear the Leverage women ask for mercy; but silence held the house. Dann grinned. "How about the furniture in the big house? How about burnin' the whole shebang down? That's what they did to the Wells."

Redmain shook his head. "Do what I told you, and make it fast." He returned to the bedroom. "Guess you ain't so far gone, Jake, but what you heard that. A little lesson in manners. It is costin' you a nice sum to buck me."

Still nobody answered him. He broke out wrathfully. "And I mean that lesson to circulate around! By Judas, I want it understood from now on I'm to be let alone! I'm stronger than the law in Yellow Hill! From now on I am the law in this county, and I'll ride out in broad sight without hindrance. You will all listen to me and like it!"

The crackle of flames sounded down the hall. Leverage's white lips twitched. Mrs. Leverage leaned down and touched him. "Don't you care, Jake," she murmured. But Eve ran

292

out to the porch swiftly to see. Redmain followed her and pointed to the fire licking through the heaped-up possessions.

"That," he said, grinding the words together, "is what pity does. Once I thought I'd risk anything and do anything for you. I know better. I don't want you. If I did I'd drag you along. I'd make you like the women at the Wells. Why should I bother? You're no better than they are. I'll stick to the women at the Wells. At least they're honest about it."

He strode from the porch, stepped into the saddle and motioned his men to do likewise. When they had assembled he turned and lifted his hat to Eve sardonically. "One more item. I won't even give you the satisfaction of thinkin' I had to kill Denver myself. I didn't. He didn't mean that much to me. I told Dann to do it."

Eve swayed back from the door and put up her hand to a rifle hanging inside. The outlaws had all turned out, and Dann's broad back was the target on which she leveled her gun. She closed her eyes, pulled the trigger, and flung the rifle defiantly to the floor. Dann's horse swirled and bucked. On the instant the whole party spread wide, guns raised. Lou Redmain charged his pony at Dann just as the latter was lifting his revolver on Eve. He knocked Dann aside, the gun exploded, and the shell ripped through the porch wall. In another slashing arm sweep Redmain forced his lieutenant's weapon down. "Get out of here — I'll attend to this!"

"Let him shoot me!" cried Eve desperately. "Why stop at that when you've done everything else?"

Redmain laughed. "Now I'll show you what will happen to the Leverage crew if any of them ever fire on my outfit again!" He spoke softly over his shoulder. A burst of shots crashed out. Eve turned her head away. Then the renegades were racing off, leaving Leverage's saddle stock slaughtered in the yard.

A half hour later Redmain, deep in the Copperhead country, halted and gave his horses a chance to blow. A part of the bunch threw themselves down as soon as they lighted. Redmain, cagy and aloof, went on to an isolated point and kept his seat. Presently a newcomer emerged from the west and rode along to Redmain's covert.

"Well?" challenged Redmain.

"Not much doubt about it. If he wasn't killed outright in Tom's Hole, then he died after they lugged him home. I crawled on my stummick till I had sight of the whole D Slash premises. They buried him just a little bit ago.

I saw the coffin go down and the earth cover it up."

Redmain nodded and called out to Dann. "Come on." So the cavalcade strung after him, this time posting north through the rugged defiles bordering the river, verging toward Sundown. Redmain's glance began to reach ahead more impatiently. And abruptly he lifted an arm by way of signal. The column halted. An inconspicuous little man with swarthy features had been standing athwart the trail in an attitude of long waiting. He came up promptly.

"I was about to conclude," said he, "you wasn't goin' to make it."

"I do what I say I'll do," jerked out Redmain morosely. "Sing your piece."

"I was told to tell yuh," recited the little man tonelessly, "that the Association busted up without no decision. The vigilantes idee ain't goin' to be carried on. Nobody wants the job of runnin' it. The little fellers won't join in. So the big fellers have decided to organize their own ridin' committees to cover their own ranges — nothin' more'n that."

Malicious satisfaction dawned on Redmain's face. "So I split 'em up. Just what I wanted to do. Anything else?"

"I was told to tell yuh to use yore judgment fer a few days."

"I reckon I'm in the habit of doin' that pretty well," remarked Redmain dryly and somewhat irritably.

The swarthy messenger cast a sidewise glance at Dann. "Steers has published his intention of goin' after yuh, Dann. He stood in Grogan's and called you a number of names. He challenged yuh to meet him anywhere, any time."

"Small potatoes," jeered Dann. "He figgers he's safe in cussin' a man that ain't able to come out in the daylight and meet him. And say, how does he know I kicked Denver over? That's what I want to know."

"It's the dope around Sundown," added the messenger.

"News seems to get published awful sudden," grunted Dann. "To hell with Steers. I ain't worried about him."

Redmain's silence began to be oppressive. He had his eyes fixed calculatingly on Dann. Presently he spoke up. "That's an idea. Why not?"

"Why not what?" Dann wanted to know.

"Go get him."

Dann turned defiant. "Yore runnin' this outfit, ain't yuh? Why don't yuh do yore own shootin' once in a while? Have I got to do all of it?"

"Afraid of Steers?" asked Redmain softly.

Dann jumped at the bait. "You know better'n that, Lou! I'm afraid of nobody that walks!"

"Considerable territory," observed Redmain in the same cool and cutting manner. "For instance, you sound like you might be includin' me. Which of course you don't mean, do you, Dann?"

Dann held Redmain's eyes until his own turned bloodshot. The messenger shifted uneasily. Redmain smiled with his lips. "You didn't include me, did you, Dann?"

Dann shifted. "Let it go," he grunted and found an excuse to look at his feet. "If yuh really want me to go get Steers —"

"I do. Go after him. Choose your time and your ground. But get him. I want Yellow Hill to understand that I hear all these challenges and that I call all bluffs. I mean to make it so this county won't dare speak about me above a whisper. Go get him."

He turned to the swarthy messenger and studied him in cool detachment. The latter felt himself being dismissed and without another word rode off. Redmain waited for a few moments and took up his talk again with Dann.

"There's more to it. You'll create a sort of side show while I'm up in the hills plannin' somethin' else. There's one more big play comin' up. One more smash this country's goin' to suffer from me. They tried to lick me — and couldn't. Now they figger to let me alone. And they can't do that either. They went too far. I remember every slight, every insult. I got all that down on the books, and I intend to pay off. What did they do to the Wells? Destroyed it! All right. I am going to destroy Sundown, Dann! And then ride out of the country!"

"When?" was Dann's swift question.

"Never mind. You'll know soon enough. Get on your horse and pull out. You've got the next three-four days to find Steers and maneuver him into position. I'll be up in the country above Sundown — out of sight and out of mind."

Dann turned back, got his horse, and rode west into the timber. Redmain watched him go, a flare of cruelty on the triangular face. He had told Dann two reasons for going after Steers; but he had not told Dann the third reason. In short, he wanted Dann to be shot down. The big man was becoming too dangerous, too boastful, too much of a malcontent. He might infect the others, he might turn treacherous. Steers, of course, was not as good a shot as Dann, but once the big outlaw was sent off alone he was apt to get foolish and betray himself — and be trapped. In any event, Redmain meant the man should never return to the party. If he did return he would never so much as get off his horse. Thus definitely did Redmain erase Stinger Dann from his plans. He signaled to the outfit and led away. The column vanished through the green thicket.

CHAPTER XVI
WHEN A MAN THINKS

For a dead man, Dave Denver exhibited singular symptoms. He lay on his bed at D Slash, a row of pillows propped to either side. His head was encased in an enormous ball of bandages that ran from crown to chest and exposed only a bruised nose, a cut mouth, and a pair of rebellious eyes. One of his arms was splinted all the way down, and nothing showed but the tips of his fingers; and at present he twiddled them one at a time, meanwhile muttering something about Sweet Adeline in a cracked voice. This was an innovation; he hadn't tried it during the preceding two days, but a man flat on his back will try anything once. Sometimes the results are gratifying. In this instance it brought Lyle Bonnet into the room on a dead run.

"What's the matter, Dave?"

Denver didn't turn his head. He couldn't turn his head. But he broke off singing. "Nothing! Why all the lather?"

"Great guns!" snorted Bonnet. "I heard yuh a-groanin' and a-sobbin' and I thought yuh had a spasm."

"I was singing. No law against it."

"No-o," reflected Bonnet. "That is, not for actual bona-fide singin'. Was I you, I believe I'd whistle instead."

"Oh, all right," muttered Dave fretfully. "I just wanted to see if my chest was in order. I guess it is. See them fingers? I can move 'em. Nothin' busted down there. Wish Doc would come. I want to get the verdict on this left arm. I wish I could get up and move my legs."

"No, cut that out. Ain't I had grief enough without arguin' with yuh? You got yore orders."

"Huh, I got no more say-so around this dump than a dish washer," opined Denver. "Lyle, ever reflect on the wonders of nature? No? Well, you ought. Improve your education. I have. See that fly on the bedpost? That's Oscar. I reckon you've always held the common misguided opinion that flies are hostile insects, ain't you? Dead wrong, Lyle. Oscar loves me. If he's kissed me once he's kissed me fifty times. And I suppose you hold that flies are unclean animals? Ain't right. Oscar washes ever' fifteen minutes. How do I know? Well, he takes a seat on my nose to do his laundry. Regular ceremony about it. First he lifts his left laig and bats himself on the nose.

301

Then he makes a swipe at his ears with the other laig —"

"Flies ain't got ears," remarked Bonnet glumly.

"Didn't I tell you folks was all haywire about flies? Biggest ears you ever saw. When he sleeps he covers his eyes with 'em. He turns himself around like a dog. On my nose, see? Two-three times. Then he squats and drops anchor. After which he lops his ears down. He's got a lullaby song, too. Kinda pretty in a flyish way —"

"Quit movin' yore head."

Denver groaned. "Some day I'm just naturally goin' to tie the can to you, Lyle."

"I wish to Gawd yuh would," muttered Bonnet. "If I take much more punishment I'll go batty. Ever since we pulled that fake burial day before yesterday your friends have been droppin' in to give me fits. Seems like everybody wanted to see yuh dead — well, I mean they sorter wanted to say so-long before we covered the coffin. I been told I had ought to of laid you out like Exhibit A. I been told I should 'a' took you to Sundown's cemetery. Steve Steers was so hog-wild when he come that I figgered he was agoin' to shoot. It's a good thing I got Doc to back me up, or I'd be accused of buryin' yuh alive."

"What's Doc tell 'em?"

"Tells 'em that if folks can't keep fresh beef from spoilin' in this weather what do they expect of a defunct human being?"

"A good answer," mused Denver, "but not nice."

"And here's another item," went on Bonnet. "I may be a hard nut, but I can't stand by and listen to any more women cryin' — like Eve did. Dave, I tell you I almost broke down and told her the truth."

Denver raised his good arm. "I know — I know. I was just as bad off, lyin' here and hearin' her out there. That's something I'm going' to carry on my conscience a long time. I don't know if she ever will forgive me when she finds out. Maybe I didn't have any business keepin' her out of the secret. It was cold blooded. But it seemed to me then — and it does now — that there is no way of getting Lou Redmain in a trap without throwin' him off completely. If he knows he's put Leverage out of the way and me out of the way he'll be apt to take longer chances. That's just what I want. And he won't be spyin' around D Slash to see what I'm up to. I had to make the idea of my being dead sound truthful. Redmain's no man's fool. Supposin' he had run into Eve right afterward. Or supposin' he's got spies around the Leverage place, as he probably has. If she seems unconcerned about me he'll get suspicious right away. No, I had to take the hard way, and may the Lord forgive me for doin' it."

"You going to tell Steve?"

"Not today or tomorrow. If he's gone hog-wild, then that's the best advertisement of my kickin' the bucket I could want. I'm not worryin' over him. He can stand the gaff."

"How about Lola Monterey?"

There was so long a silence that Bonnet figured Denver hadn't heard. Denver was staring blackly at the ceiling. After a while he spoke, never answering the question — and Bonnet knew he was not to mention the girl's name again. "Do you think we fooled Hominy Hogg and the Steele bunch?"

"I'd say so," said Bonnet. "You got to figure that when all those shots turned our attention toward Tom's Hole and we found yuh lyin' in that mess of rocks, you was in no pretty shape. Of course, yuh talked, but it wasn't no great shakes. So when we got here and put yuh in the bedroom I think the Steele bunch considered it a toss-up. Anyhow, when I walked out on the porch and said yuh was gone, they rode home with a good imitation of bein' sunk."

"To tell you the truth," revealed Denver, "I got the idea of playing dead the minute I shook the fog out of my head and found

304

I was still kickin'. I wasn't hurt as much as I gave indications of bein' in front of the bunch. I trust almost all of the Steele bunch, but there's a chance some one of them might be playing double. So I thought it best to carry out the idea. Therefore there's nobody but my own crew who knows I'm alive. And we'll keep it that way until I get wind of Redmain and have a chance of running him down. Did you do what I told you?"

"About the men? Yeah. I explained the situation. Chester Mack, Limerick Lane, and Gallup decided to play the part of havin' quit the ranch. They're to hit Sundown and indicate the ranch is breakin' up. Mack's to stay in town and keep his ears wide open. I told Limerick to ride around the hills like he was lookin' for work. Gallup is to get himself a pack horse and strike out on a prospectin' trip — keepin' to the upper Copperhead. So that covers that. What next?"

"You can't hang around the ranch too much, Lyle. There might be renegades spyin' on us."

Bonnet frowned. "There is — or was. Lee was pokin' around the east trees a little while ago and found where a fellow had beaten down the grass and brush. Apparently watchin' the house. Considerin' yore helpless I wasn't going to say anything about it."

Denver thought about this for a period.

305

"Redmain may be near by. Only one way to be sure. You start out in the morning as if to round up the stock. Beat the country pretty well. Better yet — send out some men tonight with cold grub. Put 'em where they'll cover the trails. Same system we tried before. It worked then, and it'll work now."

"That all?"

"Ahuh. Get out of here. Oscar's losin' his patience. Can't you see him fiddlin' around?"

But Bonnet had hardly departed when Doc Williamson arrived. He cast a professional glance at Denver. "Suppose you've been threshin' around the bed and cussin' everybody. Your kind always does."

"If I ever get out of here I'll never look at that ceilin' again. Going to paint it full of faces, so I can talk to 'em. Put your face in the middle and give you the devil. Meet Oscar."

"Crazy as a loon," remarked Doc Williamson and threw back the covers. "Now if this don't hurt, tell me. Otherwise keep still."

"It's a good thing you've got Pete Atkins to take care of up here, too," reflected Denver, "or I don't know how you'd manage to keep up the story of me bein' dead. Yeah, that's my foot, all right. No doubt about it."

"Think you're wise?" countered Williamson. "Givin' grief to a lot of good people —

306

and some in particular?"

"I reckon I'll pay for it later. It's a hard game, Doc, but I've got to play it out."

"Somebody's got to play it out," agreed the Doc, "or this county will be worse than when the Indians skulked through it. Now, I'm going to get a little rough."

"What do you call what you been doin' so far?" Denver wanted to know. He closed his eyes while Williamson lifted one foot and another, turning the ankles, bending the knees, all the while his sharp eyes probing Denver's face for pain. In ten minutes or so he had worked up as far as the splinted arm; taking off the bandages he continued his search, fingers gently insistent. Then he was done; and he leaned back, eyes lighting. "Well, after bouncing off every rock in Tom's Hole I still can't find any bones busted. What'd you want a doctor for? Legs are sound, ribs seem satisfactory, that arm's got a few pulled tendons, but nothing more."

Denver considered he did very well in suppressing his wild emotion of pleasure. "How about my head?"

"You got a gash in it big enough to drive a span of mules through, right over the left ear. I washed so much grit out of it the other day I thought I was prospectin'. What difference does it make? Nobody in Yellow

Hill uses a head often enough to count, any-how."

"So I can get up, uh?"

"Who said so?" grunted Doc, juggling some vile-looking pills into a glass of water.

"Well, if I'm not hurt —"

Williamson clucked his tongue in disgust. "Listen, Dave, if you were a horse I'd shoot you for bein' absolutely no good for further service. But since you're a Denver — the blackest and toughest breed of mortal fools I ever knew — I'll say you stick on your back for a week. Then you can do what you please. You will anyhow, so I might as well say it. Drink this, and don't bellyache."

Denver obeyed, shuddering as he waved the empty glass away. "You'll make me sick yet. But, listen, you cut that week down to about three-four days, Doc. As a personal favor to me."

"I'm not God," said Williamson, closing his bag. "But I'll drop around tomorrow and see if some packs and some massagin' won't work a little of the bruise out of you. Now, get some sleep."

"Sleep — I'm so full of sleep I'd float," grumbled Denver fretfully. "Go on away and leave me alone."

Williamson paused in the doorway. "Well," he mused, "I'm glad it wasn't worse." That was his only display of sentiment, his only admission of the deep concern he had felt for a man he loved. Closing the door quietly, he went out to treat Pete Atkins, who had taken a bullet through his leg in the fight.

Denver stared at the ceiling, calculating his condition. A week was a long time to be helpless while Lou Redmain raced through the hills. If the renegade would just play 'possum for a while, it would be all right. But the thought was not worth entertaining. He knew Redmain. The man was a furnace of tempers. He had tasted blood, and like all killers, low or high, he would be lusting for more. Redmain had boasted on that night in the Wells — it seemed months back — that the sky was his limit. He wouldn't know enough to stop, and there was no audacious scheme he would turn away from.

The fly, or one of its innumerable cousins, made a graceful loop through the air and came to rest on Denver's nose. Denver blew him away abstractedly. Then he lifted his sound right arm and considered it. He had the means of defense left him. Or attack either. One arm was better than no arm. And the right arm was a little better than the left one, though he had been trained from childhood to shoot with either. He waved it across from one side to another, feeling the stiff and aching resistance of his chest muscles. Changing tactics, he operated the member up and down — and woke more muscles to discomfort. There seemed to be no single square inch of his body free from hurt.

"Must of lit on all four sides at once," he gloomed. "I recall Dann pluggin' my horse. I recall goin' down that slope like somebody that'd been sent for in a hurry. I bounced. Yeah, I sure did bounce. Anyhow, I faded to the sound of music and shootin'. I bet Dann would have stood on top of the ridge and made a target out of me all day long if the boys hadn't heard the ruction from the trees and come along. I must have been within hailin' distance of them that morning when I went into Tom's Hole. There's another item Redmain had figured down to the seventh decimal. He had it doped we'd come struggling out of the brush and take the shortest road home. And so he planted himself. No, by George, a week is too long. He'll be started on a campaign of ruin before I'm up."

The renegade had uncanny perceptions of attack and defense. Denver was candid enough to admit his own mind didn't move as fast as Redmain's. Redmain was like a sharp sword, flashing in and out while he, Dave Denver, was as slow moving as a bludgeon. He didn't have the dash, the flair; he could only do as he always had done: beat doggedly ahead, take punishment, and keep going for the knockout blow. There was that difference between them; and the fight would be so waged. Until one of them got in the killing blow. No other end than that. A kill.

The fly made another landing. Denver looked crosseyed at the insect. "Oscar, I'm gettin' disgusted at you. Go play with your own friends." And he made a swipe at his nose that flexed all the mass of jangling ligaments in his body. He relaxed groaning.

Patience was not one of his virtues, and when Lyle Bonnet brought in supper he was morose and irritable. "Roll me about five hundred cigarettes, Lyle, and pile 'em on the table. I've tried to do it one-handed and wasted three sacks of heifer dust."

"Want me to spoon this nutriment into yuh?"

"No," rasped Denver, "I'll spill my own soup on my own chin."

Bonnet chuckled. "What big teeth yuh got, Grammaw. Well, I'll go eat and set half the crew to rollin' the aforesaid cigareets. There just ain't nothin' we ain't bright enough to do in this outfit."

"Go 'way and let me think."

Bonnet caught that one neatly. He raised a skeptical eyebrow. "Well, that'll be something different, anyhow." Grinning broadly, he departed.

When, an hour later, he returned, Denver lay silent on the bed. So Bonnet put the cigarettes in a row, laid out a bunch of matches, turned down the lamp, and tiptoed away with the dishes. Denver, who only had his eyes closed, heard all this; and through his morose discontent he felt a warm glow of affection. Bonnet was as tough and devil-may-care as they made them; but he was a man. In the middle of the night when he drowsed he faintly heard the latch click and somebody come in for a moment.

Next morning he was cheerful for a little while. Bonnet arrived to say he had sent out four of the outfit to settle down in convenient locations; he was taking all the rest on the ranch but five, to go out on the fake roundup.

"Why leave five here?"

Bonnet's reply was a little too casual. "Oh, just to hang around."

Denver seized upon the suspicious manner instantly. "Spit it out. You've got something in your coco."

"Shucks," grunted Bonnet and studied his cigarette. "Oh, well. If yuh got to know, I'm leavin' 'em for protection. Redmain done rode his bunch into Leverage's, scared the women, and made his brag generally. Eve — by golly, I hand it to her — took a pot shot at Dann, and Redmain burned a lot of stuff and killed off the saddle stock. That's why."

Denver's body stiffened; the violet of his eyes began to suffuse. Bonnet hurried on. "Doggone it, I knowed it would just make things worse! Cut it out and calm down. No good bustin' an artery. I give orders to the fellas stayin' behind. They camp on the porch until I'm back."

Denver thought it out, mastered his hot rage. "I can see what's smokin up now, Lyle. He'll never be satisfied at just plain revenge. Lord have mercy on the people he chooses to hurt. We've got to get busy. And we've got to have more men. Today you angle over to Steele's. Talk to Hominy. Tell him you're short handed. Tell him the D Slash estate will stand back of the wages. Argue five men out of him. These five —" and he named them — "I know are absolutely to be trusted. When we get 'em down here we can break the news."

"Good enough. Well, I'll have news by tonight."

"You better have," said Denver. Bonnet went out. Denver waited until he heard the horses being saddled. Then he got into action.

He swept away the bed covers and slowly drew his knees up, working them cautiously.

He put his good arm under him, turned half over. He kicked half a dozen pillows to the floor, rolled on his face, and settled his feet to the carpet. And again by the aid of his useful arm he pushed himself straight.

His head throbbed, his knees quivered a little. But he was up, and that was something to write home about. Supporting himself at the bedside, he stared with a thin-lipped triumph at the familiar walls. "Oscar," he grunted, "just take a look at this and tell your children. Maybe I wouldn't pass as a civilized specimen with my shirt tails a-flappin', but I guess a fellow's got a right to wear underclothes in his own bedroom."

He sneezed, rousing a headache. Specks floated around the room and disappeared. He steadied himself, waited for his vision to clear, and decided it was time to do something else. So he put a foot forward and aimed for the dresser. It was not bad at all, excepting for a particular joint in his hip that seemed to bite him at each step. Arriving at the dresser, he peered into the mirror.

"Good God, is that a face?"

Within the cowling of bandages was half a forehead with a sort of cross-hatched pattern of scars, a skinned nose, a pair of puffy lips, and two red-rimmed, groggy eyes. The eyes rolled owlishly, turned puzzled, turned cold.

Denver swung away. "I look like I've been drunk since Lincoln was shot. Now, there's one more important test. If I can sit in that chair without breakin' my back —"

He swerved, making for the bed. The door opened, and Bonnet stepped in with his mouth half open to speak. Denver stopped dead and essayed a smile — a crooked, furtive smile as of a man caught stealing chickens. Bonnet slammed the door behind him and lifted the quirt dangling on his wrist.

"Damn you, Dave Denver," he cried, hard and angry, "get back in that bed! Ain't there a lick of sense in your stubborn head? What the devil do you think Williamson's makin' a long trip out here for every day? Can't nobody tell you nothin'? Get back there! Go on. I've got a ninety per cent notion to tie yuh in."

"All right — all right, I'm goin'," muttered Denver. Getting down was harder work than rising. He made three futile attempts to lift one foot and collapse gradually. Bonnet stood by in stony silence. Denver swore and closed his mind to the inevitable hurt; he swung his good shoulder to the bed and pitched forward, rolling the rest of his body after. Very slowly he clawed the quilts around him. "All right, Simon Legree," said he, panting like an engine, "crack your whip and see if I care."

"Listen, Dave, I want yore promise not to essay that stunt again today. Either that or I don't budge. I'm gettin' all-fired tired of playin' wet nurse, and I ain't goin' to see yuh do anything that'll stretch it out. Do I get the promise?"

"You got it. What'd you come back for, anyhow?"

"Had a blamed good idea what you was up to. Saw the glitter in yore eyes."

"Well, I'll stay quiet today. But I'm a sound man, Lyle. And tomorrow I aim to get on my hoofs again. Williamson's all wrong about this week business. I can't wait a week."

"Why not?"

"I know Redmain too well. Hell's brewin' somewhere. I don't know where, and I don't know how. But I know. There never was a time of trouble in this country that I didn't get the whisper of it. The old feelin'. Somethin' passin' through the air. Medicine drums beatin'. And I'm just enough savage to feel it — hear it. Go on, Lyle. I'll stay in bed today. But when I get well I'm going to burn the cursed thing."

"Lay there, doggone yuh," said Bonnet, and went out.

"Either I fire that buzzard," decided Denver, "or I give him a quarter interest in the ranch."

A steady ache throbbed through his body. He shut his eyes, but that only seemed to bring him nearer the pain; so he opened them again and stared at the ceiling. There was a drifting crack in the plaster that reminded him a little bit of the Copperhead's meandering course. The reverse turn would be about at the lower falls. The first little offshoot was Butte Creek. Weeping Woman fell in just above. But from that point the crack curved the wrong way, and Denver had an impatient desire to get up to the ceiling and correct the error. He closed his eyes again, groaning. "If I ever get off my back I'll sleep on my stomach the rest of my life."

Once he had thought this bedroom to be a pretty nice place. After the dreary hours in it he decided he had never seen a more barren room in all his days; and suddenly it occurred to him his own life was equally barren. What sort of a game had he been playing all these years — and where did it lead? What was he fighting for, why was he building up the ranch? Who cared, other than himself, whether he had a dime or a fortune? Always until now the day and its work had been sufficient. His own energy had carried him along, from the first flush of dawn until dark. Up and away in the saddle, riding the trails, standing over the hot brand fire, full in the brawl of the dusty, bellowing herds. Into town to watch his accounts, to meet with the Association, to drink and joke awhile among men of his kind. And home to eat and sleep. That was all the ranch house meant — a place to go to and to depart from. Nothing more.

In such a day there was no time for reflection, no need of long brown thoughts. Nor was he a man given to introspection. His own vitality, his own love of rough life sufficed; the primitive pleasure of feeling the rain slash his cheeks or the sight of the sun exploding riotously into a crimson setting — these things were enough for a pagan. They had filled his day.

Until now. The house was too quiet, too empty. The cook's footfalls echoed too blankly. With a growing uneasiness he reflected that his own career was much the same — full of sounds echoing into blank corners. It surprised him to find he had blank corners. He thought he had done very well by himself. It surprised him to find this strange disquietude running through his body. Actually it was like hunger, a hunger for something he had never had — something he couldn't even place.

His turning thoughts skipped the gap, and he recalled the evenings he now and then spent at Leverage's. Jake Leverage seemed to mellow and take his ease inside the walls of that pleasantly warm and comfortable house. No blank corners there — none whatsoever. And in another abrupt jump Denver saw Eve standing at the door, smiling out of her steady eyes, the fragrance of perfume in her hair faintly crossing the shadowed porch to perplex him. A serene, boyish figure with lurking laughter about her; yet this was the Eve who had taken a gun to fire on Dann. Denver closed his fists and glowered at the ceiling.

"That pack of dogs has got to be wiped off the earth," he muttered. "They might have hurt her. I've been the Lord's worst fool to stand aside all this time and let Redmain get enough power in his hands to be able to do that. Leverage was right. It didn't make any difference to him if there was crooked influences back of the vigilante idea. He was fightin' to keep his women safe. Bein' married, bein' a father made him see that. I didn't. I'm just a half-wild rider, nothin' more. Good God, I wish I was up!"

His head was so tangled with all this thinking that he lost trace of what he was trying to unravel. He closed his eyes, and the extra exertion of the morning put him to sleep.

When he awoke, alert and startled, there was the sound of singing out in the big room. A woman singing. He had no need to guess;

only Lola Monterey's voice carried that husky, infinitely sad pitch — only Lola had the power of throwing herself into words until the very air vibrated with her personality. The song was in Spanish, and the melody of it seemed to blend all the ancient wisdom of love and life and tragedy. It swayed hauntingly, fell to a whisper, and rose like a clear call. And suddenly broke off, to leave the silence bleak and tense. Denver lay immovable. A quick step tapped over the big room's floor. She spoke.

"David."

She was at his door, her hand brushing it lightly. Denver watched the knob, suspended between a desire to call and the grim need of being silent. But he never had the opportunity of deciding. Lola cried, "David!" again. The door flew open. She paused, tall and beautiful and supremely moved. Then she threw herself into the room and fell beside him, head on his chest, choking out her words.

"David — I sang to wherever you were! To call you back, my love! And then I knew you were not dead!"

One of the hands appeared in the door and motioned apologetically. "She jest wanted —"

"Get out of here," said Dave. He put his hand on the jet and shining head. Saying nothing for a while, knowing nothing ought to be said. The pound of her heart lessened; the trembling of her body died away, and it was as if she slept, hands tight on his shoulders. He had no idea how long a time passed, for his thoughts traveled the old bitter pathway backward, and he was lost in a memory that was fire and flame, laughter and quarrel — like sunlight flashing intermittently through storm clouds. Then Lola sprang up, tipped her chin; and through the film of tears her eyes were smiling.

"So I live always, David. From hurt to joy. Never even, never serene. Why did you do it — why did you?"

He shook his head. "I can't tell you, Lola. All I say now is that when you go out of this house you've got to carry yourself just the same as when you came in. Not by a single look or thought or word must you be changed. I'm publicly dead — and so I remain until —"

"There is only one reason," said Lola, whose eyes never left his face. "You hope to get Lou Redmain."

He had no reply. Lola spoke swiftly. "Lou is deadly."

"I'm not exactly skimmed milk, Lola. Wasn't there a time when you called me a hard man?"

"I know, but Lou never gave anybody a fair chance in all his life — except me. There's something in him that warps every good impulse. He will tell you he is your friend. He will actually mean to be honest and fair and straight. But after a little while he turns aside. I never realized that until I had thought back from the very beginning of when I'd known him. He tricked you up in the hills, didn't he? Dave, he will do it again. And you'll go straight ahead, as you always do, and —"

"Not with Redmain," grunted Denver. "I fight him as dirty as he fights me. I expect nothin' and I give nothin'."

She was silent a moment. Then: "Does Eve know —"

"Lord forgive me, no! She thinks I'm dead."

Very softly she added a question: "And how about me, David? Did it occur to you I might be hurt too?"

"I reckon I've always hurt you, Lola."

"The light of day," said she in a half whisper, "died out." But she shifted to gayety on the instant. "I must not carry on. Who wants to see Lola Monterey in tears? Only women who are loved can afford to show unhappiness. David, my dear, get well. You are scowling because you can't be on your feet, because you are not the old domineering David Denver."

"Not sure," he mused. "A man does some powerful thinkin', flat on his back. The little round world don't look the same. Maybe I've been a fool. Maybe I've rode alone too long. It's lonely."

"Then there is hope for you," said she, her red lips dimpling at the corners. "And perhaps some hope even for me." Leaning swiftly down she kissed him. "For old times, David. Be good."

"You've got to forget I'm alive," he warned her. "You've got to hide your feelings."

"What have I been an actress for all my life? Isn't that just what I always must do — seem sad when I'm so happy I want to cry out, and seem glad when there's nothing in me but an ache?"

She went out, trailing grace and vivid color. And the room was again four shabby walls.

Doc Williamson, returning in the late afternoon, found his patient locked in gray rebellion.

"You've got to fix me up," said Denver.

"What with?" was Williamson's sarcastic rejoinder.

"What do I care? Use dope, or balin' wire, or an ax. But you've got to do it. You're a doctor, ain't you? Then get busy."

"For that," promised Williamson, "I'm going to rub you so hard you'll yell like a dyin' Comanche."

"Go ahead. Try and make me yell."

"Wait'll I get some hot and cold water."

Williamson was just rolling down his cuffs and looking rather more tired than usual when Lyle Bonnet returned. Bonnet grinned.

"Did yuh give him the works, Doc? That sucker horsed himself outa bed this mornin' and tried to walk."

"Sure, all lunatics are like that," said Williamson.

"What's the news?" was Denver's impatient interruption.

"The most important item is," reflected Bonnet, "that Steve Steers has posted his intentions of gettin' Dann, and has challenged Dann to meet him any place, at any time."

Denver swore in round, blistering phrases. "That damn idiot! He can't do it — Dann's too fast for him. We've got to stop it. Listen, you race a man over to Nightingale's. Use any excuse to get Steve here. I'll break the news. I didn't want to do it for another couple days, but we've got to haul him around, or he'll get shot cold. Hurry up."

CHAPTER XVII
THE DUEL

Stinger Dann kicked the ashes of his small fire together and ground them out. Sunlight streamed into the glade, the odor of bacon and coffee lingered faintly on — and Redmain's right-hand gunman greeted his fourth day of lone hunting with an accumulated moroseness.

There were two sides to Dann, neither of them any credit to him. In a pitched engagement, such as with the vigilantes and Denver, he let himself go with an unreasoning and tigerish fury, never considering safety, never slacking off in his desire to destroy and inflict pain. But in this present affair with Steers he was a different man altogether, stolidly patient enough to wait all year for his chance, and avoiding every false move. He might have forced the issue sooner, for he had seen Steve Steers two or three times from afar, and he recognized the fact that Steers was advertising his position and issuing a challenge. In each instance Dann recoiled from the setting, thinking a trap to exist, or considering the odds uneven. So he held back, waiting for the time when Steers, tired of the crossplay, would become reckless. Dann knew the occasion would arise. Because of that belief he kept to the high levels, out of the traveled areas, and changed locations each night. He had waited behind Shoshone Dome, watching the stage road. He had taken a covert position near the Copperhead bridge. Then, shifting his position, he had settled down near Nightingale's ranch. But of all places this was the least profitable. Steers was not using the ranch as a base. Therefore Dann moved south of Starlight and took to his present position, which was on a wooded butte commanding the end of Sundown Valley, the stage road, a half dozen forking trails, and the prairie.

He had another definite reason for holding off. Not being a fool, he knew no man in Redmain's shoes was to be trusted; in this illicit kind of a life it was dog eat dog, with no scruples shown. During the hours of solitude it had been borne upon Dann that he was practically stationed between two fires. No longer did he have the mass protection of the wild bunch. He was on his own, an isolated outlaw to be shot at. And what was to prevent the bullet from coming out of the wrong direction — Redmain's? Such things happened. He had been a valuable man to

Redmain, but the chief treated him scurvily.

"He's afraid of me," grunted Dann to himself, watching the road below. "He's runnin' the bunch, and he don't want me to interfere. Higher they get, the more nervous they get. I can tell. He's took to watchin' his shadder — and that ain't healthy for anybody that crosses his path. But I was a sucker to leave. He meant somethin' by it. It wasn't just no case of gettin' Steers. Anybody could get that washed-out runt. Why pick me? Yeah, he had an idea, the slippery rat."

The sun rose higher, melting morning's dew. Three Leverage riders came around one side of the butte, patrolled as far as Starlight, and circled toward their ranch. Dann felt a strong desire to scatter them with his rifle, such being the rankling, surly state of his mind. And momentarily his resentment grew.

"I was a sucker to leave," he repeated. "Who's done all the hard work for Lou Redmain? Me. He gets the credit. And still he plays his own hand well enough to tell the wide world I shot Denver. I had ought to of stayed. It was smokin' up to a fight between me and him — and it only needed one bullet to settle him. That's my crowd, not his. He's afraid of me, that's what. Well, I'll get this job over with and go back. And we'll see who's —"

327

His roving glance came to focus. Beyond Starlight, a rider pursued the Sundown-Ysabel Junction road with a free gait. Dann crouched closer to the earth, sidling a little to keep the approaching man in view. He reached back for his rifle, considered the distance from butte to road, and slowly sent the bolt home on a shell. Tentatively he settled the gun to his shoulder. But in the very act of rehearsing the forthcoming scene he let the gun fall and scurried off to get a view of the reverse slope. The Leverage riders were still in sight. Dann watched them drift along, a scowl deepening on his red face. Then he returned to his original location and swept the green timber on the far side of the road, all the way up to the mouth of Starlight. That canyon was a tricky stretch of country. Denver country with Denver men in it; and the solitary rider had all that to his back as he loped ahead.

It was Steve Steers. Dann had recognized him at the first far glance. Steers rode with a peculiar flopping of elbows and a distinct swaying in the saddle; moreover, Steers had a favorite horse, colored like a blanket — a small horse that lifted his feet high. Dann leveled his gun on Steers, still engaged in the debate with himself. There was such a thing as missing his target, considering the distance; there was also the ever present possibility of a trap. Dann never forgot that item. And while he tarried, keeping his sight on Steers, the latter went rocketing through the throat of the hills, fell down the long grade, and was beyond reach. Dann cursed slowly, flipping over the rifle's safety. He watched Steers settle to a long straight course southward.

"He's goin' to the Junction," decided Dann. "And that's the chance I been waitin' for. Once he's out of these hills I know blamed well there ain't anybody helpin' him. Now I got him just like I want!"

He rode down the butte side, shot across the road, and gained cover once more. Fifteen minutes later he appeared on the edge of the prairie, away off to the left rear of Steers, who had become a bobbing point in the distance. An arroyo stretched over the undulating land like an avenue; into the protection of this Dann descended, whipping his horse.

Steve Steers never rode abroad without unconsciously absorbing the details of the land. This was range training. And recently he had been especially vigilant because of his challenge to Dann. Whether or not Dann was gunning for him, he couldn't tell, for in all his roundabout riding during the last four days he had found no sign of the burly outlaw. But today he crossed the prairie in a fairly relaxed frame of mind. Outside of the broken stretch of country called the Sugar Loaves half way to the Junction and the Mogul canyon slightly farther on, there was no place for an ambusher to hide. These two geographical man-traps he put behind without accident. Once, quite a few miles to his left rear, he had picked up a moving object and then rather suddenly lost it, but it was like a ship sighting another ship down the horizon and he paid scant attention. Two hours from Starlight he reined in at the Junction and dismounted, a little dry, a little drowsy, and expecting nothing. The only definite thoughts he had in mind related to his errand, which was to send a telegram up to Salt Lake to a certain gentleman who specialized in doing detective work around stockyards. He had talked the matter over with Niland, and they had agreed it might be illuminating to have the man look into Fear Langdell's shipments as they arrived, more especially studying the flesh side of the brands after the steers had been skinned.

He walked toward the station house, contemplating the utter desolation of this pin point upon the map. A dripping water tank dominated Ysabel Junction, which was half the reason for there being a railroad stop here at all. The other half rested on the presence of a long series of cattle pens and loading chutes that ran the full length of about eighteen hundred yards of siding. There were also three bilious colored section shanties, now quite empty of life, and a few flimsy sheds. And this was the scene. Steve ambled through the open door of the station house with an increasing sense of weariness. The telegraph clacked crisply through the droning air, but when he passed from the waiting room into the agent's combined office and living quarters he found nobody present.

"A large and busy life," he reflected, easing himself into a chair. "I'd go nuts if I didn't have nothin' to do but watch the trains pass by. This and sheep herdin' is my idea of absolute zero in human activity. Now I wonder where that gazook has done gone and lost himself?"

He rolled a cigarette and tilted the chair against the wall, considering it easier to wait than to go out and shout. A fly buzzed around his head, and he closed his eyes. The telegraph chattered companionably for a while, then fell silent. The world was large, and there was plenty of time, a seasonable share of which slid painlessly by before Steve took cognizance of it. The telegraph rattled again, and though Steve knew absolutely nothing about Morse code, he thought he detected a regular sequence in the call. The reiteration of it made

331

him slightly uneasy; rising, he walked along the walls and studied the pictures tacked profusely thereon, most of them women out of magazines. Some had clothes on.

"Mama," grinned Steve, knocking back his hat, "come save your son! This fella has got taste."

After a while even the undeniable novelty of art appreciation waned. Steve considered. "His hat's here, his coat's here, and so's his gun. There's his pipe. Well, I guess he's got more time than I have, so I better look. Funny thing, but the less a man's got to do the harder he is to find."

He went back through the waiting room and stepped to the cindered runway. Not a soul stood against the hard bright day. Outside of the Mexican houses and the open sheds there was no place of refuge available to the agent. Steve began to resent the cosmic indifference sweltering around him. He opened his mouth and emitted a strident bellow.

"Hey!"

No reply. Not even an echo. It appeared there was no power sufficiently strong to dent the overwhelming vacantness. Steve considered the water tank thoughtfully. "Wonder if he climbed up there to take a bath and couldn't get out? HEY!"

He swore mildly and started for the Mexican

houses. "Well, if I got to find him, I got to find him. But the type of help this railroad company employs shore is scandalous." His boots ground audibly into the cinders, then struck soft sand. The first Mexican house lay a hundred yards down the track, while a short fifty feet to the left stood the gaunt ribs of the first loading pen. Steers reached for his tobacco and had grasped the package in his fingers when a shaft of hard cold warning plunged through the lethargy of his mind. His hand froze to the tobacco sack, his feet faltered. But an impulse raced like lightning to his lagging muscles, and he pressed on, keeping the same tempo. There could be no turning back to the shelter of the station house now. He was a broad, fair target, and no safety presented itself short of the loading pen, which in that same interval had drawn a thousand miles off. Sweat prickled his skin; then he was cold and nerveless. He felt his face cracking under the strain of maintaining it lazily indifferent. And the end window of the nearest Mexican shanty stared at him like the eye of death.

"Trapped, yuh lousy fool!" he cried to himself. "One move out of place and yore dead as a last year's snake skin! My God, why don't yuh *think!* Now, now — keep goin' — a little more — a little more! Don't run for it yet! Don't — run — for — it —yet!" And while

333

he kept cautioning himself and throttling the impulse to panic it seemed he was standing dead still. The apertures between the corral bars were like so many mouths jeering at him. The silence of Ysabel Junction had drawn to an awful thinness, ready to burst with a roar like the crack of doom when Dann's gun spoke. And for every yard he gained to safety there was also a yard shortened between himself and the unseen weapon.

A small voice inside his brain said distinctly, "Now!" Steve leaped aside, lunged for the corral, leaped again, and heard a gun's fury booming out of the section house. He fell to the ground, rolled against the base of the corral, sucking dust into his lungs. Bullets ripped madly through the posts, knocked off splinters, sent up sand sprays a foot beyond his head. Steve weathered through it. The shots ran out. Dann cried furious from the shanty, "Yuh wanted this, Steers! Stand up and get it!"

"No more shells in the rifle," thought Steve and jumped to his feet. Dann leaped through the door of the shanty and crossed the open area to the side of the corral before Steve could set himself for an answer. The outlaw had resorted to his revolver; he sent another bullet over the compound but it ripped the wood behind Steve.

"That's one," muttered Steve and retreated to the back line of the corrals. Dann was retreating also, ducking under the loading chutes. Steve paralleled him. Dann stopped and dropped down. Steve did likewise.

"If he's tryin' to draw me into them corrals," grunted Steve, tasting sweat, "he's got another guess comin'. But —"

He crawled on and came to a narrow alley. Dann was waiting there and opened up again. Steve rolled back. "That's numbers two and three — too close."

"Steers — I'll meet yuh out in the open, at yonder end!"

Steers said nothing. He passed his arm into the open, drew the fourth bullet, and heard Dann retreating again on the run.

"Tryin' to get far enough off to load — damn him!" He delayed only a moment longer, or until he sighted Dann through the bars. Rising, he took the alleyway on a gallop. Dann whirled back, fired, and came to a stand. Steers thought, "He's got me hipped again. He's all set and aimed. Well, what of it?" And he fell out of the alley. Dann's last bullet ripped through the fullness of Steve's coat; and then Steve stopped and faced Dann directly.

"Steers," said Dann, throwing open the cylinder of his gun, "I'm out of cartridges.

If yuh want to be a man —"

"Yeah?" was Steve's toneless answer. He lifted his weapon, aimed, and fired.

Dann trembled, fell to his knees. He tried to hold himself up by his hands. They gave way under him. He struck on a shoulder point and tipped to his side. Steve walked up, looking at the outlaw without the trace of feeling, with no more compassion or consideration, than he would have given to a fallen leaf.

"Dyin', Dann?"

"Cashin' in — by God!" breathed Dann. All the ruddiness faded before that final gray of death.

"Good. It won't be necessary to waste another shot. Die quick. I despise lookin' at yuh."

"Framed," coughed Dann. "Me. I made a mistake. Listen — I'll square it with Lou Redmain. Listen. He's goin' to burn Sundown."

"When?" said Steve. But Dann was dead, and as his muscles gave way and he settled on his stomach he seemed to shake his head.

Steve turned around. The station agent stood half in and half out of the Mexican shanty. Catching the scene he ran toward the station, calling back, "Dann held me in there — and that condemned key's been tappin' for half an hour!"

Going by the shanty, Steve saw Dann's horse also crowded inside. He led it out and left it beside his own. Automatically he reached up for his tobacco and then remembered he had flung it down beside the corner of the corral. He went back; it had been a full square sack once, but there was nothing left now but a few shreds of fabric and a ball of tobacco bearing his finger marks. He kicked it away and walked into the station. The agent's nerves were jerking him around in a sort of St. Vitus's dance. "I'm quittin'," he told Steve. "Feel bad? Of course I feel bad. You'd feel bad, too, if you lived in a joint where nothin' moved except your pulse — then all of a sudden something like this hit you in the face. I'm through! Here — this just came over the wire. You goin' to Sundown? Well, take it in. Save waitin' three hours for the stage. It's to Ed Storm at the bank. He'll want to know. Pay-day money shipment comin' to him."

Steve looked at the shaky symbols on the open sheet of paper. There were only four of them, reading as follows:

ABACUS SIN EULOGIZE HAROLD

"How do yuh know?" inquired Steve.
"Because I know. Now, what about that

337

fellow — Dann?"

"Here's somethin' I want yuh to send over the wire for me," said Steve. "I wrote it down."

"Listen — I won't stay around here with that body out there! I won't touch him!"

"There's the message," said Steve, laying it on the agent's table. "Here's two dollars. And if a thing like that upsets yuh, friend, Yellow Hill is sure no place for you."

"Ain't you got any nerves?"

"Nerves?" grunted Steve. His voice began to grow thin on him. "Yeah, but I ain't proud of 'em. They don't help atall. A man in this country with nerves ain't got no more chance than a snowball in hell."

"I almost went bughouse," said the agent, squirming in his chair. "Him a pushin' me against the wall of that shanty with his gun! Say, he was a cold cucumber! I heard you, and there I was, not able to do a single thing but listen for you to die!"

"Well," said Steve, "it's pretty simple. You die or he dies. And there ain't no great amount of time decidin' who is who. If yuh live there's nothin' to worry about. Otherwise yuh can't worry. Say, you got a drink around here, a drink of hard liquor? No? All right, I reckon I can stagger home without it. I'm leavin' Dann's pony. If the wild bunch don't come

338

along tonight the sheriff will. Send the message through."

He rolled out to his horse and turned north across the prairie, eyes half closed to the glare of the sun. Unconsciously, he began to sway in the saddle, moving his arm from side to side, screwing up his face, touching the butt of his gun. Not until his dragging spurs set the pony to curvetting did Steve realize what he was doing; he quelled himself sternly.

"Here, here. This is all over with. Why fight the battle again? He's dead. I'm alive. He missed me with twelve slugs, and I killed him with one, which I never expected to do. He could beat me to the play any day in the week, any hour in the day. If he'd stood right out to plain sight, announced himself, and walked forward on even ground, I'd be dead now. But no. He had to make a sure thing out of it. He had to foller his sneakin', treacherous nature. And so here I am, safe and sound — and a million years old."

Lassitude crept through his body, he sat in the saddle like a half-filled sack of meal. His cigarette had no taste to it, and his senses refused to reach out into the world as they were wont to do. Never in the twenty-five years of his life had he felt more weary. "Gettin' a touch of the grippe," he surmised, not knowing that in the few minutes of action by Ysabel

Junction he had used up the energy of a week's hard labor. And so sluggish were his thoughts that he had passed Mogul Canyon before they broke out of this furrow of reasoning into another.

"I never thought," he mused, "I could ever stand over a man and find pleasure in watchin' him die. Never thought I'd ever reach the point of holdin' a gun on him for a second shot in case the first wasn't enough. Starin' at him with no more feelin' than 'sif he was a snake. Glad to see him go — and tellin' him so. Man's got to be pretty far along to do a thing like that. I reckon I must be different than I figgered I was. Worse or better — the Lord knows. But I'll never ride as light and easy. Not no more." And long afterward, as he entered the first lip of the hills and felt the shadow of the pines fall on him, he added, "What difference does it make? What good have I gone an' done? Denver's no more. Redmain still rides — and here I am."

He pulled himself from these dismal reflections with effort. He was approaching Starlight, approaching a horseman who jogged out of the timbered slopes of the canyon. The horseman stopped on the road and turned, waiting. Steve considered this suspiciously but kept his gait. Presently he discovered it was Lyle Bonnet. Lyle lifted a hand and swept forward, reining abreast. Enormous relief registered on his face.

"Yuh feather-footed, sword-swallerin' brush jumper. Where yuh been? Where ain't yuh been? I been pokin' into every prairie-dog hole, bear den, and holler stump in the country. I been lookin' for yuh. Tell a man!"

"Here I am," said Steve and sat silent.

Lyle Bonnet looked at the man more closely. This was not the same Steve. No flicker of harum-scarum humor moved in the pale blue eyes, no drawling melody played through the answer. This fellow who rested woodenly in the saddle and stared back mirthlessly, mouth pinched together, was an uncomfortable stranger; and Lyle Bonnet had the queer sensation of seeing somebody who was Steve's counterpart.

"Yeah, there yuh are," grumbled Bonnet, "and I reckon it don't mean nothin' to yuh that I've just naturally trotted the hocks off six horses tryin' to locate yuh. Looks to me like yuh ain't had no sleep since the Fourth of July, 1887. Where was yuh?"

"Doin' a chore," said Steve and again let the silence fall.

"My, my," observed Bonnet. "Talkative cuss. Well, come on to the ranch."

"What for?"

"There's been some developments," was

341

Bonnet's evasive answer. "In fact, there's a sorta meetin' to discuss topics of mutual benefit and interest."

Steve considered it and nodded. "Let's go, then," was all he said.

Bonnet led him up Starlight at a rapid clip. Once he drew away from Steve and turned to discover the man lagging beside the canyon, head lifted as if scanning the far ridge. But Steve came on, and presently they arrived at the crest overlooking the D Slash yard. Right beside the trail was the fresh rectangle of earth marking Denver's false grave. Steve passed it hurriedly, cheeks like stone, and trotted up to the house porch.

"Who's at this meetin'?" he wanted to know.

Bonnet indicated the house negligently. "Go on in."

Steve pushed the door open, started to cross the sill, and stopped like a man shot through the heart. Denver stood in the center of the room, supporting himself with a cane; and Denver attacked him instantly, bluntly, severely.

"Where in the name of common sense have you been? What business have you got ridin' like a wild man through the country, challengin' all the tough eggs as if you were Wild Bill in person? Don't leer at me like that. It's a fine situation when a man can't find his friends in time of need without sending a posse out. Come in and shut the door."

Bonnet was directly behind Steve. Steve swung on his heels, pushed Bonnet aside with a curse, and walked to the far end of the porch. Bonnet went inside.

"It looks to me," he remarked, "as if you was goin' to get both ears chawed off in a minute."

Denver grinned wryly. "Well, I had to say somethin' to take the edge off this reunion, didn't I? I suppose he'll give me fits, and I suppose I've got to grin and bear it."

A weird honking sound came from the porch. "What's that?" demanded Bonnet, starting out.

Denver checked him. "No, stay here. Steve's just blowin' his nose. Sentiment seems to affect his breathin'. Where'd you find him?"

"Comin' out of the prairie, lookin' like Israel's last child, like the sole survivor of the flood, like the fella who'd forgot his name. What I mean, he was sorta that way, if yuh gather me."

"In parts and by slow stages," grunted Denver. "Stick with me and don't let him strike a cripple. Here he comes."

Steve stood in the doorway, thumbs hooked in his belt. His face was drawn together in an enormous scowl.

"So yuh come back, Mister Denver?" he stated coldly. "They didn't have no wings in heaven yore size, and hell wouldn't let yuh in. Just a big overgrown practical joker, that's what. My, my, I thought I'd die of laughin' when I heard you'd kicked the bucket. Listen, Denver, you got no title to have any friends. In so far as I'm concerned yuh might just as well climb back in the grave. Imagine a man —"

"It's his voice," opined Denver, nodding to Bonnet. "But that face ain't familiar."

"Never mind my face," snapped Steve. "Yores won't bear much daylight, Mister Denver."

"Think of that, Bonnet," grieved Dave. "Think of that kind of talk from a man I practically raised from poverty."

Steve yelled, "What in the name o' Jupiter did yuh go and do it for?"

Denver smiled — a rare and warming smile that drew the resentment out of Steve like a poultice. "I know it hurts. But somebody had to be hurt. I wanted it thoroughly advertised around this country I was dead. And I think you made a pretty good advertisement."

"So I wasn't to be trusted?" Steve grumbled.

"You had a part to play, Steve."

"Never do that again," warned the puncher.

344

"You hear? Never do that again."

"All right," agreed Denver. "I'm lucky to get off like that. But what's this foolishness I hear about you?"

"That's more of the part I was to play," retorted Steve.

"Well, don't go gunning for Dann," admonished Denver. "When we take him into camp it will be along with the rest."

"You won't never take him to camp, Dave," said Steve gently.

Bonnet and Denver looked more closely at Steve. Bonnet said, "Say, was that why yuh come up from the prairie lookin' like yu'd swallowed a lemon?"

"You met him?" challenged Denver.

"Yeah," muttered Steve. "At Ysabel Junction. He laid a trap, and I walked into it like a fool kid. He took twelve shots. I got him with one. And laughed in his face when he died."

Quiet came to the room. Denver tapped his cane on the floor, lips compressing. "You took a whale of a chance, Steve," he said finally.

"Consider that next time you play dead on me," replied Steve. Then his puckered face was swept up in a grin. He walked forward and struck Denver on the chest. "Yuh wildcat, they got to use dynamite to remove yuh from this mortal map! Well, here I am — and what's next?"

Denver smiled again. "Bonnet, here's our Stevie back home again."

"Listen," added Steve, "I got somethin' to say. Dann died thinkin' Redmain had framed him. So he squealed, and you can take it for what it may be worth. He said Redmain was plannin' to hit Sundown and burn it to the sills."

"When?" demanded Denver and Bonnet in unison.

"He died on me and didn't tell."

Denver limped around the room. "I wish I knew where Redmain was hiding. None of the boys are able to pick up a smell. We've got to find out. We've got to do it, in a hurry. Burn Sundown? If that's in his head, he'll never stop short of fillin' his promise. Not Lou Redmain. He'll destroy right and left."

Steve put a hand in his coat pocket and pulled out the station agent's telegram. For a moment he puzzled over it. "Oh, yeah," he murmured. "I've got to drag into town with this. Agent said it was somethin' for Ed Storm. Money comin' in for the pay days."

Denver stopped in his tracks. "When?"

"This is code, but the agent seemed to know. He said Saturday."

Denver drew a deep breath. "All right. If

we can't find Redmain's date of attack, we'll make one. We'll make it worth his while to come in on Saturday — after the money arrives. You go give the message to Ed. Then go get a few drinks —"

Steve lifted a protesting hand. "I never want to see liquor any more."

"— Get a few drinks and let your tongue waggle. Mention about the money in Grogan's. Mention the date. The news will get to Redmain. Never worry about that. And it'll be all the bait he needs to set off his raid."

"Then what?" insisted Steve.

"Then you go back to Nightingale's and mind your business until I send you word to come. When I do, waste no time."

"What'm I goin' to tell Ed Storm? He won't like it."

"Al Niland knows Storm. Have Al explain."

"Explain what?" Steve wanted to know. "And do yuh put the job of tellin' Al yore still alive on me? Ain't I had trouble aplenty?"

"Tell Al the whole story. But get him off in a private place to do it. Then, when he stops swearin', you tell him this: He is to go to Storm, explain that the news of the shipment has leaked. He is to ask Storm to take absolutely no step toward extra defense of the bank, nor to take any measure that would draw suspicion. Everything is to go on as before. But when Redmain comes to town that day, I will be there — with men."

Bonnet broke in. "That's drawin' things down to a fine point, Dave. Supposin' Redmain don't wait for the money to get to the bank. Supposin' he holds up the stage out in the hills?"

"If he has set his mind to destroy Sundown," said Denver, "he will do it. And it's my belief he'd wait until the money was in the bank and so be able to kill two birds with one stone."

"Burnin' Sundown sounds to me like the dream of a wild man," said Bonnet. "I don't see how he figures to have the chance of a one-armed Chinaman."

"He will ride into town with more than thirty men," Denver answered. "Who would try to stop him?"

Steve agreed. "An organized party always has got the bulge. People in town will sit tight and say nothin' — hopin' the trouble will blow over."

"That's it," said Denver. "They will be covered in a hurry. Redmain will hit the bank, drop a half dozen matches and be on his way. And when a substantial fire starts through those buildings Sundown is gone."

"I still think yore drawin' things too fine,"

objected Bonnet. "A single leak — and blooey for us."

"It will be a gamble," said Denver, eyes narrowing. "But that's the best we can do. If we don't do it I'm afraid of the consequences. Better ride, Steve. It's gettin' late. And try to look sad."

"That ain't hard," opined Steve, "considerin' I got to tell Niland yore alive."

Bonnet still doubted.

"And how you goin' to get near Sundown on Saturday without bein' seen?"

"That's the gamble," replied Denver.

"I know a bigger one," reflected Bonnet. "Which is you tryin' to fight in your present shape. Foolish."

"Forty-eight hours from now I'll be a well man," stated Denver.

"And mebbe stone dead on the forty-ninth," said Bonnet moodily. "This fella Redmain never answers to reason. That's why I think somethin's haywire in all this schemin'. It don't sound right."

Denver shrugged his shoulders. "Either Redmain's makin' a mistake or I am. We'll soon find out."

CHAPTER XVIII
THE MISTAKE

The little man of the olive skin who faded so successfully into the background of Sundown sat on a bench by the Palace and smoked his black paper cigarette puff at a time. He looked up to the large stars, thinking whatever sly and secretive thoughts his little head permitted; and he looked again to the dusty, lamp-patterned street and saw Steve Steers enter town. Very carefully the little man pinched out his smoke, crouched back, and waited. Steers went directly to the bank, tapped on the window, and was let in; five minutes later Steers came out, teetered between the restaurant and Grogan's, and succumbed to obvious temptation. The little man rose, crossed the street by a dark lane, and followed into the saloon, slouching against a wall. Steers was drinking. Beside him stood Al Niland, another citizen the little man found time to watch. The two were talking. The little man sidled forward.

"Can't I drink?" Steve was asking Niland.

"Don't baptize yourself in it again," warned Niland.

Grogan leaned over the bar in his striped silk shirt sleeves. "As a personal favor to me, Steers, go light on the liquor and I'll supply it free."

"It ain't worth the price, even gratis," observed Steve and won for himself a black regard. "Money in the bank. I wonder who gets it all?"

"What money?" asked Niland.

"I'm a regular Wells-Fargo messenger," muttered Steve mysteriously. "I brought a telegram today from the Junction to Storm. Code, accordin' to the station agent. Money comin' to the bank."

"Don't spend any of it here," warned Grogan. "That last jamboree won't bear repeatin'. I took all I ever will from you. We'll consider the slate clean. But don't try it no more. Just accept the advice of a kindly spirit. What money was you talkin' about?"

"Fatherly," grunted Steve. "You'd put a knife in me if yuh could, Grogan. I know. But don't worry. I didn't say it was my money, did I? It's the bank's, or will be when it comes Saturday."

Niland found a dozen interested listeners roundabout. He jogged Steve's elbow. "You've got no right peddlin' the contents of private telegrams, Steve. That applies double to bank affairs. Don't you know? Hush up

351

and come get a steak."

"What's the harm?" Steve wanted to know. "Bank's a public institution. Money's common currency."

"Just so," agreed Niland. "Sometimes too commonly current. Ever hear the story about the man that held up the stage? Listen, are you coming after that steak or do I bring it to you in a sling shot?"

There was some friendly wrangling between them. The little man drank his glass down to the last neat drop, paid for it, and slid out of Grogan's just as inconspicuously as he had entered. On the street he paused to relight his black paper cigarette. Impulse, or perhaps a cautious desire to check what he heard, turned him toward the bank. Passing it he squinted through the window and saw Ed Storm locking up; a little farther on he drifted against Steve's horse and tentatively rubbed the animal's chest, feeling the crust of sweat and dirt. With these gleanings he drifted down an alley, skirted the back of the Palace and ascended upon Langdell's stairway. He listened, applied his eye to the keyhole, tapped discreetly. Langdell didn't call but the little man entered anyhow, with one swift and sliding motion.

Langdell looked up from his desk. The little man murmured, "You want me, Colonel?"

"No. Get out. I'm busy."

"Thought you wanted me."

Langdell straightened, slipped off his eye-shade and motioned the little man to stand farther from the windows. "Well, if you've got something let's hear it."

"Why should I?" parried the little man and fastened a hungry glance on Langdell's bottle locker. It seemed to be a ceremony Langdell had to endure. He nodded his head and the little man indulged himself in a full glass. "But I do know somethin'," he added. "Steers is in town."

"Not worth the drink," said Langdell. "I'd found it out myself soon enough."

"Him and Niland has got their heads together at Grogan's."

"What of it?"

"Steers is publishin' the fact he carried a telegram to Ed Storm. Money bein' shipped in Saturday."

"That telegram," grunted Langdell, "is always in code. How does he know? What right's he got to talk about it if he does know? Blabbin' is a fool caper. It's the bank's business."

"I thought I'd tell."

"Well, don't keep runnin' to me with stuff I can't use."

"You don't want me to see Redmain pritty

353

soon?" persisted the little man.

"No," said Langdell. "Get out." He swung his chair back to the desk and bent his head. His pen made a flourish and stopped in the air; kicking the chair around again he stared at the little man who stood like a shadow in the corner. "What put that in your mind?" snapped Langdell.

"What?"

"Don't bluff. You know Redmain very well, don't you?"

"Not bein' allowed to talk much," said the little man, "I use my eyes and ears considerable."

"You think he'd try that?"

"He's et raw meat and likes the taste of it," averred the little man. "He might try this, if he was told to. Mebbe would anyhow, told to or not."

"You're too cursed wise," said Langdell, frowning. "You know too much."

"If you want him to, I had better go see him. If you don't want him to, I better see him also. What am I to do?"

Langdell rose and poured himself a drink; when he lifted his face a cold, sea-green light flashed against the lamp rays. "He's eaten too much raw meat to be of much use to me these days. I'll have to talk to him. Say nothing about the money. Tell him I'll be at the Fish

Creek crossing Friday. He's to be there."

"I thought you might want to see him," said the little man and slipped away. The door closed soundlessly, leaving Langdell in the center of the room, frowning at his empty glass.

As for the little man, he found his horse in a back shed and rode out of Sundown. Twice he turned, shifted direction, and curled back on his trail. He came to a bridge but avoided it and forded the creek at a dark eddy. More than an hour from Sundown he caught the flicker of camp light and approached it directly. There was no hesitation about him, no groping. One moment he stood in the dangerous outer darkness; next moment he was stepping down from the saddle beside the fire, gravely eying the men who sprang up.

"The chief?" he murmured, comforting himself with a cigarette. There was a long delay. Men murmured; a soft call went out. Boots slid around the little man; Redmain stepped into sight.

"Some of these days," said Redmain, "you're going to get shot so full of holes you won't hold baled hay. You sift in here too easy. How did you know I'd changed camp?"

"I knew," said the little man and held his peace.

"What's up?"

"This is news," said the little man. "There is money coming to the bank. And a certain person wants to see you at the Fish Creek crossin'."

"He told you to tell me about the money?" demanded Redmain, interest sharpening his face.

"No. I'm tellin' you about the money. You want to know things, don't you?"

Redmain put out his arm and hauled the little man nearer the light. He studied the passive face carefully. "You're a nosey little rat. Who told you about any money?"

"Overheard Steers tellin' it," remarked the little man. "He brought a message from the Junction to Storm at the bank. It was in the saloon. Steers was drinkin' a little."

"Pay-day money," reflected Redmain and seemed to harden with suspicion. "But what's Steers got to do with it?"

"Couldn't say. I felt his horse. Seemed likely he'd come from the Junction, though. Horse crusted some with sweat and prairie grit."

"When is this to be?"

"Money comes Friday. He wants to see you at Fish Creek crossin' Saturday."

Redmain moved his head. The little man got on his horse and merged with the night, not realizing he had twisted his dates.

Redmain stood by the fire a long while afterward, looking into the heart of the flickering coals. "I don't trust him, and I don't trust Langdell," he muttered. "I don't trust anybody. But if that is true, by the livin' Judas, I'll wring Sundown dry before I set it ablaze. Here — Hugo, Slats, Mexico — come over here. I want you to ride tonight."

The men came nearer. Redmain spoke in quick phrases. "If this is bait, I'll find out. One of you camp near Nightingale's all day tomorrow and until Friday afternoon. Keep an eye open for riders movin' away. Hugo, do that. Slats, same around the Denver outfit. Mexico, ride on the hill above Sundown and see if that joint gets heavy with any undue population."

"Leverage?" queried one of the men.

"Leverage's out," stated Redmain. "And I'll do the thinkin' for this camp. Go on, you men. If it's straight, we're due for a young fortune — and a bonfire like you never have seen before!"

"How do yuh feel?" inquired Lyle Bonnet, facing Denver in the big room of the D Slash house.

"That's the fourth time you've asked me in the last half hour," said Denver. "I look sound, don't I? Well, that's the way I feel."

"I wish yuh didn't limp thataway," muttered Bonnet, "and I wish that left arm wasn't tied in no sling. It's bound to affect yore speed."

"If you keep harpin' on disaster much longer, Lyle, I'll tie crêpe on your arm. Stop squintin' out of the window. What do you see, anyhow?"

"A blamed dark day," gloomed Bonnet. "It's goin' to rain before night. That mebbe don't mean a thing, but it's funny it should cloud up just before we move against Redmain."

"The sooner dark falls tonight the better."

"Yeah? Say, do yuh realize that this is Friday and it falls on the thirteenth? I ain't got a lick of superstition in me, but I don't see the necessity of goin' outa our way to borrow trouble."

"Get out of here before you break down and cry," said Denver. He looked at his watch. "Time to roll the ball. I guess we're organized right. There's ten men along the Copperhead on roundup. Seven out draggin' the Little Bull Canyon for strays. Four left here. Five scouting for sign of Redmain. That's twenty-six. The three boys that took their walkin' papers brings it to twenty-nine. All of 'em nicely scattered. That's the big point, Lyle. We can't go toward Sundown in a bunch. You managed to get word to the fellows on scout?"

"They're to drift toward Sundown," said Lyle Bonnet, "and meet in the timber back of Lola Monterey's house. Ahuh."

"That's right. The seven in Little Bull Canyon will wait until dusk and ride for the same place. But the bunch on the Copperhead will come to the ranch, eat supper, and walk around the yard. Then sift off one by one. We can get away with that. If anybody's watchin' us from the brush they won't be the wiser, for there'll be about five to stay behind and act as a sort of blind. We should all be behind Lola's house by eight o'clock and ready to move."

"Leavin' them five behind pulls us down to twenty-four," observed Bonnet. "And if I can't get in touch with Gallup and Limerick Lane durin' the afternoon that'll reduce us to twenty-two. Ain't enough."

"Plenty, if things go right," returned Denver.

"Supposin' things don't go right," Bonnet wanted to know.

"Did you ever hear of anything absolutely sure and certain in this crooked universe, Lyle?"

"Death an' taxes," grumbled Bonnet. "And the trickiness of Lou Redmain."

"Time for you to pull out. When you get

to the Copperhead, send one man over to Nightingale's and tell Steve to be behind Sundown by seven o'clock."

"That helps," said Bonnet. "How are yuh feelin'?"

"Get out of here!"

Bonnet departed. Denver took up a slow tramp about the room, trying to work the stiffness from his muscles; trying to suppress the wild impatience feeding into his veins.

Hank Munn, who had been dispatched by Lyle Bonnet to warn Steve, reached Nightingale's about noon and found the home part of the crew eating. Both Nightingale and Steve were at the table and Munn drew up a chair willingly. Not until he had quieted his appetite and risen from the table did he speak of business, and then it was in a very casual way.

"We got nine o' yore strays held out for yuh, Steve."

"I'll send a couple hands right over," said Steve and idly walked with Munn to the latter's horse. Munn swung up, observed that they were beyond earshot, and murmured, "Denver says to be in the little clearin' above Lola Monterey's house around seven o'clock tonight. That's all." And he rode away.

Steve built himself a cigarette and walked for the porch. En route, he called two of his men over and told them to lope after the strays. Then he settled himself on the porch steps and waited until Nightingale came from the table.

"I think," mused Steve, "I had ought to hit Sundown this aft'noon."

"You're the boss," agreed Nightingale.

"I mebbe won't be back till late."

Nightingale stuffed his pipe, azure glance flickering along the back of the foreman's neck. "The world will meanwhile toss along its accustomed orbit," he observed.

"In fact, I dunno just when I will be back."

Nightingale's match waved gently across the pipe bowl. There was a prolonged silence. "One would infer," the Englishman presently reflected, "that the nature of your business is vague to the border of doubt."

"Ahuh," said Steve. "Just so, only more so."

"One is led to wonder," proceeded the Englishman with the same indifferent calm, "whether or not there might be some mystical connection between the D Slash gentleman's arrival and your departure."

"Was it that plain?" grunted Steve, turning to his boss. Alarm showed on his face.

"Not so," said the Englishman. "I was merely applying the ineluctable law of physics. Action and reaction. The little pebble dropped into the pool produces ripples that run their concentric course."

"No doubt yore right," agreed Steve. "Anyhow, it sounds like it ought to be somethin' swell."

"Old fellow," said the Englishman, "don't be so dashed shy. Y'know, you are not as hard to read as a Babylonian tablet. Two and two do not always make four, but it is a safe thing to count it so. I should not wish to pry into your affairs, but I will remind you I liked Denver. And I've had no huntin', no fishin' durin' the age of an extr'ord'n'ly mature coon."

Steve faced the Englishman. "All right. I'll say it. Denver ain't dead."

"My sacred aunt," said Nightingale, hauling the pipe from his mouth. The ruddy angular face did not bend to every passing emotion, and it scarcely showed astonishment now; but there was a brightening of the blue eyes.

"I said worse than that when I found out," said Steve. "Well, he ain't dead. He's only played 'possum to throw Redmain off. And he's got a plan to get Lou. It ain't for me to say how or when. Only, I'm ridin' to Sundown, and yuh'll see me when yuh see me."

The Englishman carefully knocked out his ashes, rose to his full length, and turned into the house. *"Ad interim,"* he called back, "remain as you were."

Steve gloomed into the distance. "Some of these days I'm goin' to get a toe holt on one o' them outlandish words and pin it to the mat. Meanwhile I just look intelligent and hope he ain't swearin' at me. It goes to show how ignorant folks can be. Here I been all these years thinkin' Englishmen talked the same language as us."

Nightingale returned, hat on, and gun strapped to his hip. "All we need to complete this tale of border warfare is a set of heathenish bagpipes. You may like it or not, my estimable superintendent, but whither thou goest I shall follow. Lead on."

Steve got up. "Mr. Nightingale, this ain't goin' to be no joke. God only knows —"

"The disposition of Providence," said the Englishman gravely, "is not to be questioned. One prays and follows the light of conscience."

Steve got in the saddle. Nightingale swung beside him, and together they cantered northwest. Steve found his first admiration of the man strongly kindled. He never pretended to understand the Bucket owner's moods. Humor and gravity were too closely blended; the man's thoughts were too contained, never breaking out into the broad wild fancies of the range. Sometimes Steve was certain Nightingale caught very little of what went on; and at other times, such as the present one, he

363

had the uncomfortable feeling the cattleman's aloof indifference covered a sharp and penetrating mind. But, nevertheless, Steve usually felt at ease with Nightingale, for something about the Englishman kept reminding him of Denver.

They ran down the trail without a word between them, crossed the open flats of the upper Bucket range, and went over the Helen Creek ford. Beyond a ridge they pursued a broad wagon leading by Lunt's home quarters. Steve intended to turn aside, but abreast the house he heard his name called in that crisp, assured manner so familiar. Instantly he checked in. Nightingale overran him and looked questioningly back. Steve grinned and muttered, "Be with yuh in a minute," and cantered to the ranch gate.

Debbie Lunt came down the path, her pretty, sharply defined face studying him.

"Were you going by without stopping in?"

"Sort of busy today, Debbie."

"I haven't seen you since the afternoon in Sundown."

"Been all over the map meanwhile."

"Apparently so," said Debbie. "I sent Bill over yesterday, but you weren't around."

"Whistled for Rover but he wouldn't come, uh?"

"That's not funny, Steve," said Debbie with

increasing force. "I don't like that kind of humor, if you meant it as humor. If it was sarcasm, you ought to be ashamed. I wanted to see you yesterday. I have heard something. Can't you come to the house a minute?"

Steve shifted in the saddle, looked at Nightingale waiting in the distance, and shook his head. "Debbie, I can't do it now."

Debbie moved her shoulders impatiently. "I suppose I shouldn't insist. But you will have to listen to me. Steve, I have heard a horrible story, and I don't believe it. Dad was in Sundown yesterday and somebody told him a ghastly lie. That you had shot Dann."

Steve waited. Debbie kept her eyes on him and finally said, "Well?"

"No lie. I shot him."

"Steve!"

She drew back, put a hand to her face; and suddenly the color on her cheeks faded. She stared at him as if he were a stranger. A quick breath came out of her. "I don't believe it."

"I told you, Debbie."

"Oh, Steve! Why — why?"

"Because I said I would," answered Steve.

The girl clenched her palms together — a sign he knew of old, a sign he dreaded. Debbie's anger cut deep.

"Because of Dave Denver?"

"That's right."

"So you dirtied your hands, made a killer out of yourself — because of him! What right does a dead man have to make you do a thing like that? I know he was your friend! What of it? I never liked him, and I don't now! The man despised me! And he could wrap you around his finger any time he chose! A friend! How far do you go for your friends?"

Steve sat like a rock, taking the punishment without a change of expression. "As far as a friend would go for me. As far as Dave would have gone — which was all the way to hell if I'd asked him."

"You thought more of Denver than you thought of me!" cried Debbie. "You do now!"

"If you'd think straight," replied Steve, "you wouldn't say that. It's the same as sayin' a beefsteak tastes better than a rose smells. The things ain't the same."

She flung back her head. "We must fight this out, Steve! We must settle it! I'll be expecting you for supper tonight."

Steve sighed. "Debbie, it seems like yore askin' me to do things today I can't. I'll be in Sundown tonight."

Debbie looked away, stormy eyed. She bit her lips, moved restlessly. "I suppose I must wait, then. If it is ranch business it comes before me. At least I'm glad to know you've got business to keep you from running idle through the hills."

Steve said nothing, and Debbie challenged him swiftly. "It is ranch business, isn't it?"

He seemed to debate his answer. "I ain't in the habit of lyin'. No, it's not."

There was only one alternative in so far as Debbie was concerned. "Does it have anything to do with Denver — or Redmain?"

"Right now," said Steve, "I can't answer you, Debbie. Next time I come back I will."

"Then it does!" exclaimed Debbie. "You are going down there to mix up in Denver's quarrels again! Steve, I refuse to let you! The man's dead! Lou Redmain's done nothing to you! You've no business keeping up the fight. I refuse to let you, do you hear?"

Very slowly Steve answered: "I reckon you don't own the right to tell me whether I can go or stay, Debbie."

"Oh, don't I?" Debbie drew herself together. "Listen to me, Steve! If you don't come back here for supper you need never come back at all!"

A slow, brick-red mantle crawled up Steve's neck. "Mean that, Debbie?"

"You know I mean it! You be here!"

Steve startled her into stiff silence by the changed pitch of his talk. "You fool girl, I wish the Lord had given yuh enough sense to get in outa the rain. I've been pushed around, led around, shoved around by you and yore family until it's a wonder I still wear pants. Who ever told you a man could be cussed into shape? It's about time you learned your limits. I'm no Santy Claus, and I'm no Lord Fauntleroy. There's lots of things about me dead wrong, and I've got sense enough to know it. As regards them, you can have your say any day in the week. But when it's a question of how I conduct myself with men, how far I'm to ride, when I'm to draw out, what I'm to say, neither you nor any other woman that breathes has got the right of tellin' me a thing. I do my work, I'll take care of my own conscience without help. And I don't propose to be humbled in my own estimation or go around with Jim Coldfoot's whipped-dog air. You seem to want a dummy for a husband. Ain't you satisfied to be a woman without tryin' to be a man likewise? Who taught you how to treat a man, anyhow? Yuh been actin' like a nine-year-old girl who was afraid somebody was goin' to steal her dolly. Grow up and get some average common sense. You've sorta indicated durin' the last six months that 'most everything about me was haywire. All right, I admit it. I've had to do a man's work ever since I was ten years old, and Yellow Hill is no place to get the education of a scholar and a gentleman. As for Dave Denver, he's a better man than me any time, any place. And I owe him too blamed much to let the Lunt family interfere, which includes yore maw and paw, yore brothers and sisters, yore aunts and uncles and cousins, and all the rest of the tribe which has offered free advice on my conduct. If I'm the total loss yuh seem to think, I'll relieve you of the burden here and now. Don't expect me tonight or any other night. Ma'm, I'll bid you good-day."

He tipped his hat, turned, and spurred off. Nightingale joined him, and they galloped across the meadow. As the trees reached out to close them in Steve looked around; Debbie still stood by the gate, crying. Steve groaned, said, "Aw, hell!" and shot past the astonished Englishman.

They reached town near the middle of the afternoon, racking their horses in front of the hotel. Nightingale cocked his blue eyes on Steve for further information.

"I tell you," decided Steve. "You better bed down somewhere so not to draw too much attention. Nothin's booked to happen till after seven."

"Well enough," said the Englishman. "I shall get whatever newspapers are available and settle right yonder in the porch rocking chair for some leisurely reading. Give me the appropriate gesture when you are ready."

"Read?" grunted Steve, whose increasing nervous tension would not let him be still. "Imagine that!"

"Well, yes," murmured Nightingale, sauntering away. "People have been known to do it."

Steve rolled to the nearest building wall and leaned against it. Under the pretext of building a smoke he ran his glance from one end of the street to the other. Sundown seemed unduly empty until he caught partial sight of a crowd inside the courthouse. Promptly he strolled across and went in, his entry marked by a sharp gavel tap. The judge was speaking.

". . . Thus with all the evidence before me, I am bound to render decision. Litigants will remember that while the broad and noble structure of the law incorporates and irradiates the sum of human wisdom and human error of the toiling centuries, it is not meet to say that it represents always infallible justice. The law is both an embodiment of common sense and arbitrary rule, without which confusion would reign sans end. The law is an increasingly crystallized thing, a thing of tangible substance, form, and shape. The forms of the law are, as it were, the ribs which hold in the essence of the social body, and if, perchance, some of that essence should trickle through those ribs and fall wasted to the receptive earth, we can only say that nothing conceived by mortal man is perfect, and nothing conceived by mortal man will ever cover the infinite vagaries of social experience and the multitudinous variations of human conduct. With that in mind this court made the attempt to bring plaintiff and defendant into harmony before trial. Failing, this action ensued, dragging its weary lucubrations over the diurnal face of the calendar."

The court paused and scratched its judicial nose. Up from the packed and stricken silence wavered a faint cry. "True, brother, true." Sheriff Ortez leaned against Steve and whispered, "All this fer a six-dollar pony on the aidge of nervous breakdown. Nobuddy can say the judge ain't give 'em their money's worth."

"*In re* Wilgus *versus* Tuggs," stated the court, "concerning the identity and ownership of one male horse of problematical age, unknown antecedents, and endless branding, we find for the plaintiff. So entered."

Wilgus rose grinning from his seat and yelled. "I said it was my hoss all the time and I could of told you in the beginning! What's mine's mine, and I'll have it! Let that be a lesson to you, Tuggs!"

The gavel slammed down. "Five dollars for

contempt of this court," said the judge.

Wilgus subsided, muttering. Fear Langdell rose. "Your honor, may I thank you for the just verdict? To my client this represents a sweeping corroboration of a principle. And now I should like to present the bill of costs, to be entered against the defendant for payment."

"You bet," mumbled Wilgus. "He lost. Let him pay."

"The clerk will read the bill of costs," said the court.

The clerk accepted the statement from Langdell, shifted his tobacco and read without emotion.

" '. . . Do swear the following items have been personally and beforehand paid by plaintiff, as follows:

'To stable rent at Grover's
  two weeks . . . .$ 15.00
To extra feed 37.75
To 45 bales hay, extra bed-
  ding on acc't feeble condition
  of animal in question 22.50
To carpenter work, knocking
  out stall for extra space, also
  on acc't feeble condition 12.50
To material, same 8.30
To damage to Grover's stable,

knocking out stall	11.00
To lost rent on stall so knocked out	15.00
To special stable hand to care for horse in lieu of sheriff . .	12.50
To veterinarian's calls, 14 @ $5 per each	70.00
To medicine, same	16.20
To veterinarian's night calls, 4 @ $10	40.00
To ten witnesses, 1 day @ $3 . .	3.00
To four witnesses, 2 days @ $3	24.00
To state veterinarian, subpœnaed to testify as to brands of horse; witness fee, 1 day @ $3	3.00
To state veterinarian, travel exp.	36.37
To same, board and lodging same	41.40
To incidentals	19.60
To same	1.00
Total	$416.12' "

The court looked at Al Niland, found no objections, and said, "So entered."

Wilgus could be heard again, murmuring his shocked surprise to Langdell. "Great guns,

Fear, you sure did lay it out. I told yuh to go ahead, but I never did think it would come that high. Supposin' I'd lost and had to pay?"

All through the courtroom was a mutter of discontent. The gallery gods found this an unhappy ending to the thus far splendid entertainment. Tuggs sat miserably downcast. But Al Niland rose, smiling in that tight and gleaming manner Sundown knew presaged trouble. The silence became absolute again. Niland cleared his throat and made a generous gesture toward Wilgus. "I congratulate you in having won a victory of principle. To such a man of principle as all Yellow Hill knows you to be, the verdict must be especially pleasing. There seems at this juncture nothing for the defendant to do but pay the bill and bear up. In so far as Tuggs is able to do these things he will. Fortunately we spent very little on the case, having little to spend. I think our costs will run about twelve dollars. A kind friend of Tuggs's was generous enough to pay this. As to the bill just rendered by the plaintiff, we will willingly pay all that we are able, and to that end Tuggs has itemized for me a list of all his earthly possessions. They include, two blankets, three quilts, some dishes, the suits of clothes he wears, a mouth organ, and one valise. Estimated value, five dollars at forced sale, excluding the suit of clothes, which by law he is entitled to keep. Therefore, your honor, we will pay over the five dollars readily, leaving Mr. Wilgus out of pocket only $411.12."

The ensuing roar almost lifted the ceiling of the room. The judge stood up and banged his gavel viciously; and above all this turmoil and fury rose the agonized screech of Fleabite Wilgus. "I'll see about that! It ain't so! I won't stand a penny of it! I'll slap an attachment, a lien on every gol-blasted thing he's got! There's stock — there's implements — !"

"Silence in this court!" bellowed the judge.

"You can't skin me!" cried Wilgus, and shook his fist at the judge. "You neither, you mealy-mouthed son-of-a-gun!"

"Twenty-five dollars for contempt!" said his honor.

Niland still stood and still smiled. His answering words quieted the room. "For a man of principle, Mr. Wilgus, you should not object to the price. If you can find anything to attach other than the aforementioned articles, go to it. Tuggs rents the place he lives on. He rents the implements, the harness, the very wood he lights his fire with. He had five head of milk stock, which by strange coincidence he sold twenty-four hours before the papers in this suit were filed. He has one horse, loaned to him by the late David Denver. Other than that he has nothing. The horse you might have bought for twenty dollars now costs you better than four hundred. It's the principle of the thing, Mr. Wilgus."

Wilgus shook his fist at his attorney. "Yore a fine lawyer! Why didn't you tell me he didn't have nothin'? What made you run up them bills so high, anyhow?"

Through all this Langdell had remained aloof and very faintly amused. He stopped Wilgus curtly. "I said you might be better off buying the horse, Wilgus. I said you would gain nothing otherwise. Please be kind enough to stop moving your fist in my face!"

"You paid them bills out of your own pocket!" shouted Wilgus. "Just try and get any money outa me! You'll see!"

"The money," said Langdell, so quietly that only the front rows heard it, "has already been deducted from the sum I owe you on livestock purchases. Including my attorney's fee of $150. Stop scolding your own lawyer, you fool."

Wilgus extricated himself from the fore part of the courtroom and started out. At that same moment Grover, the livery stable man, came in.

"Y'honor," he called, "whose horse have I got, anyhow?"

"Turn it over to Wilgus," directed the court.

"Fine enough," grunted Grover. "Git yuh a team, Wilgus, and drag him outa my place. He died on me, twenty minutes ago."

The courtroom became a weird scene of thirty or more men collapsing on the benches; and the howling laughter started a runaway down Main Street.

Steve shouldered to the street, for the moment at ease in mind. Langdell emerged with graven irony; then Wilgus came leaping after, stopped Langdell, and cursed him. "Listen, you! I'll have yuh disbarred for this! Don't think I won't!"

"I have wound up my affairs with you, Wilgus," said Langdell, cold as ice. "I wish to have no more to do with you. You disregarded my first advice. I took your case in doubt. Now that it is over I am free to say I'm not sorry at the result. I despise your hypocritical manner, you dirty codger. Take this warning from me: If ever you address me again in the same terms you have just used, I shall challenge you on the street. Get out of here!"

Wilgus glared at him and shambled swiftly off. The last Sundown saw of the man was a pair of coat tails streaming down Prairie Street on top of a fast traveling horse. Langdell drew out a handkerchief, wiped a fleck of dust from his sleeve, and turned in the direction of his office, throwing a noncommittal glance at Steve. Directly afterward Niland strolled through the courthouse door. And then the ominous weight of oncoming events dropped down on Steve's shoulders with an actual physical hurt. Niland's eyes warned him. Together they walked as far as the hotel.

"Anything more?" murmured Niland.

"He's collectin' the boys. Seven o'clock up behind Lola Monterey's."

"What am I to do?"

"No instructions. Wait till then and duck up there."

"Careful — careful," said Niland. "There's Redmain men in this town. Not his riders, but sympathizers. What's Dave aim to do?"

"Have to ask him. I wish I had a drink."

"Not now," said Niland quickly. "By the Lord, this thing either goes off right, or it'll be the worst mess ever come to pass. Frankly, I'm nervous. How does he figure to hold twenty or more men just outside of Sundown all of tonight and most of tomorrow without being seen? That's just the kind of a situation Redmain loves."

"I know. What time is it?"

Niland looked at his watch. "Four-thirty."

Steve let out an enormous breath. "Great guns —"

Both of them drew up by the hotel. A rider came in slowly.

"Limerick Lane," muttered Steve. "And he either knows somethin' we ought to know, or we know somethin' he ought."

"I'm going back to the office. Shouldn't be herdin' up like this. See you later."

Niland turned away. Limerick edged his horse toward the sidewalk and looked down at Steve.

"Got a match?"

Steve supplied it. Limerick lighted his cigarette and tossed the match away with an easy glance all around the street. "What you know these days, Steve?"

"That ain't the question," grunted Steve. "I know what you know, up to noon today. What comes next?"

Limerick grinned cheerfully for the benefit of the world, but his quiet words expressed trouble. "That's it. I thought you was in this. I ain't got in touch with Bonnet for two days. I found somethin' a few hours back, and I'm afraid to take the risk of ridin' over to the ranch and bein' traced. I ain't supposed to belong to D Slash any more. Those hard nuts have got the country speckled with eyes. What'm I goin' to do?"

The street darkened unaccountably; Limerick's body grew gray. Steve looked up to a

379

sky filling with black; a far-off clap of thunder sent its running warning across the heavens.

"What's your information?" inquired Steve, more and more uneasy.

"Just about two hours ago I cut across an old worn-out trail north of here. A whole slew of tracks on it, warm enough to cook eggs. I think it was Redmain, borin' for the south at a fast clip. Understand? South is D Slash, Nightingale's, Steele's, Leverage's. Hell, south might be anything."

"Listen," said Steve earnestly, "you ease out of here slow and put the prod after you get into the trees. Dave ought to know that. He's figgered Redmain different."

"I was told not to go back there," mused Limerick. "I was told to stick here and pass word to any D Slash man I saw."

"Never mind — you go. And don't let any dust settle on yuh, Limerick. Denver will be on his way here in another hour!"

Limerick considered it, forgetting to smile. "I suppose," he muttered. "Well, I'll have to get a drink and make a stab at lookin' lazy for a few minutes."

"If you can manage anythin' resemblin' a look o' laziness," said Steve, "yore a better man than me. I got a case o' swamp fever right now."

Limerick nodded and rode off. Steve felt

a heavy drop of rain strike his hat. Nightingale was on the porch, buried in the folds of a paper. Steve drew himself together and headed for the restaurant. "If Redmain's caught wind of anything and intends to catch Dave on the flank again —" He cursed under his breath. "I don't dare move for fear of upsettin' the apple cart. It's Dave's game, and I got to stick tight!"

CHAPTER XIX
THE MEDICINE DRUM SPEAKS

That first small clap of thunder heard in Sundown reached also to D Slash. Standing behind a window, Denver saw the vortex of the storm swing in from the prairie. The vanguard of rain pattered on the porch roof, and then day had prematurely gone. At five o'clock the lamps were lighted. At half-past, when Doc Williamson came, the world was quite dark, and a wet, tempestuous night had set in. Williamson shook off his slicker and stood a moment by the open fire, regarding Denver.

"We also serve," he said with calm humor, "who only ride around and get soaked. You look like you're up to something."

Denver nodded. "This left arm of mine's no good, is it?"

"Not for a month, Dave."

"Then I want you to bandage it tight to my chest. Tight enough so I can't move it. I don't want it in my road."

Williamson opened his bag. "All right, Dave. This is a very funny world — and that's the full sum of knowledge I have gained in sixty some years. Seems little enough. Must be some order about this universe, but it's hard to find. Maybe Yellow Hill's outside the scheme of things. Sit down."

Neither Denver nor Williamson said anything during the bandaging and prying about. Later, as the doctor was putting on his slicker, the crew returned from the Copperhead. Bonnet entered, water cascading from him. "So far, so good," he commented. "But no signs. And no more to be had now."

"Get your supper," said Denver. Bonnet went out, leaving Williamson standing thoughtfully in the center of the room. Something in the mind of this weathered shepherd moved toward expression but never came out. Denver broke the silence.

"You'll be going to Leverage's next?"

"Just so."

Denver reached into his pocket and handed Williamson a letter. "Will you give this to Eve? Something I want her to know."

Williamson accepted it incuriously.

"I believe I'll not hand it to her until I am ready to leave the Leverage home. I have no wish to see her face when she reads it, Dave."

"I know," said Denver. "That's one of the things on my conscience. I reckon I've got a lot of things to answer for. And may soon stand in need of answerin'."

"Bad as that?"

Denver pointed toward the outside. A far-off flash of lightning threw a faint glow through the window; the long, rolling blast of thunder rocketed across the pit of night. "Hear that, Doc? Medicine drums talking." Standing across from Williamson, he seemed to swell with the dark fires of his inner nature; seemed to grow taller, more somber. The cheek bones of his rugged face stood out; his tousled head gleamed in a black radiance. Light flashed from his eyes as he turned his head, and then they were pools of shadow in the deep recesses. "Nothing of very much importance has ever happened in this country that I haven't felt coming. This troubled land seems to use me as a sounding board. It's been like that too many times. I've heard it one way or another — like that thunder out there, or the sound of the Copperhead on the rise, or in the absolute silence of a summer night. Invisible telegraph. Medicine drums. Whatever you please to call it. But the warning is there — as it is now. I've lived too close to the country, and I've fought it too long to ever make a mistake about its temper. I'm about half a savage, I guess."

"Personal warning?" asked Williamson quietly.

"No-no, I can't draw it that fine. But a man

can sometimes feel the bulk of something ahead of him, the premonition of events about to happen. I will say this to you, Doc. Redmain and I have been pointing at each other over a pretty long time, and I would be willing to swear in absolute sincerity that one of us will die at the hands of the other. I'm not upset over it. There's the fact, neither more nor less. I'm not even overly curious about the result. It's just one of those things a man's got to face and take in his stride. What comes will come. I've had about as many lucky breaks of fortune as anybody could expect; there's always a time when the break goes the other way. It's always been my belief that the country would some day get me. Whether Redmain's the instrument to do it or not, I don't know. But wherever he is, the man's dangerous."

"Agreed on that point," said Williamson. He sighed and looked wistfully at the fire. "Some of these days I think I'll retire, sit a week in front of a blaze like that and give in."

"Don't do it for a few days yet," drawled Denver. "You've got customers comin' up."

"New ones, I hope, if there must be any at all. I get tired of going over my old patches. That applies to you. Be careful."

He went out and was lost in the driving

elements. Denver walked to the gun case, slipped the black-holstered gun from its peg. The last time he had reached for it, he remembered, he had been like a furnace, ablaze with the desire to kill. Tonight no similar whirlwind of emotion moved him. Rather he was gripped by a sense of being inevitably pushed on toward a long-prepared-for crisis of his life — a crisis made not by man but by a force beyond man's control. It was as if the finger of destiny in writing out the chart of his life had reached a point and the voice behind that finger had said, "Here David Denver reaches a turn. We will wait and see, nor write more till then." Wedging one end of the belt between his hip and the wall, he buckled it and shook the gun to its rightful position. Bonnet came back.

"I started the boys off already, one by one. They're about half gone. Not a chance of anybody seein' down here tonight."

"Good enough," said Denver. "But we'll keep to the original idea of spreadin' them out. And five will stay behind."

"Arranged for. Yore horse is under the shed."

"All right. You'd better drift."

Bonnet nodded impassively and left. Denver went to the fireplace, kicked back a log, and entered his bedroom. He rather awkwardly pulled on his slicker and turned out the lamp. A side door led him to the porch, beyond the flare of kitchen lights. So he stood for several minutes, catching here and there the dim figure of one or another man shifting away from the yard. Presently he crossed through the rain to his waiting horse, climbed to the saddle and fared into the night.

All along the road he was wrapped in the same untouched calm; all along it his thoughts revolved about the certainties of his life. Here a regret and there a glow of deep pride; past and present running queerly together. A song of Lola's in the old days, still carrying to his inner ear the vibration of her feeling. The still fresh memory of a time far back when he had walked blindly down the dusk-ridden road feeling the grip of his father's hand, hearing his father say, "She's gone now, Son, and we'll just have to get along somehow." Eve's level eyes shining at him in lazy humor or in soberness, but always straight and clear. And through all these images, like a recurring thread breaking across a pattern, moved the figure of Redmain: of Redmain forever facing him with a flare of hatred, with passion and lust to kill on the triangular face. Thus Denver rode north while wind and rain whipped through the forest and the shuttering lightning flashes revealed a tormented world. And so he caught the lights of Sundown all blurred and glimmering from the southern ridge. Working around, he aimed at the bright window of Lola's cabin, passed back of it, and came within the silent circle of his own men. Bonnet's voice checked off names sibilantly; occasionally a groping rider challenged softly. Otherwise nobody spoke. Time dragged; Denver's eyes held to Lola's windows, and when her shadow passed across them he struggled with memories he had long before willed to be buried.

Somebody said, "Steve — and Niland. Dave come yet?"

"Here," muttered Denver.

They were afoot, and they steadied themselves beside his horse. He dismounted. "Listen," said Steve, "did Limerick Lane get to you?"

"No. Why?"

"Good God!" muttered Steve. "About four he came to town. He had located Redmain's tracks — fresh and headed south."

Denver said nothing. Steve prompted him. "Don't that mean nothin' to yuh, Dave? It means —"

"It might mean anything, Steve," murmured Denver. "It might mean he's caught wind, as he did before. It might mean he's off to burn the lower end of the country. It might mean I've got no more ranch now than a jackrabbit. Or it might mean he's in Sundown at present, waitin' for me. No man knows what Lou Redmain holds in his head."

"Well, what do you figure on?" interjected Niland.

Once again the silence fell. But when Denver broke it Niland recalled what Cal Steele had said on a certain day in Grogan's. "While you and I doubt ourselves, Dave never falters. He drives ahead, and nothing will stop him." Standing there in the miserable night, filled with foreboding and half fear, Al Niland felt the supporting, comforting power of Denver's presence and words.

"Do what I have planned to do," Denver was saying. "It seemed a good idea yesterday, and it seems good now. I can't play up to Lou Redmain's feints, I can't expect to read his mind. It moves too fast for me. We'll go ahead per schedule."

Bonnet called the roll again and announced the result. "We're all here, Dave."

"Crowd around," said Denver, and waited a brief moment. "Now, this is it. We are going to drift into Sundown on foot, few at a time and without being seen. We are going to crawl into a dozen hidin' places I have in mind, stay there all of tonight and all of tomorrow — until Redmain shows up. Not a sound, not a move until then. When Redmain and his party enters Sundown and are completely between the two rows of buildings, Niland will walk to the courthouse firebell and ring it. At that stage we move in and go to work. I depend on this being carried out. Not a stray move in those hiding places. There must be no giveaway. And, Al, you'll have to stay close to your office during this time in order to reach that bell. Is it understood?"

A murmur of assent ran round the circle. Denver went on, pairing off men, naming the places he wanted them. "Munn and Jackson, you will go to the back of the empty bakeshop, climb to the second-story front room. Nick and Bonnet, Phil Blaney and Phil Jewel, you four hit the hay loft of the stable. Be careful about that. Grover's night man is half deaf, but his sight's good." He ran through the list, ending with a lone and youthful puncher by the name of Kalispell. "Sorry, Kalispell, but you've got the worst job in the lot. You're to bunch up the horses and take them all the way back to the ranch."

Kalispell made no comment, and the darkness hid his feelings. Denver said, "Munn and Jackson go first. Keep out of the light, keep off the trail. We'll start the next pair in a couple minutes."

Boots sloshed through the mud, and for one

brief moment the forms of the departing punchers stood against Lola Monterey's house light. Niland spoke to Denver hardly above a whisper. "I found something about Lang—"

Denver drew him away. "Considering what other name is mixed up with him, be careful."

"You'll never prove this in any court," said Niland, "but there were three men in the deal. You and I know the one we've been worryin' about. Sorry, but it seems to be so. Langdell's the second. As for Redmain, I have no written evidence of his being the third, but what difference does that make? It works out."

Denver said, "Wait a minute," and walked back to the huddled punchers. "Four for the barn, go ahead," said he, then returned to Niland. "All right. But how did you make this?"

"A slip of paper in the desk of — the man we liked. It had figures, representing cattle money. These figures are usually divided by three. I went to Storm. I asked him as his friend to answer certain questions. Never mind what he did or didn't answer, or how I got my information, but Langdell's account — in the bank at the state capital — shows where one of these thirds went."

"Al, you are certain enough of that to hang him on it?"

Niland's reply was short. "Yes, or I'd say nothing now."

Denver took Niland by the shoulder. "If we get through this, Al, we'll take care of him. Damn his heart, he'll get off easy because we can't do anything to drag in the name of a better man than he'll ever be. Come on. We're too slow."

He closed up to the punchers again. "All right. About six of you this time."

"I'll pull out too," said Niland.

"Go ahead. You know what you're to do."

The wind brought up from the town muted fragments of piano music out of the Palace. Denver listened for it, with nothing better to do and no other means of keeping from his mind the descending chilling feeling of disaster. Lola crossed the window again, and from her chimney shot a shower of sparks that streamed instantly askew and were snuffed out. The smell of wood smoke came on; a crashing reverberation shook the sky. Steve's voice was faint and seemingly distant. "The Lord's horses shore are runnin' away —"

Out of Sundown rose the report of a sudden firing.

It struck Denver like the blow of a sledge, and he stood rooted in his boots, saying, "It's Redmain, and he's caught me again. My men are scattered all over hell." Then he was racing down the slope, rage searing him at the thought of once more being tricked — that

392

battering rage of a solid fighter maddened beyond belief by the jabs and slashes and swift parrying of an always elusive antagonist. He cursed his way through the trees, never realizing what black epithets he hurled ahead of him. Steve ran beside him and yelled, "Go slow, Dave, go slow!" The remnant of his men came after, slipping in the soft mud of the trail, breathing hard at his heels. He passed Lola's house as the door sprang open. She was in the doorway, a swaying silhouette calling into the uncertain darkness. On down the grade he ran, veering to catch the end of the street, Steve repeating again and again, "Dave, damn yore soul, go slow!" Firing beat more heavily out of the town, seeming strongest by Grogan's. Considering this he swung again and came up to the back of the Palace. Without a word he sprang down the alley, knocked some fugitive townsman flat to the earth, and reached the street.

He checked himself, his men spreading to either side. Steve muttered, "Good God, the town's lousy with 'em! Watch out, they're in the Palace, too!"

The outlaw bunch had split into sections. They were by the hotel, by Grogan's, in the shadow of the courthouse; they flashed across the lanes of light and into blackness again, they made swift forays, turned and charged back;

and the crackling detonation of the guns drowned all else. Muzzle lights flickered weirdly. A woman in the Palace screamed. The report of two shots shuddered through the door of the place; a man rode out of it, straight against Denver. Denver lifted his weapon and emptied the saddle, while starting toward Grogan's.

"Knock down that fellow on Prairie!" he shouted. "And come on!"

The courthouse bell clanged violently. From the east end of town Redmain's men swept along in close-packed ranks. Denver and his followers were in the dead center of the street, facing the charge; there they stood, pouring fire into the massed target. Horses went down; riders careened, jammed up, and cursed clear. Steve's voice lifted wildly, ran through Sundown like a tocsin of battle, and from the yawning mouth of Grover's stable came Lyle Bonnet's reply. The plunging Redmain riders swept forward. Denver leaped aside, taking deliberate aim. Glass shattered on the porch roof of the bakeshop, and the crash of a timed volley sailed over his head, beating at the whirling horsemen; a rider fell to the ground and knocked Denver flat. Denver rose and pointed his gun to the mud. But the man was dead.

The renegades veered into the protection

of Prairie Street and turned. Back they swept, raking the walks. At the same time the courthouse corridors flung out the hollow booming of some solitary duel; then Redmain's men were dismounted by the hotel and there making a stand. Denver considered the situation briefly. Behind him was clear ground. Prairie Street was empty and the Palace quiet. Two doors to his right front lay Grogan's saloon, as still as a grave. Across, on his other flank, the courthouse duel had dropped to significant silence. So then Redmain had elected to draw back to the west end of town and fight from a stationary position. And behind that screen of guns was Ed Storm's bank with the door wide open.

A lull fell, both parties were recoiling for breath; shots rang between the buildings sporadically. Munn and Jackson jumped from the bakeshop second story and landed in the mud.

"Get down," muttered Denver. His own men were lined in the black angles of either street side. Bonnet's party, in the stable, kept up a sultry, persistent fusillade. On the far side of the renegades some isolated D Slash man was potting away. Rain sluiced down in great ropes; a pale blue flare of lightning fitfully illuminated the town, and he saw Redmain's henchmen crouched by the hotel. In the succeeding deep dark the play of shots rose higher. Denver came to a decision.

"Come on, D Slash!"

Bonnet's party caught the idea instantly and opened a stiff covering fire on the porch. Denver ran along the walk; D Slash fighters sprang out of their shelters and ran with him. Steve's answering yell emerged from the courthouse opposite. The gunplay from the stable stopped suddenly, and Denver heard the converging tramp of their boots as he plunged over the loose boards. A solid row of muzzle lights flickered from the porch; the blast of the volley cracked his drums. All around him was the racking reply of his men. Steve shouted, and the challenge caught hold and carried D Slash onward against the porch.

"Back side!" cried Denver. "They've left the hotel! Don't go down that alley! Go around!"

He raced forward, then whirled and cut out of the crowd. A figure had crossed the yellow lane of the bank light. Reaching the door, he saw a black Stetson rise suddenly from behind the counter. Redmain faced him. Redmain saw him, and Redmain's gun raked the door. Denver drew aside and hooked his weapon around the sill, answering. A door slammed in the rear. Redmain had fled.

Denver hurled himself in, vaulted the counter, smashed out the wall lamp with a passing blow of the gun barrel, and ripped the door open, stepping aside again. A single slug splintered the sill by him. He pitched through, crouched in the absolute darkness. Redmain's boots sloshed through soft ground. The man was laughing bitterly; and then ceased to laugh. The sound of his steps died.

Denver marked the last point he had heard them and stumbled through a pile of junk. He cut himself on a snarl of barbed wire, cleared it, and aimed into the dripping trees. Over Sundown's housetops came the staccato and ragged echo of the fighting; dying to lesser anger. Denver stopped again, hearing nothing from the foreground. He went on, cleared the trees, and tramped up the trail to Lola's. Her lights shone out through the crystal beads of rain; her door opened, and a man passed through. Denver cursed out Redmain's name and lunged on. He heard Lola crying even above the rush of the storm, and when he reached the door he wrenched it wide and sprang forward without thought of the trap awaiting him. Redmain was backing away slowly, his gun raised. Every feature on that triangular face was distorted to a point almost past recognition: a bloodless, demoniac face with flaring eyes pouring out the amassed and brooding hatred of a lifetime. Lola screamed. "David, watch!" and sprang out of her corner, hands stretched forth as if to check the inevitable bullet. Redmain shouted, "Damn you, there will be no mistake this time!" The small room shuddered to the explosions following, and the lamplight guttered down to a choked, dismal glow. Lola was on her knees, both hands slipping away from Denver.

"Lola!" cried Dave. "My God, what have — !"

The light flared. Lou Redmain lay dead beyond the stove. Lola swayed against Denver's body, speaking softly.

"What other way could there be for me, David?"

"Lola, hold on to me!"

"No — don't pick me up. There's no time. I want to say —" She stopped. The pale oval of her face tipped back, and the soft mass of her hair rested in his arm. She closed her eyes, lips parting, and he thought she was slipping silently away. But she roused after a moment, and from the deeps of her being glowed that vibrant, haunting emotion he knew so well. It was as if by that glance she gave to him all that remained worth giving; telling him again of the changeless flame of love that always had been for him and would so remain to eternity. Denver shook the mist from his eyes, bent over and kissed her.

"I pay for my sins, David," she murmured. "But I am not sad. Beloved, good-bye." When she died there was the curve of a smile on her lips.

Denver remembered carrying her to the bed; remembered catching up Redmain in his one good arm and throwing the outlaw into the mud beyond her door; and remembered closing that door on the sad, sweet silence pervading the room. But there was a passage of time in that night which seemed blank; and when he called himself back from the depths he stood at the street end of Sundown, the water coursing over his bare head. Very quietly and definitely he placed all the treasure she had given him into a chamber of his heart and locked it. . . .

There was no more firing in Sundown. The lights flared high again and people of the town roamed restlessly through the street. D Slash men came lagging back from the southern edge of town. Steve ran out of the hotel, calling anxiously, "Dave?"

"Here, Steve."

Steve turned like a terrier. "Where yuh been?"

"Settling accounts with Redmain, Steve."

Steve said nothing for a minute. A vast sigh came out of him, and presently he began to talk like a parrot. "Well, that is those and them there. We collared about three quarters of 'em. The rest won't stop runnin' short of

Old Mexico. The jail's full."

"That ends one part of our job," said Denver. "Now let the jury take care of the wild bunch. Where's Niland?"

"In the hotel," said Steve and grinned. "Look behind yuh. See all them chairs piled up? Nightingale was readin' on the porch when Redmain come in. After the fireworks started, the Englishman hauled all that furniture beside the hotel and forted up. I counted seventeen empty shells on the ground. And where do yuh suppose he is now? He found a paper in the hotel he hadn't read. So that's what he's doin'. Imagine it!"

"Steve," asked Denver, after a long pause, "who got hurt?"

"Munn," said the puncher slowly. "Some others got hit. But Munn — he's gone."

They found no more to say. Niland walked across the hotel porch. Denver went over and called him. "There's another thing left for us to do, Al."

"I saw him go to Grogan's," said Niland. He swung beside Denver, and the two started for the saloon. But before reaching it they discovered Langdell coming from the courthouse; he paused, looked around, and went into the stable. Niland and Denver followed. Langdell came out in time to confront them. It brought him to an abrupt halt; the lean face tipped back as if better to watch. "Where's Redmain?" he demanded.

"Dead, Fear," answered Denver. "But it won't help you any."

"Be careful, Denver."

"For reasons you know as well as we do," stated Denver, "the less said the better. We'll stand behind the name of a good man and do nothing to dirty it. You are getting off easy. Leave town in ten hours and don't come back ever."

Langdell smiled, cold and thin. "I have bluffed some in my time, and I recognize a bluff when I see it."

"There will be no court action," was Denver's even rejoinder. "Does that penetrate your crooked head? If not, look about and see what's been happening to other crooks tonight. I said, leave town. Never step inside the lines of this county again."

Langdell stood still. A pair of horsemen galloped up Prairie and into Main. Denver turned. Williamson was passing by, and beside him rode Eve Leverage. They were looking straight ahead and so missed seeing him, but Denver watched Eve until she had dismounted and gone into the hotel, and when he shifted his attention back to Langdell it was with impatience.

"That's time enough."

"I'll go," said Langdell. He passed them as if they were nonexistent and walked to his office. Niland spoke irritably.

"It's a damned shame we can't hook him harder. There goes the brains of the wild bunch."

"It's not in the power of human beings to produce full justice," reflected Denver. "That's in the hands of a better judge."

"So be it," agreed Niland. "I'll say now what I wouldn't ordinarily say — and probably never will say again. It was a lonely day for me, Dave, when I heard you were dead."

Denver put his hand on Niland's shoulder. "I've always been blessed with fine friends, Al. May it continue to the end of the chapter." They stood a moment, studying each other, a little embarrassed. Denver turned away. "There's an empty place in the circle, Al. I'm suggesting a name for it."

Niland chuckled and supplied that name. "Almaric St. Jennifer Crevecœur Nightingale. I vote yes."

Denver walked to the hotel with a quickening pace. Steve was in the doorway talking to a youth in no humble tones. "Bill, I don't like you. That clear? Yore Debbie's brother, but I don't like you. And I won't like yuh until you change yore manners."

"Listen," pleaded Bill, "what've I got to

do with it? Debbie said —"

"All right. What did she say?"

"She told me to tell you she was waitin' for you, any time and any place. That it didn't make any difference to her."

"I ain't comin' up to any geedee Lunt supper table," was Steve's flat refusal.

"She said she didn't expect you'd want to," agreed Bill. "You tell me where you want her to come. Shucks, Mr. Steers —"

Denver broke in. "Steve, get out of the doorway and I won't have to listen to your family troubles."

But Steve didn't move. "All right, Bill. Tell her this. Tell her I'm awful doggoned sorry for what I said. But I meant it then and I mean it now. Tell her she can be the boss inside the house and I'll be boss outside the house. And the house is my house. Tell her to pack a grip and come down here tomorrow morning and we'll be married. Tell her not to bring any of her relations, near or remote. Tell her I'm sorry she sees anything in me worth marryin', but glad she does. Now get out of here, you little pup, and I don't want to see no more of yuh for about a month. Mebbe I'll get to like yuh meanwhile."

"She'll be here," said Bill and hurried away. Steve frowned at Denver. "Am I right — or am I right?"

"I'll love her like a sister," said Denver, "if she'll let me."

"Say," exclaimed Steve eagerly, "I'll tell her that! Only, be doggone shore it don't get beyond the stage o' brotherly interest. Great guns, I thought I'd lost her!"

Denver, moved by impatience, went into the hotel lobby. Through the crowd he saw Eve — and through that same lane Eve saw him. She rose from her chair, faced him, and stood gravely waiting. Denver crossed the room. Williamson came out of an inner door, and Dave, checking his stride, spoke quietly.

"Doc, I want you to go to Lola's cabin."

Williamson looked sad. "Is she hurt?"

"I want you to take care of her — for the last time."

Williamson showed shock. Eve stepped forward with a quick intake of breath. "Dave!"

Denver nodded and said nothing. Williamson's mouth compressed, and he walked away slowly.

"She was so beautiful," said Eve. "Beautiful and — a woman."

Denver lifted his head. Eve's features were clear in the lamplight; clear and honest. Some veil of reserve lifted from her eyes and he saw the deep promise in them.

"I meant what I said in that letter, Eve."

"If I had not believed it, Dave, I should not be here. But because I do believe it, nothing on earth could keep me away!"

"I'm a Denver," he mused, "a black Denver. But if you'll have me —"

"That is all I ask for," said Eve, and suddenly light came to her eyes, vital and glowing.

Ernest Haycox during his lifetime was considered the dean among authors of Western fiction. When the Western Writers of America was first organized in 1953, what became the Golden Spur Award for outstanding achievement in writing Western fiction was first going to be called the "Erny" in homage to Haycox. He was born in Portland, Oregon and, while still an undergraduate at the University of Oregon in Eugene, sold his first short story to the OVERLAND MONTHLY. His name soon became established in all the leading pulp magazines of the day, including Street and Smith's WESTERN STORY MAGAZINE and Doubleday's WEST MAGAZINE. His first novel, FREE GRASS, was published in book form in 1929. In 1931 he broke into the pages of COLLIER'S and from that time on was regularly featured in this magazine, either with a short story or a serial that was later published as a novel. In the 1940s his serials began appearing in THE SATURDAY EVENING POST and it was there that modern classics such as BUGLES IN THE AFTERNOON (1944) and CANYON PASSAGE (1945) were first published. Both of these novels were also made into major motion pictures although, perhaps, the film most loved and remembered is STAGECOACH (United Artists, 1939) directed by John Ford and starring John Wayne, based on Haycox's short story "Stage to Lordsburg." No history of the Western story in the 20th Century would be possible without reference to Haycox's fiction and his tremendous influence on other writers of stature, such as Peter Dawson, Norman A. Fox, Wayne D. Overholser, and Luke Short, among many. During his last years, before his premature death from abdominal carcinoma, he set himself the task of writing historical fiction which he felt would provide a fitting legacy and the consummation of his life's work. He almost always has an involving story to tell and one in which there is something not so readily definable that raises it above its time, an image possibly, a turn of phrase, or even a sensation, the smell of dust after rain or the solitude of an Arizona night. Haycox was an author whose Western fiction has made an abiding contribution to world literature.

The employees of THORNDIKE PRESS hope you have enjoyed this Large Print book. All our Large Print books are designed for easy reading — and they're made to last.

Other Thorndike Large Print books are available at your library, through selected bookstores, or directly from us. Suggestions for books you would like to see in Large Print are always welcome.

For more information about current and upcoming titles, please call or mail your name and address to:

THORNDIKE PRESS
PO Box 159
Thorndike, Maine 04986
800/223-6121
207/948-2962